THE GIRL AND THE UNLUCKY 13

A.J. RIVERS

D1738936

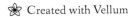 Created with Vellum

PROLOGUE

Remember who you are.
Remember where you come from.
Always remember.
Nothing will ever matter more.

SHE KEPT the words running through her head as she made her way across the coarse, dry grass. The sun dropped toward the pale blue horizon as if it was sagging under the heat of the day. It stung the back of her neck; made sweat drip down in beads that rode the ridges of her spine pressed up against skin pulled taut over her bones.

She couldn't let it slow her down. She was exposed. The field stretched around her at every angle. Her tunnel vision made it feel as if it went on forever. There was nothing else but the grass, made crunchy and painful against her feet by that brutal sun.

Remember who you are.
Remember where you came from.
Always remember.
Nothing will ever matter more.

The words kept running through her mind and occasionally

tumbling down into her mouth. The further she made it away from the building behind her, the faster the words fell through her throat to become sounds dropping from her lips.

The sun was trying to do to her what it had already done to the building. Once-pristine bright white paint shriveled in the unrelenting glare until it curled in on itself and flaked away, exposing the wood beneath. Shutters that had been deep, rich black now looked rubbed with charcoal, barely clinging in place on their hinges.

It wanted to dry her up and break her down. It was in good company.

Remember who you are.

Remember where you came from.

Always remember.

Nothing will ever matter more.

That was true. Nothing had ever been as important as grasping hard to those thoughts and keeping them tight against the hollow of her chest. She scraped the corners of her mind and brought out everything she could.

Red.

Leona.

Fireworks over the picnic grounds.

A black cat and a pink sweater.

Sandcastles connected with a path of shells and surrounded by a deep moat.

Lemonade.

Pumpkin pie.

Those words would protect her. The field wouldn't swallow her up if she kept saying them. She would never have to see it again. Not if she didn't want to. Not without her say. Never again would people take her mind from her; make her mind their own. Never again would she let anyone tell her who she was. Where she came from.

That was for her to say now.

She wasn't theirs. She was her own.

If she could get through the field. If she could get out of the sun.

They were behind her somewhere. She wouldn't look over her shoulder to see if they were coming. She wanted to listen for the sound of their feet on the dry grass, but she stopped herself. If they were coming for her, let them come.

She wouldn't cower. Not this time.

This time, she knew who she was. She knew where she was going.

She only needed to get there.

TIME PASSED, BUT SHE DIDN'T KNOW HOW MUCH. THE SUN WAS traveling down the second half of the sky. The white-hot pressure of the temperature had broken, breathing softer on her skin as she made her way beyond the fields and onto a road. She'd seen the road before. She didn't know what it was called or which direction she was going, but it would bring her somewhere. From there, she would find her way.

Night came, bringing with it the same fear it always did. Only this time there was nothing to fulfill it. It was shadow fear, the kind cast by something horrible but that could only darken her eyes and make her skin tingle. It couldn't touch her. Nothing could. Not anymore.

She fought the fear with more of the tumbling words.

Remember who you are.
Remember where you came from.
Red checked curtains pulled back with a wide red ribbon.
The favorite blanket. Beautiful shades of cream and taupe folded over the arm of a chair. A book hidden in the folds.
Banana splits with extra pineapple.
Paul Charles Middle School. Soccer Field. Noon.

She walked through the night until she couldn't move her feet anymore. Until she could do nothing but sink down onto the ground and feel grateful that some of the day's heat still warmed the moss and soil beneath the trees. She'd ducked away from the road when piercing headlights caught her eyes, but none stopped.

The morning had to catch up with her. She was already moving again before the sun lightened the path in front of her. She walked by the force of sheer will rather than memory. She didn't think she had come this way before. Maybe she had.

A car slowed beside her. She wouldn't let herself be afraid to look through the window. That fear belonged to them. It wasn't hers.

The face that stared back at her didn't register. She hoped she'd never seen it. She climbed into the seat beside the driver and closed the door, blocking out the world behind her.

Paul Charles Middle School. Soccer Field. Noon.

She closed her eyes to feel the wheels move beneath her. It felt as if they were creating the road. As if nothing was there until she was.

They could only take her so far, but it was far enough. Any distance was far enough.

She was drawn across softer grass, toward the tall chain-link fence in front of her. A sea of red lay just beyond. One hand wrapped around the metal, gripping until the uneven edge cut into her skin, she leaned forward to rest her head against it.

She released years of held breath.

ONE

Four weeks earlier...

Leaning back in my office chair, I intertwine my fingers behind my head and close my eyes. It's been a long couple of weeks and I'm lost in thoughts about a case that won't leave me while I prepare for undercover work in the days ahead.

"Am I interrupting?" Sam's voice comes from the doorway.

I straighten up and look over to where he's leaning in the door, a smile on his lips as he watches me.

"Of course not," I grin.

He walks into the office and gives me a kiss before setting a folder in front of me and tapping it with his fingertips.

"What's this?" I ask, turning the folder toward me and opening it so I can look at the documents inside.

"We identified her," he says just as I'm looking at the first picture.

It's an image that I've seen many times before by now. One that is etched in my mind. The body of a girl curled in the corner of a cavern, wearing one shoe. The other shoe had already been found long before.

"The girl in the cavern?" I ask. "With the shoe?"

Sam nods, leaning back against the edge of my desk.

"Her name is Delaney Mendoza. She was twelve years old. She wasn't from the area. She had been abducted two states over and brought to Sherando Ridge," he tells me.

I can hear the emotion in his voice. It's hard to describe what it feels like to come to this moment. Finding a body is a moment that changes you. I've encountered dozens of bodies in my years of service to the FBI. There's a point when you're able to turn off the humanity of it for long enough to get through without the trauma.

Rather than seeing the blood, the gore, the tragedy of that life being ripped away, I see a puzzle. I'm able to remove myself from that harsh truth enough that I can push forward through the details and find out what happened.

It's harder when there's no name. When I know who the person is, or at least have some way to identify the victim, it's a stepping stone. That information is valuable to understand what happened. It gives me the focus to work through the case. That's when the humanity returns. Once I've processed the scene and started working through the puzzle of understanding what happened, knowing who the person was drives me.

When I don't know, there's a hollow feeling. It's still a person, a human being taken from life, but without that name, that connection to the life he or she lived. It's deeply sad and infuriating at the same time. The entire concept of murder is so arrogant. So unbelievably entitled. To believe yourself so important you have the right to determine another person's life and death, just on a whim, is something I can't understand. It completely disgusts me.

I've been put in positions when I've had to take the life of another human being. But it's never done lightly. It wasn't because I just wanted them to die, or thought it would be a fun, thrilling way to pass the day. It was a necessity. I never once endowed myself with the right to destroy that life, or thought to myself that it was perfectly fine that I did. Just because those deaths were justifiable and essential to my own survival, the weight of those moments never escapes me.

Finding a body and not having an identity to attach to it is painful, sad, angering, and frustrating. But then there's a strange reversal when the body is finally identified. There's happiness and relief, but there's also a renewed sense of sadness and finality. You finally have a name and a face. A life to attach to that body. And the sense of grief, that this victim has gone without those things and without true mourners, can come down hard.

There's a picture of Delaney in the folder and I look down at a pretty girl with big eyes and a smile on her face that said she believed the world was at her feet. She was only twelve years old. A little girl with so much life ahead of her. Then someone snatched it away. The very worst type of entitlement. The kind that says a child is his to hunt, and if he can catch her, his to keep and use as he pleases.

Even I have a hard time pushing away my rage at those monsters.

"What's going to happen to her?" I ask.

"Her family will need to be contacted," he says. "Then we'll decide from there."

"I'll do it," I say. "They should hear it from me, because I'm the one who found her."

"That would be great," he says. "I think it'll be comforting hearing it from you."

It's not an aspect of my job I enjoy, but one I take seriously. The responsibility of taking away the hope of a parent and replacing it with gut-wrenching despair and fury is a heavy one. These calls and visits never get easier. They are always painful and uncomfortable. But they aren't about me. I'd rather they get the news from someone who cares, someone who has been a part of the case from the beginning than a generic officer who has no insight and no connection.

It might not make that much of a difference. And I've had cases when the families were angry at me when I came to tell them. They felt I'd betrayed them in some way. But if there's a single person I can make feel a little better in this horrible time, that's what I want to do.

Looking at the girl brings my mind back to the woods, and a phone call the police got when the news first emerged of the bodies rising up out of the lake.

"Wait. If the body was Delaney Mendoza, what about Ashley Stevenson?" I ask. "Her family said she went missing five years ago and was in that area. They found a few of her belongings chained in the bottom of the lake."

"All the remains have been accounted for," Sam says. "They've all been tested. Besides, her age doesn't line up. She would have been thirteen five years ago. Much too young."

"So, she's not on the campgrounds?" I ask.

"No," Sam clarifies. "Still missing."

Three days later ...

I uncross my legs and shift in the hard wooden chair. For a restaurant wanting customers to enjoy their meals, it is decidedly uncomfortable. But that doesn't really matter right now. I'm not here to be comfortable. I'm also not here for the mediocre bowl of soggy pasta swimming in weak tomato sauce sitting in front of me.

Shifting to the other side, I uncross my legs again and cross them the other way. I check my watch, noting the time, then pick up my phone and swipe through a couple of screens. I'm not looking at it. My focus is out of the corner of my left eye, to the shadowy back corner of the dining room. I'm waiting for the slice of light to come from the opening of the door there.

I shift again and set down my phone. Every movement is carefully measured. I take a sip of water and swirl my fork around in my bowl, hazarding a bite so the waiter doesn't come by again to check on me. He's been hovering not too far away, trying to make himself look busy by rolling flatware in dark purple linen napkins.

By the look of the number of tables in the restaurant, he just pre-rolled about three weeks' worth of flatware. Maybe I'm missing something.

What I'm not missing is the figures scurrying back and forth across the back of the room, moving in and out of the kitchen so fast I can't even see their faces. That's why I'm here.

I shift again. I pick up my phone and scroll through. Not because I'm really looking at anything. In all honesty, I'm flipping through the weather and caught up with some nonsense complaints on a write-in advice column. The point isn't entertainment. Two other agents are watching me. Every movement I make means something to them.

This case has been hanging over me for the last two months. I started as a consultant, just helping with research and giving insight from experiences I've had with other cases. But I haven't been able to stop thinking about it, and the further it progressed without resolution, the more I needed to step up.

It's not the rest of the team's fault. They weren't doing anything wrong, exactly. It was Creagan's mistake to develop a team without anyone who had handled a captivity and forced-labor case. They aren't easy. They're gut-wrenching and infuriating, not the least reason for which being how hard they can be to prove in court.

This restaurant is a classic example of that. People want to think they'd be able to recognize it when other people are being held against their will and forced to do the bidding of someone else. In the simplest terms, slaves. The assumption is at least that the people being held involuntarily would do absolutely everything in their power to get out.

That's the thing people don't understand. In these situations, the captives' power is taken from them. What little they have left is only enough to keep their hearts beating and their lungs pumping air in and out. From the outside, there seem to be so many ways out. An open door. Dozens of people around them. Lights that go out at night. Phones.

But those things don't exist to the ones held captive.

To them, doors could lead to terror, because at least they can see what's around them where they are. It's familiar. For all they know, a door could lead somewhere worse. They see people they can't trust, because they once trusted a new face and it betrayed them.

It isn't that easy. And is the mistaken belief that it's that easy is why people are left to suffer.

Not on my watch.

The information the team was able to collect was instrumental in uncovering how the owners of this restaurant weaseled their way into the lives of three people in dark, challenging times in their lives, then manipulated them into servitude. This isn't the first time they've done it, and we have strong reason to believe there are others in various locations.

Some no longer living.

These criminals need to be stopped.

Together we identified key locations, gathered evidence, and prepared for the moment when it would all end, both for those who caused so much pain and those who lived in it.

It all led to this moment.

Heat prickles the back of my neck. Adrenaline surges inside me as I work my mind up and prepare my body for the intense burst of energy I'm going to need to blast through this. It's not going to be simple. It's not going to be pretty. But it's going to be effective. And if we do it right, it doesn't have to be deadly.

Looking at my watch again, I make a move as if I'm adjusting its position on my wrist. Instead, I'm activating a button that connects me with the ground crew outside, so I can mutter the few words they need to hear every so often to know everything is still going as planned.

They're waiting to surround the building. If the perpetrators try to flee, no matter which direction they go, they'll end up running right into our waiting arms. And the line of fire.

But we're also taking precautions. As critical as it is to get these victims out of this situation as fast as possible, we can't forget that we are in a restaurant that's still open to the public. The place is fairly empty, but there are a few patrons around. Right outside, parked right next to the van containing other agents and law enforcement, are people who have absolutely nothing to do with this, who have no idea what's going on. They shouldn't be caught up in it if it is at all avoidable.

Patience is one of the greatest challenges of orchestrating an operation like this. Sometimes when out in the field, I get to rush into a situation and everything happens in a split second. I get to kick down doors and storm rooms within moments of actually getting to a place. But not always. A lot of times it ends up just like this: long stretches trying to not look suspicious while waiting for everything to fall into place.

And then it all suddenly happens.

Out of the corner of my eye, I see the sliver of light appear and the movement I've been waiting for. I run my fingers back through my hair, and seconds later, three more agents walk through the front door. They move with smooth confidence to the nearest table of patrons, acting as if they know them.

They don't want to bring any attention to themselves as they subtly let the people know they need to get out of the restaurant. I continue to watch the shadowy space, making sure I have my eyes on the doors as well as the figures moving back there.

It takes a few minutes for the agents to convince the customers at the nearest tables to leave. There's only one table left, and when I look up, the two people sitting at it make eye contact with me. I don't know if it's because they've caught on to the fact that I've been sitting there for so long, or simply because I'm the only other human in this space other than the waiter, and they want to make sure I see what's happening.

I shouldn't give myself away. But it's obvious they aren't comfortable with being there. I give as subtle but convincing a nod as I can and tilt my head toward the door. It's a compelling enough move and they get up, tossing money onto the table before leaving. The waiter tries to stop them, but the agents follow right after.

Then I'm the only one left. He starts toward me, and I don't like the look in his eye. My watch makes a subtle sound that tells me everyone is in place around the building.

Let's do this.

I give the final signal. Seconds later, a cacophony of shouts erupts from the back of the building. I get up to my feet, push away from the table, and reach for my gun. The waiter immediately heads for the door, but the other agents are waiting.

From there, everything happens in a blur. The adrenaline and sheer fury push me through. By the time I'm standing with my foot in the middle of the back of a handcuffed man, my gun pointed toward his head, I more than remember why I started doing this.

There have definitely been times that I've doubted my place in the FBI. I tend to buck tradition and err on the side of my feelings and intuitions, rather than always precisely following the rules and procedures. It used to get me in trouble fairly often. At the worst point, it landed me behind a desk and out of the field for six months.

Last year, I went through a difficult time and I didn't know if I could stay in the Bureau. Clashing with my supervisor and struggling to be respected and properly recognized by others drove me to the edge. As much as being an agent had been everything I'd worked for since I was eighteen years old, I just didn't feel the same satisfaction and fulfillment anymore.

It only took one case that threw me into the depths of human darkness to remind me of who I am. Challenges and clashes or not, I'm an FBI agent.

My career isn't the same as it used to be. But I'm not the same as I used to be, either.

For a while I worked purely as a consultant, while also working with my fiancé, Sheriff Samuel Johnson, in the Sherwood, Virginia police department. Then I got involved in some private investigative work with my cousin Dean Steele. He's a licensed private investigator and is constantly on my back, reminding me that I can't refer to myself as a PI or say that I was doing any private investigating until I go through the training, get tested, and get my license just as he did.

But I've been telling him that, as the young folks are saying these days, I ain't got time for that.

Nope, still can't pull it off. If I have the compulsion to preface something with "as the young folks are", and then add in some sort of action word, such as eating, drinking, doing, or saying, I just need to take a step back and tell myself "no." No good is going to come of this.

Dean doesn't know I've been working my way through the training. I'm actually just about to finish the course. I haven't wanted to tell him and build it up too much. He wants me out of the Bureau and working with him full-time, but now I realize I can't do that. At least not at this time.

I've been easing back into the field more and more and I'm not ready to leave it. I can't do as much as I used to. The notoriety that's come from my recent jobs has made it much more likely for me to be recognized. I'll probably never be able to go undercover again. But there's still plenty of work to be done. Too many smaller elements of larger crime rings I busted were either never identified or have gotten out of jail. They're not going to hit the straight-and-narrow and start living choir boy lives.

It isn't likely, anyway. Not that I don't believe in the concept of redemption and rehabilitation. Dean is the perfect example to prove that doing bad things doesn't automatically imply a bad person. He made choices when he was younger that left his life in tatters. But he took those tatters and mended them back together, becoming a special forces veteran and warrior for what is right.

It would be naïve to think that will happen for everyone. Many more will go right back to the illegal activities and the people who got them in trouble. Instead of working harder to be better human beings, they work harder to be better criminals. And that includes burning undercovers. If there's any way they can recognize an agent, they'll make sure everyone knows about it.

Since my face has been splashed all over the news at a frankly uncomfortable frequency throughout the last few years, there's enough risk that some of them could pinpoint me that I have to stay away from those roles.

This case was a risk, but I felt passionate about it. We did enough preliminary work for me to feel confident they didn't have strong ties to any of the large drug or crime syndicates still being dismantled. Their twisted, disturbing crimes were all their own, which meant I got the distinct pleasure of being here to bring them down.

One day, maybe, I'll decide it's time to settle down and retire from the Bureau. My upcoming marriage and my little chosen family's getting bigger, with the any-day-now birth of Bellamy's baby girl, have given me a glimpse of another kind of life in my future. But it's not set in stone. There's no reason I can't have both lives for as long as I want. My marriage certificate isn't going to double as debriefing papers. Having a new baby in my life just means renewed purpose and a stronger desire to make this world safer and more beautiful for her.

I'll wear my wedding ring and carry Sam with me into battle, work alongside Dean and Xavier on cases that need us all to unravel, help keep down crime in Sherwood, and still be home to bake cinnamon rolls and have Game Night with Paul and Janet across the street. People have doubted me in the past. I've doubted myself in the past. But no more. If Barbie can do it, so can I. Bitches, beware.

TWO

"You wanted to see me?" I ask, dipping my head into Creagan's office.

"Griffin, yeah, come in. Sit down." Creagan gestures to the chair across the desk from him and I close the door before taking the seat. "How are you feeling?"

Shit. It's never good when he starts down this path. It's the same one that got me stuck behind a desk years ago after an undercover job almost imploded. It's the same one that ended with me stretched out on a therapist's couch picking apart my life when I really didn't want to. And it's the same one that forced me into medical leave that nearly led to my losing my mind.

In the end, all of those situations worked out, but I'm not looking forward to what it's going to lead to this time.

"Doing fine," I say carefully. "I've got a couple bumps and bruises, but nothing serious."

"Good," he nods. "You did a great job out there. This whole job. That couple is going to go away for a long time, and their victims are going to have a chance now."

I give a single nod. "That was the goal."

"And you did it."

"Thank you." Well, this is awkward as hell. Creagan isn't the best at being loving and supportive. For the most part, he's a hard-ass who'd rather plow through anything having to do with emotion, good or bad. And I'm feeling on guard. So, I decide to plunge ahead into a conversation I've been meaning to have with him anyway. "I'm actually glad you asked, because I have something I want to talk to you about."

"Oh?" Creagan asks. "What is it?"

"I want Greg's files," I say.

It's blunt and to the point. I already have a feeling this is going to be a bit of a struggle, so I saved my breath and explanations for when he starts being difficult about it.

"Why do you want his files? You already have the information given to you during the investigation."

"The investigation is still ongoing. We don't know who killed him or why. And I do have pieces of the case files, but not everything. I want more of the crime scene photos and unredacted reports."

"You know my feelings on your being involved in the investigation into his murder," Creagan replies. "Considering your relationship and your inheritance of his estate..."

"Those things are exactly why I want access. And I want to be involved in his investigation. There's no excuse for our not having solved this by now. Greg was one of our own. My relationship with him aside, he was an agent. A loyal and talented agent who was instrumental in solving several high-profile cases. Including uncovering the depths of Leviathan and ensuring Jonah Griffin never sees the light of day again. He deserves better than to be covered by the energy and effort equivalent of a side chick," I say.

"A side chick?" he raises an eyebrow.

"A... on the back burner," I attempt to clarify.

"Griffin, I fully understand the importance Greg had in this organization, and I appreciate your wanting to uncover the truth, but I think you're way off in your characterization of the work being done to find out who's responsible. It's a challenging and complicated case."

"I know it is. So, let me put an extra set of eyes on it. From the very beginning, I've been the one who's been able to provide the most information. I know you think I'm too emotionally involved, but maybe that's what this needs. His death makes no sense. You know that yourself. He hated water. He had just started what could have turned into a relationship with the investigator Lydia Walsh. He'd just recovered from what Jonah did to him. Why would he have Lydia come meet him at the hospital only to break off from her and go to the beach?

"And what about the time in between? It took three days to find him, Creagan. Three. And he wasn't dead for that whole time. The medical report proves that."

"What do you mean the medical report proves that?" he frowns.

"He didn't show the signs of being dead and exposed to water for that many hours."

"I think you're wrong about that," Creagan says.

His insistence is a little strange, but I don't push him on it. The truth is, I have suspicions. Strong, complicated suspicions that have been creeping and tangling in my mind like vines for the past few weeks.

"Then let me have full access to the case files so I can see that. Either way, there's still the question of who killed him and how they managed to do it without anyone's seeing them. He was supposedly shot in broad daylight. And there were no signs in the sand that he struggled or fought back in any way. According to the way his footprints were positioned and the way his body fell, it looks as if he didn't even turn around. How could that possibly be?" I ask.

"I don't know, Griffin. It's something we're all trying to figure out," Creagan says.

"And I should be allowed to help more than I have been. You cut me off from official involvement in the case too soon," I say.

"I removed you from the task force because you are too close to the situation."

"I was too close to my mother's death and I got the answers to that," I point out. "I arrested my own uncle after he spent my entire life stalking me. That's too close, Creagan. But I did it because it needed to be done. And so does this. Another year shouldn't go by with Greg's still not having justice."

Creagan still looks as if he's waffling on the request. Even if he won't relent and give it to me today, I'll keep asking. The partial files I have are a start, but they don't give the full picture. There's information missing. Pictures missing. I need to have all the crime scene photos, rather than just a few snaps Eric was able to get for me.

Something has been bothering me about the ones I have, but I can't figure out exactly what it is. It's sticking in the back of my mind and won't let go. I might have made a connection, but it doesn't make sense. Not yet. Those pictures aren't enough to give me the full idea of what happened. They all seem to be lacking something. I don't know what, but each one feels incomplete. I feel that I need to see other angles. I Ii think if I could look at these still images differently, I will see what I need to know.

"I'll consider it," he finally relents. It's a start. I'll keep bothering him about it until I get the answer I want. He probably already knows that. "But for right now, I asked you here because I need to talk to you about something."

"What is it?" I ask, back to the hesitant feeling.

This doesn't sound the same as when he started trying to poke around in my mind and figure out what made it click; when he decided I needed to stretch out and stare at a ceiling while a woman whose name I wouldn't even say for several months cracked me open and explored around.

"Your work in Harlan," he says.

That's not what I was expecting. But maybe I should have. Creagan doesn't like the way it looks when a case he all but dismissed explodes into something huge and complex. And then doesn't have a resolution. That's what happened in Harlan.

Looking back, it's hard to identify how it actually started, because it all became intertwined so quickly. Dean had been investigating the disappearance of a man after a bizarre set of actions, including filling and emptying his bank account a couple of times and marrying a woman no one had ever met or heard of. At the same time, I was drawn into the case of a missing internet celebrity, Lakyn Monroe, who was last seen leaving an appearance and seemed to have simply vanished.

That's what brought Xavier Renton into my path. Or, more accurately, brought me into his path. Xavier doesn't come into people's lives. He exists in his own sphere and some people are fortunate enough to get absorbed into it. Lakyn was almost there. Xavier was imprisoned for eight years, accused of the grisly murder of his best friend, and was only getting more isolated and unpredictable as time went on.

According to what she shared with the public, Lakyn was working toward illuminating Xavier's plight and getting him released. We later found out she was delving deep into the case and angering people who didn't handle being angered well. This is where the cases really started to spiral and twist onto each other until they were strangling the small town.

In the end, lives were brutally lost, and a horrific organization known as The Order of Prometheus was uncovered. They were the ones who killed Xavier's friend and framed him for it; they were the ones who murdered Lakyn; they were the ones responsible for the mysterious disappearance in Dean's case and a host of other murders besides. They manipulated and controlled practically every aspect of the town and carried out cult-like rituals. They even tried to sacrifice me.

I came out of it all with Xavier as a new part of my chosen family, and complete enmity and bitterness toward the members of The

Order who ensured he spent so much time in captivity and tormented him throughout it.

Though we pieced together some of the truth, The Order members disappeared before they could be brought up on any charges. They left behind their cavernous meeting hall full of secrets and lingering questions. Especially when we accidentally uncovered a powerful connection to the Dragon, a drug lord I brought down years ago. And had thought to be dead.

The aftermath left Harlan bloody and reeling. And we still don't have all the answers. Creagan didn't even want to get involved. When Lakyn disappeared and things started to unravel, he pushed back against letting me investigate as an agent. But then he realized just how big the situation was, and suddenly it became about his reputation. He wanted to be able to bask in the attention, holding press conferences and doing interviews to talk about justice and the world being a little safer.

There isn't anywhere near as much glory in having to talk about a case that's still ongoing. Or to admit we still don't have all the pieces. It frustrates the hell out of me that I can't figure out why some of the players were involved or how some of the crimes were committed. I hate that we can't find The Order or the Dragon. But I'm really not in the mood to get lectured about it. Especially considering there's literally nothing he could say that I haven't thought of myself or that will make a difference.

"We are still actively investigating those cases. My father's undercover work wrapped recently, and we are going over the information he collected. We're doing everything we can."

"I know you are. It's a complicated case and there's a lot to be done on it. Which is why I think this is the perfect opportunity," he says.

It feels as if I missed something. As if he told me something important and I didn't process it all the way through. Or maybe he thinks he told me something and just skimmed past, hoping I won't realize I don't have all the details.

"You think *what* is the perfect opportunity?" I ask.

"The new agent," he says with a hint of false confusion in his voice.

Yep. That is exactly what he thought he did. He tried to slide this into the conversation so I would think I just missed his saying it and wouldn't ask. Which certainly won't be happening.

"Which new agent?" I ask.

"Agent James. She recently finished her training and will be entering the field. She's located in the Harlan area and has expressed a tremendous amount of interest in you and your work. She could be helpful to you and you could mentor her."

It's all I can do to prevent myself from rolling my eyes. "Creagan," I start, but he cuts me off with a look.

"You ain't getting out of this one, Griffin."

THREE

"WHAT THE HELL does he mean, 'mentor her'?" I ask Sam over speakerphone as I drive away from the headquarters a few minutes later. "How old does he think I am? I am not at mentor age."

Sam laughs. "You don't have to be old to be a mentor, honey. You just have to be good at what you do. And you're the best of the best. He just wants to have more like you. Or as close to you as possible, since he's not going to get another Emma Griffin."

"I'm an FBI agent. Not a kindergarten teacher. I don't need to be responsible for some baby agent who doesn't know what she's doing. And I definitely don't need her getting in my way in one of the biggest and most complicated investigations of my career," I argue. "Obvious exceptions excluded."

"I know. But he could be right. She could be helpful. Especially while you're handling other investigations. You're still working the Arrow Lake case, and it isn't easy for you to juggle cases that far apart. She could do some of the groundwork for you."

"How am I supposed to trust her with something that important? I don't even know her," I say.

"Immediately after meeting him, you trusted Dean with helping to investigate your mother's murder. While a serial killer was stalking you," he points out flatly.

"Dean is my cousin," I protest.

"You didn't know that at the time," Sam counters. "You just saw that he had skill and was able to help you figure things out. Maybe this woman will prove herself to be useful. And you know how hard it can be for a woman in the Bureau. Your presence could make a huge difference in her career."

"Are you pulling the 'sisters are doing it for themselves' card on me?" I ask.

"I'm just saying maybe you should give her a chance. See what she's made of. If she's got the skills, utilize them. If she can't hack it, she'll figure it out quickly enough. At least you will have done your part to help and be a good role model," he says.

He's right. Of course, he is. Sam is too good for my own good sometimes. A lot of the time. It doesn't mean I like it. And I guess she's made it this far. There has to be something in her to get her through training. That isn't easy.

"Alright," I say with a sigh. "I'm pretty well done with the 'feeling old' portion of the day. Let's talk about something else. How is everything in Sherwood?"

I've come back to Quantico to stay at my father's house while Bellamy and Eric are on baby watch. I want to be here when their daughter is born, and this is a good opportunity for me to spend some time with Dad. He's been undercover trying to flush out the missing members of The Order from other chapters. It was an incredible shock when I found out he, my grandfather, and my great-grandfather were all a part of the very same mysterious and deadly organization.

That was before I realized the chapter in Harlan had gone rogue, engaging in activities and rituals that have absolutely nothing to do with the ideals of the true Order of Prometheus. The organization is intended to lift up promising members of society.

Just as the Titan god of fire who gave the organization its name crafted humanity from clay and stole fire from the gods to give to the humans, The Order of Prometheus, in its purest form, is meant to give opportunities and offer support and guidance to men they think have potential. They move through society unnamed and unnoticed, pulling strings, using connections, and flowing money to create paths for these people and ensure success. At least, that's how Dad describes it.

Somewhere along the line, the chapter in Harlan lost its way. Rather than being about encouraging and supporting the next generation of leaders and influencers in society, they became a frightening pack of imposing, generally wealthy, men who literally wielded the power of life and death over those around them. They created blood pacts that bonded them together. They saw it as creating loyalty and strength. In reality, it was nothing but a savage series of killings designed to promote servitude and fear among those not in the highest tier of the hierarchy.

I haven't seen much of my father in the last several months because of his work, even missing the holidays with him, so I'm glad to have at least a couple of weeks. Even if it does mean being away from Sam. That's the only thing that gives me pause. I hate being away from him. But as sheriff of the small town of Sherwood where we live, he can't just leave for long stretches of time. They need him there to keep order and protect the people and community he loves.

He's planning to come when the baby is born, but right now he's saving up his time off as much as possible. With our wedding sometime in the near future, his sights are set on a long honeymoon when we can just disentangle ourselves from the rest of the world and be together.

It sounds like heaven. But one thing at a time.

I listen as he updates me on everything going on in town. It's only been a few days since I left, but it feels as if I'm missing everything. Fortunately, that doesn't include a tremendous amount of crime. For the most part, Sherwood is an incredibly safe, wonderful place to live. It has the smaller crimes you'd expect in any small town: theft, bar fights, vandalism, disorderly conduct, traffic issues. Then there are the more difficult situations he sometimes has to deal with, such as domestic violence and other abuse. Serious crimes like murder are rare, but it was just that situation that brought me back after seven years away from the town where I spent more of my unpredictable childhood than anywhere else.

Right now, there isn't anything that dramatic happening around town. His update focuses more on the people and everything they're up to.

"Bianca is really looking forward to your class at the community center," Sam says. "She's gotten a lot of interest for it."

"We don't even know exactly what the class is going to be about," I say.

"It doesn't matter. People want to hear from you. They are interested in your experiences and expertise. Whenever the sign up goes live, I have a feeling all these slots are going to fill up quickly. Maybe you'll have to start teaching several classes there."

"How did I start today as an FBI agent and finish it as a mentor and schoolteacher?" I groan.

Sam laughs. "If there's anybody in this world who can pull that off, it's you."

"I think that's a compliment. If it's not, don't tell me. Just let Bianca know I'm finalizing a couple of different courses and I'll show the options to her once the baby gets here. Then we can figure out when to actually offer the class."

I've been working with the director of the Sherwood Community Center for several months now with putting together a class I can teach. We haven't been able to nail down exactly what I'm teaching, whether it will be basics of criminal justice or more focused on true crime and the cases I've worked. Either way, it's important to me to include elements of self-defense and safety. Especially for people living in a small town with little crime, they can get lulled into a sense of complacency and think nothing bad could ever happen to them.

Unfortunately, I know for a fact that's not the case. Awful things can happen anywhere, and it's critical to be as prepared as possible to respond when they do.

I've never particularly understood the common saying that bad things happen when you least expect them. That's not always true. Some people know when they are in danger and will need to be able to protect themselves. As for the others, of course, they don't expect it. That makes it even more important to be armed with knowledge and skill that can bring a terrifying and disorienting situation a bit more under control.

My investigations have forced me to delay the class a couple of times, so at least it's good to hear Bianca hasn't given up on me.

"How about you? How are you? I miss you," I say.

"I miss you, too. It's hard here fending for myself."

I laugh. This is coming from the man who has lived his entire adult life unmarried and on his own. Not to mention one who has a freezer full of meals and cinnamon rolls ready to put in the oven whenever his heart desires.

"I think you'll survive."

"Are you almost back at your dad's place?"

"I have to stop at the store really fast, then I'll be there. I'm actually about to pull into the parking lot."

"Alright. I'll call you tonight. I love you."

"I love you."

We get off the phone and I take a second to let myself be sad. It isn't as if Sam and I are never apart. When I'm on a case, I might be gone for several days at a time. But this feels different. There's an open-ended element to it that makes it even harder to be away from him.

I go through the store quickly, then head to my father's house. Part of me feels that it should be strange to consider the house his again. Technically, it's mine. My name is on the deed, and it has been since I was eighteen years old. I lived there alone for the ten years my father was missing out of my life. It was my house, but as soon as he resurfaced, it became his again. He moved back in and the interior shifted back to being more like it was when we lived there together during my college years than it was when I lived there alone as an adult.

But there are parts of it that are the same as they were before I left that house to go to Sherwood. Including my bedroom. He kept it the exact same way, so I can come and go as I please. I go there right after dropping the groceries off in the kitchen. I can't wait to get out of the heels and pantyhose I wore to headquarters.

Once I'm comfortable again, I go back into the kitchen to make a late lunch that I carry into the living room to eat on the couch while I research on my laptop.

FOUR

"Do you ever take a break?"

I'm mid-bite and almost choke on the mashed chickpea salad sandwich when he comes into the room.

"I didn't realize you were here," I say, wiping my mouth with a napkin.

He gestures down the hall toward his room. "I was lying down for a bit. The heat gave me a headache. What are you eating?"

"Chickpea salad on multigrain bread. There's a bowl of it in the refrigerator for you."

"Thanks, sweetie," he says.

He heads into the kitchen and comes back a few moments later with a thick sandwich piled high with the creamy salad, a few big leaves of lettuce, and thick slices of tomato. The other half of his plate is a small mountain of potato chips. Have to balance out all those health benefits. I wish I'd thought of it.

I reach over and snag one of his chips. "Are you feeling better?"

"Yeah. But I'm definitely looking forward to the summer weather being over," he says.

I chuckle. "It's July. You've got some time ahead of you."

"I know. But I can start dreaming." He takes a bite of his sandwich that looks as though he's trying to devour half of it in one go. It takes him a few seconds to chew and swallow. "How was your meeting with Creagan?"

I sigh and take a sip of water. "Well, he started the conversation by telling me I did a good job on the takedown yesterday."

"That's great. That was a really tough case, and it's good to hear he's giving you the recognition you deserve," Dad says.

"Then he told me he wants me to mentor a new agent," I say.

Dad shrugs and takes another bite of his sandwich. "That's not all that unusual, I guess. I don't think I've ever heard of a supervisor's directly asking an agent to do it, but I've known plenty of established agents taking new ones under their wings."

"What if I don't want her under my wing?" I asked.

Dad laughs. "What's wrong with helping out a new agent?"

"I have too much to do to babysit," I say. "If she got this far, take it from there. And if she needs help, she'll find people in her area who can help her. I don't understand why Creagan decided I need to be the one to hold her hand and guide her through the career she chose."

"Maybe because you're the best example of a woman in the Bureau he can possibly think of," Dad offers.

I shake my head. "Creagan would never say that. Today was the first time I can remember when he actually complimented me on how I did during a job. He can do a little congratulatory comment about its going well or a good resolution for the case. But he's never just said I did a good job or I handled it well. That would be far too close to admitting he's not the one who controls everything and makes everything happen. There's something else behind this," I say.

"Like what?" Dad asks.

"I don't know. But I feel off about it," I tell him. "Besides, I don't think he has suddenly had some sort of come-to-Jesus moment and he's going to recognize the contribution I made. And anyway, I'm too busy making said contribution to mama-bird someone else into everything. I don't have a problem with meeting this woman or being on a team with her if there's a case I'm working. But, the way he's talking, it sounds as if he just wants her to shadow me. As if she's supposed to just follow me around and watch what I do."

"He's going to have to understand you're busy. The cases you're handling are intense and require as much attention as you can possibly give them. He can't expect you to just drop everything to spend time with her."

"No," I say. "But he thinks she'd be a great help." I can't mask the sarcasm in my voice. "Sam seems to think so, too. He thinks that I should be open to letting her do some of the groundwork for the investigation in Harlan while I'm dealing with Arrow Lake."

"That might not be the worst idea," Dad nods. "You've been trying to go back and forth. That's got to be exhausting."

"But she doesn't know the case. She doesn't know what happened or what any of that means. She doesn't know the people involved. How is she supposed to make a valuable contribution?"

"You tell her the things she needs to know. Or you have her do things that don't necessarily require her to have all the details right off the bat. You could also ask her to assist Dean when the two of you aren't working on something together. Having FBI clearance can be more influential than being a private investigator. You know that. Even if he's the one doing the bulk of the work, just having her credentials to get more information or better access would be extremely helpful," he says.

"I guess I really don't have much of a choice. Especially since Creagan's holding hostage the case files I need," I admit.

Dad looks at me questioningly. "What do you mean? Which case files?"

"I want to look at the full files about Greg's death," I tell him. "I have some of the information and some pictures Eric was able to get me. But Creagan hasn't wanted me involved in the investigation, so I don't have all the details."

"Why do you want them?" Dad asks. "Has he changed his mind and is going to let you investigate?"

"I don't think so," I say. "He should, but he's still insisting I'm too close to it. But I need to see the actual pictures. I need the medical examiner's report and evidence collected on the beach."

"You've figured something out," Dad observes.

"Maybe," I say, letting out a breath. "I'm not sure what it is yet. It feels as if there are connections that are right there, right at the tips of my fingers. I just have to figure them out."

FIVE

"Do you still think Greg's death has connections with The Order?" Dad asks.

"I think the thread is there," I nod. "You said that nobody you spoke to in any of the other chapters had ever heard of him?"

"No," Dad says. "None of them has ever heard his name. At least, that's what they say."

"Do you trust them?" I ask.

"I do," Dad says. "The men I interacted with in those chapters were straightforward. They had nothing to hide. As soon as I confirmed my membership, they brought me in, and nothing was held back. It wasn't as though they made me aware of rituals or special meetings that I wasn't allowed access to or anything. And from what you told me about that chapter in Harlan, they wanted people to participate in the killings. They wanted the power. At some point during my time with the other chapters, if they had connections, I would have been made aware of this other side. And for the most part, I had no indication something like that was going on."

"What do you mean, 'for the most part?'" I ask.

"It's not that there was anything specifically said or done. There were just a couple of men in one particular chapter who weren't as forthcoming as everybody else. They were a little more standoffish and seemed very entitled. They felt more important than the other people who were there. That seems more like a character flaw than an indication that they might have been a part of something else," he explains.

"But you aren't completely convinced of that," I say. "I can see it in your eyes."

"It might have been something else. I can't say for certain it's not. I'm still working on them. I focused on gaining their trust and getting closer to them. It didn't open them up completely, but that was actually my point. I wanted to see if they would pursue me. So, as soon as it felt as if I was starting to crack the surface and make headway with them, I left the chapter. I made sure they knew how to get in touch with me and suggested I might not be finding everything I wanted in that particular chapter. I didn't come right out and say I wanted something else, but I left the breadcrumbs."

"Have you heard from them?" I ask.

"I didn't for the first couple of weeks after I left, but one of them actually reached out to me earlier today. It was nothing of note, just saying it was good to meet me and they were checking in. But that's a stab. Putting out feelers. So, I'm going to continue down that path and see if it comes up with anything," he tells me.

I'm doing my best not to be frustrated. I know how difficult undercover work can be. It's not so easy as just walking into a situation and thinking everything's going to fall at your feet. My father has been doing everything he can to help. I just hate that I haven't found the answers yet. I feel that by now, I should have been able to connect the dots. I should have been able to hunt these men down. But I haven't.

"I guess I can't hope that they'll send you a postcard inviting you to a party to meet their friend the Dragon," I crack.

Dad lets out a short laugh and shakes his head. "I don't think so."

"I just don't understand how they're linked. That's what brings

Greg into it. He was so invested in not letting Lydia investigate the Dragon further. He knew how dangerous that man was. And he thought just as I did that the Dragon was dead. He believed Darren Blackwell died while serving his prison term. If he needed something else, why didn't he tell me where to find Darren? Or what Darren has been doing over the last several years?

"And where do the paths of The Order and The Dragon inter-sect? When Dean and I were standing there in that temple and they were three seconds from killing me, Dean pulled out the name "Dragon" from information Lydia sent to us. I didn't even know what was going on."

"And they clearly knew who he was talking about," Dad says.

I nod. "They were terrified. None of them said anything specific, but it was obvious they were very afraid and weren't going to do anything that could possibly cross him. But why? Why would they make that association? What do they owe him? And they disappeared at right about the same time. I can't help but think that's related."

"We are getting there," Dad says. "You're chipping away at it. You'll find your way."

Before I can answer, my phone rings on the table in front of me. I pick it up, expecting it to be Sam. Instead, it's Dean.

"Hey," I say, holding the phone between my ear and shoulder so I can keep eating. "What's up?"

"How did everything go?" he asks.

"Fine," I say, not wanting to talk about the new agent anymore. "I'm glad that case is finally done. Or at least it's close. There's still the trial to be had, but after investigation and take down, that should be a cakewalk. We found so much evidence, there's no way they're going to be able to talk their way out of it."

"That's great," my cousin says. "Does that mean you're at your dad's house?"

"Yep," I say. "Still on official baby watch. I have Arrow Lake in a couple of days, but other than that, I'm here."

"Do you mind if we come up there tomorrow?" he asks.

"Sure," I say. "It'll be good to see you. I know Dad would like to see you guys, too. Everything okay?"

"Yeah," Dean says. "There's just something I want to talk to you about."

"Okay," I say. "Around lunchtime?"

"Sounds good. See you then," Dean says.

"Tell Ian not to forget about the bag ties or the meat cooler," Xavier calls from somewhere in the background.

"Did you hear that?" Dean asks.

"I did."

"Talk to you tomorrow."

I hang up and look over at my father. "It truly scares the living hell out of me to relay this to you, but Xavier says not to forget about the bag ties or the meat cooler."

Dad gives me a look that tells me Xavier's comment sparked something. His eyes widen and he nods as he finishes a bite of sandwich and puts his plate on the table in front of him. Standing, he goes to the shelves on the other side of the room and picks up a notebook and pen. I watch him scribble what I'm assuming is the note from Xavier before he comes back and sits back down.

I stare at him for a few more seconds, waiting for him to give me some sort of explanation, but he doesn't.

It's finally happened. Xavier has officially gotten to my father.

SIX

THE NEXT DAY, food from my favorite Thai restaurant, one of the couple things I long for now that I live in Sherwood, arrives just before Dean and Xavier. When they get there, I open the door and give each a hug before Xavier makes a beeline across the living room toward my father.

"Do different brands count as the same item?" he starts. "And what about those little signs sticking out from different shelves saying items are on sale? Are they actually on sale? If somebody picked those up would they be worth less than if somebody picked a different brand? Even if its original brand was worth more originally? Or is it all a ruse?"

I look over at Dean. "Do you know what that's all about?"

Dean shakes his head. "Xavier says it has something to do with a game and investigative journalism. A book that's going to blow the lid off nineties culture."

I glance across the room toward the shelves to find the two men in deep conversation over the notebook my father wrote in yesterday. As he flips through the book, I can see many pages full of notes and diagrams. I look back at Dean.

"Is this something that's real or that Xavier made up and my father is just going along with because he loves a good delusion?" I ask.

"I wish I had an answer to that."

"Well, I guess we'll find out eventually. Food's here. Want to grab some, then we'll talk?" I ask.

Dean nods and we go over to the dining room table, where I've spread out all the containers of takeout food so they're easy to access. We each get a plate and start scooping out bits of everything. Dad and Xavier have taken their conversation into my father's office by the time Dean and I get back into the living room. Eventually, they'll come up for air and get something to eat, but if they've adjourned there, we might be in for the long haul with whatever has wrapped them up.

I drop down into my favorite corner of the couch and settle my plate on my folded legs. This has always been my favorite corner of the couch for no particular reason. I'm sure the other corner is perfectly comfortable. I've had my toes wedged in it plenty of times when stretched out sleeping right here during nights I couldn't bear to go into my bedroom.

There were more of those than I cared to count in the weeks and months after my father disappeared. And then again when my uncle was stalking me.

But this has always been the corner I've gone to. Reading, homework, pizza night, TV. I know it well. It's another of the things I sometimes miss when I'm at home in Sherwood. But amazing Thai food and a well-worn couch corner aren't enough to lure me back.

"How are you doing?" I ask after my first bite.

It's one of those questions that doesn't always mean anything. People ask it and don't expect a response. They'll throw it out when walking past somebody they vaguely recognize on the sidewalk, or when they're starting a conversation with somebody they don't necessarily want to be in a conversation with over the phone but have to be.

This is the opposite. This time I actually want a response, but the question is heavily loaded and layered. I'm not just asking how he's feeling or what's going through his mind. The last few weeks haven't been easy for Dean. In truth, things haven't been easy for him at any point in his life. I'm still learning about my cousin and the lives we lived in so many ways side by side and yet completely unaware of each other. And through that, I'm learning about everything he experienced and how it made him into the man he is today.

But I didn't learn about one of the biggest factors that influenced his life until we were drawn into a years-old mystery that brought us to an abandoned campground and face-to-face with his past. It gave me significant insight into him, but also made me worry about him more than I ever had.

"I'm doing okay," he tells me.

"Really?"

He meets my eyes and holds them. "I'll get there."

"That's good enough," I say.

We go back to eating for a few seconds before he speaks again.

"That's actually what I want to talk to you about," he says.

"What is?" I ask.

"I can't stop thinking about everything that happened at the campground," he says.

"I know," I nod. "It was a lot and it couldn't have been easy for you."

"It wasn't," he says. "It was one of the hardest things I've ever had to go through. But I can't get it out of my mind. All those people. Ones we still don't know. And they're just the beginning."

"I know," I nod again. "The investigation is still going. That's why I'm going up there in a couple of days. The Bureau sent in a task force I'm heading up. We're working to piece together who the unidentified victims are, where they came from and when they died. We're also focusing our efforts on trying to locate the remains of the ones we know were victims but haven't been found yet."

Dean nods. "I know. And I am totally available to be as big of a part of that investigation as you want me to be. But that's actually not what I was thinking about."

"Oh? What is it, then?"

"We know there are still victims who are out there. Ones whose names we know, and we know when they were probably killed. And others whose bodies we have but who we are still trying to connect with missing persons cases. Bodies that don't have anything to do with Aaron or his family," he says.

"There are," I acknowledge. "Unfortunately, there's never a shortage of missing persons cases."

"One of them is really sticking with me, though," Dean says.

"Which one?" I ask, leaning over sideways to pick up my drink and take a sip so I don't have to look away from Dean.

"Ashley Stevenson."

"The girl whose family came forward when the media started talking about the additional victims," I say.

"Yes," Dean confirms. "The details of her disappearance seemed to line up with what we knew about the murders in and around the campground at the time. Her last-known location was in the park near that campground. She hasn't been seen or heard from in five years. But then we figured out she couldn't have been a victim."

"Her age ruled her out. She was only thirteen when she disappeared five years ago, which was too young for Laura or Rodney Mitchell to have gone after her. Which means if that area really was the last place she was alive, something else happened to her there," I say. "Yeah. She's been on my mind, too. She was so young. I hate to think what might have happened to her, but her family deserves to know."

"Well, that's why I'm here. I've been thinking maybe we should look into it together. Not as part of the FBI investigation, but in a private investigation capacity," he offers.

"Are you going to let me call myself a private investigator?" I raise an eyebrow.

"Do you have a license?"

"No."

"Then you know the answer," he says.

"Alright."

"Alright, you'll stop trying to call yourself a PI,' or alright you're in for the investigation?" he asks.

"I'm in. The Bureau is focusing specifically on Laura's and Rodney's victims, so no attention is being given to Ashley or the other missing persons who don't align with the methodology of those murders. Doing a private investigation is probably the family's best bet at getting any answers," I say.

"That's what I was thinking, too. Which is why I've been in contact with the family," Dean says.

"You have?" I ask.

"Yes. After not being able to stop thinking about it for more than a week, I decided I needed to know as much as I could. She was thirteen, Emma. It sounds so young, but it's also the age I was when I was starting to get into trouble and was then accused of murder. I got wrapped up in finding out about her and her case, so I started doing some research."

"What did you find out?" I ask.

"Not much. There isn't much media coverage of it. A few brief articles from when she first went missing. They all give basically the same information. She went out with friends and didn't come back. There are a couple of interviews with her mother. I was able to find her last yearbook and a couple of mentions of her in school publications. But it didn't seem as if there was a lot of attention given to it. The general consensus was that she must have been a runaway," Dean tells me.

"What do you think?" I ask.

"That a thirteen-year-old runaway isn't going to get very far in the days of ID verification for everything, social media, and security everywhere. There would be no way for her to start a life of her own.

Whatever happened after she was last seen, there was someone else involved," Dean says.

"I agree. So, what's next? How does the family feel about our investigating?" I ask.

"They want to meet with us," he says. "They're ready to talk and actually have people listen."

SEVEN

DEAN AND XAVIER stay the night, as they usually do when visiting either my father's house or Sherwood. The next morning, as Dean gets in touch with Ashley's family to arrange our meeting, I check in on Bellamy and Eric.

As much as I've wanted to visit with her and do everything I can to help in these last couple of weeks of her pregnancy, I've been trying to step back a bit. In a lot of ways, I'm still used to its being Bellamy and me, and Eric and me.

My friendships with both of them developed separately, and I always considered them my best friends, even when they didn't particularly get along with each other. Which was a considerable portion of my twenties. They clashed over just about everything. Sometimes it was hard to even be in the room with them. Which was fine, since I had different bonds with each of them.

It wasn't until everything happened with Greg that the two of them really started getting along. I didn't even realize it was happening at first. Then when I was sent on my first undercover assignment after being taken off desk duty, I found out that not only were they communicating, but they seemed to be forming a new closeness.

The rest, as the old folks say, is history. I feel a lot more comfortable saying that. Which might be giving me a clue as to why I'm suddenly being called up into the FBI Big Brothers/Big Sisters program.

Things weren't smooth and easy between Eric and Bellamy right off the bat. There was a lot of back-and-forth and pretending they weren't feeling what they so obviously were. I can't necessarily say it felt right for the two of them to end up together, but it was so obvious when they interacted, I couldn't deny it. It took a brutal case for them to finally realize what they could have with each other was worth so much more than the fear of ruining a friendship.

Now they're expecting their first child any day, and I'm having to remind myself that the baby is theirs. They are there for each other and should be experiencing this together. Not that I shouldn't be a part of it at all, but I also don't want to encroach on them as they're nesting and enjoying the anticipation of becoming a family of three.

Both of them know I'm here. At any given second, they could call and I would drop everything to do whatever they need. It's hard not to see Bellamy all the time or spend hours talking over cases with Eric. This is the new place our life has found us. We really are grown up.

We are family and nothing is going to change that. It's just that a new chapter has begun and we have to figure out what that means for all of us. Right now, that means everyone is eagerly waiting for the first sign that the baby, the first in a new generation, is coming.

"How's everything going?" I ask.

We are almost at the point in Bellamy's pregnancy where she could say the baby could be here literally at any moment. It's been interesting to watch her go through each of the stages of her pregnancy and see how she's handled it. As graceful, beautiful, and generally peaceful as Bellamy has always been, I wouldn't go so far as to say those qualities have translated all the way over into her pregnancy. There have been times when she's been downright cranky. Which is putting it kindly, but I don't want to speak ill of the procreating. The woman is growing another human being. She gets a lot of leeway. I copped an attitude with my garden when I was just trying to grow some begonias.

"I'm exhausted," Bellamy huffs. "I feel as if I weigh about forty thousand pounds and my hips don't work anymore."

"Your hips don't work anymore?" I ask, confused and maybe just a hint horrified.

"Remember when I told you a few weeks back that my hips were hurting so much all the time? Even when I hadn't done anything?" she asks.

"Yeah," I say. "You said it constantly felt as though you'd worked out for hours."

"Exactly. Well, apparently that was gearing up for all the tendons loosening. My doctor said the hormones in mid to late pregnancy signal the body to start preparing for birth. Which includes the tendons in my hips letting go so that it's easier for the baby to pass through. In theory, that sounds like an awesome thing. Making me as stretchy and pliable as possible seems like a great way to make labor easier. However, in practice during these days when I'm not actively giving birth, it's just leaving me with floppy hips. I'm waddling all over the place. It feels as though any second, I'm going to slide on something and hit one of those terrifying Barbie doll splits where her feet go up to her shoulders from the front and back."

"Please don't do that. It doesn't sound good for you or the baby," I say.

"I'm doing my very best to avoid it."

"How about other than that?" I ask. "How are you feeling? What are you thinking?"

"I'm everything. I'm nervous and excited. Really uncomfortable but more in love with my body than ever. Anxious and eager to meet her, but not really ready to give up being pregnant," she says.

"How about Eric?" I ask.

"He's doing so great," Bellamy says.

"He's in the room with you, isn't he?" I ask, immediately able to recognize the inflection in her voice.

"Yep," she chirps.

"And he's actually freaking the hell out?"

"So much," Bellamy says.

I laugh. That sounds like Eric. He would do his best to stay calm and collected, but not being in control or able to determine how this happens would push him right to the edge. Eric is great at computers, numbers, organization. He's not so great at uncertainty and having to just wait for things to happen the way they're going to.

"Well, it won't be too much longer. But then he gets to start freaking out about raising the baby," I say. "So maybe you should just get used to this general state of his existence."

Bellamy laughs. "Perfect. You're still coming by today, right?"

"Absolutely. I'll be over tonight."

"Good."

We finish talking and I'm getting off the phone as Dean comes back into the room.

"How's Bellamy?" he asks.

"Very pregnant," I say. "Ready for the baby to be born and not wanting to not be pregnant."

"Sounds about right," Dean says.

"Where's Xavier?" I ask, realizing I haven't seen him yet this morning.

"He got up early and had breakfast and he's been in the office with your father since. When I walked by, I heard them mention something about inflatables being the far superior bonus option, but the potential that they could contribute to a helium crisis, resulting in the advent of more practical items," he says.

"Still no clue?" I ask.

He shakes his head. "I've got nothing."

"What did Ashley's family say?"

"I talked to Misty Stevenson, Ashley's mother. She's ready to set something up whenever we are," he says.

"Great. Well, as I said, I'm going to be going down to the campground in a couple days. Since they live in the area, we can find a time to get with them then," I say.

"Actually, they happen to be in this area today and tomorrow. They're visiting potential colleges for their older daughter. Apparently, she graduated high school a couple years ago, but wasn't ready to go to college yet. She thought she might want to go right into a career. Now she's changing her mind and might want to go to school, so they've started touring around different ones that caught her attention. They're looking at a few within an hour of here," he says. "So, they're available to meet up any time this afternoon."

"Great," I nod. "Call them back. Set it up."

EIGHT

"THANK you so much for meeting with us," Dean says as we walk into the hotel suite. "I'm Dean Steele."

"Of course," says a slight brunette woman with tired, aged eyes, reaching her hand out to shake Dean's. "I'm Misty Stevenson. This is my husband John. Our daughter Leona is spending some time exploring the campus and surrounding areas to see how she feels about it."

"We'll meet her another time," Dean says. He steps further into the room and gestures toward me. "This is the cousin I told you about, Emma Griffin."

"Agent Griffin," Misty says, sounding almost relieved to see me here, rather than just Dean.

"Emma," I insist, shaking her hand. "Thank you for having us."

This is another one of those odd social exchanges, right up there with asking people how they're doing. She didn't invite us over for coffee or a pleasant chat. We are here to discuss the details surrounding her teenage daughter's disappearance five years ago. It's not a social call or something we should be happy about doing. We are the ones here to work on her behalf. And yet, I have the compulsion to thank her.

I've noticed I've become even more aware of, and critical of, basic day-to-day social interactions since meeting Xavier. There are things that have always stood out to me as being odd, but I went along with them without much thought because it's just the way people engage with each other.

Now after getting to know Xavier and trying to understand how he interacts with the world, these things stand out to me even more.

Finishing the somewhat awkward dance of introductions with people who have already talked on the phone or have heard about one another, we move further into the room. Misty gestures at the sitting area in the living room portion of the suite. It's separated from the bedroom by a door, which makes it less uncomfortable.

"Please," she says, "sit down."

Dean and I each take one of the overstuffed armchairs while Misty and her husband sit side-by-side on the small couch.

They both look at us hopefully, and Dean and I realize they aren't going to start this conversation. Dean slides toward the edge of his seat cushion and leans slightly toward them.

"I've gone over some of the case with Emma, and she's agreed to be a part of the investigation," he starts.

"Thank you so much," John says. "I know you are incredibly busy with your FBI career."

I give a hint of a nod of acknowledgment, but want to reassure them.

"This case has really spoken to me," I say. "I'm still actively investigating the campground and the incidents that happened there. But Ashley's case in particular stood out to me and I believe it deserves resolution. Your family deserves resolution."

"Thank you," Misty says. "It's good to actually hear somebody say that. The police aren't doing anything at the moment. Not that they've done terribly much since Ashley disappeared."

"What involvement have you had from the police in this matter?" Dean asks.

He's treading carefully, as he should. In cases like this, it's important not to interfere in a way that could compromise a police investigation that's still going on. Often families feel that nothing is happening because they aren't being continuously updated, or they haven't seen massive strides being made in the case. What they don't realize is that steps are being taken and progress is being made that can't be openly discussed, to protect the integrity of the investigation.

"When she first went missing, there was some action. Of course, plenty of the officers immediately jumped to the conclusion that she was a runaway. She was thirteen years old and going through what most thirteen-year-old girls do. Testing some boundaries. Wanting to be more independent. But she wasn't a runaway," Misty explains.

"She never went out without your knowing that she was going?" I ask. "Or was gone longer than she said she'd be?"

"No," John shakes his head. "Never. She had an attitude sometimes. She didn't always get the best grades when she was having a fight with her friends. But she was a good girl. She wouldn't have just run off. There was no reason for her to. And that's what we told the police."

"Do you think they believed you?" Dean asks.

"Some of them," Misty says. "And some of them dismissed us. Now, they seem to have lost interest in her completely. There was some movement when I reached out to the detectives to point out she was last seen in the area of all the disappearances and murders. But after that was eliminated as a possibility, they just stopped. It's as if she doesn't matter as much because she isn't part of a massive crime."

"You say there was movement in the beginning," Dean says, trying to keep them focused. "But then it drifted off. What type of investigation did they do?"

"They performed a fairly cursory search of the area," Misty shrugs. "They interviewed Ashley's friends. That's really it."

"Why didn't you push any more?" I ask.

Misty looks at me, her eyes narrowing slightly as if she's confused. "What do you mean?" she asks.

"Your daughter disappeared five years ago. You say you don't have any more information and the police aren't interested anymore. Why didn't you press more about her disappearance during those five years?" I ask.

"We did," Misty says, sounding almost offended by my question. "No one would listen. I just told you, they said she was a runaway. That she had gotten into some sort of argument with us or was mad that she couldn't do something. They concluded she wasn't happy at home. So, she ran off.

"That's really what they wanted us to believe. It didn't matter what evidence there was or who our daughter was as a person, once they decided she had run away, that was that. This has been awful for us, and for Leona," Misty says.

"I understand that," I say, "but..."

"No," she cuts me off, shaking her head. "You don't understand that. You can't. We spent all this time having no idea what happened to our daughter. Finding out about the murders gave us almost this kind of hope. Do you have any idea what that's like? To hope your child was murdered and chained to the bottom of the lake just so you know where she is? So you know she isn't being starved or tortured?"

I feel my heart constrict. I shake my head. "No. I don't."

"You have children, Emma?" she asks.

"No," I tell her.

"Then you can't possibly come close to understanding. Don't judge us, please."

"I'm not here to judge you," I say. "I'm here only to help."

The woman locks her eyes on mine intensely. "Then help."

A beat of silence passes. I give a solemn nod.

"Tell us what happened the day Ashley disappeared," I say.

Misty and John exchange glances. They both draw in breaths before looking back at us.

"She was spending time with her two best friends, Vivian

McLemore and Allison Miller. The three of them were practically inseparable. They were a year or two older than she was, but Ashley had always been very mature for her age, so they got along perfectly. It had been raining for several days and when the weather cleared up, Ashley wanted to get outside with her friends. She was feeling cooped up," John says.

"It was summer," Misty adds. "That's when kids want to be out playing and having fun all the time. They don't want to sit at home with their families." She lets out a painful-sounding laugh. "She told us they were going to go to the park and hike."

"You were okay with her going to such a big park by herself?" Dean asks. "Is that something she had done before?"

Misty shakes her head. "No. We didn't think she was going by herself. Vivian's family camped all the time. The girls had gone with them on several occasions, so we just assumed she was going with them again. We didn't ask."

I nod. "Go on. Ashley told you she was going to the park to hike. Did she tell you what area she was going to be in?"

"She mentioned the name of one of the trails. It was the same hiking loop they usually did. From what I understand, it's not too far from the campground. As I always did, I told her to be safe. I said to make sure they were paying attention and didn't get in the way of any bikers. That they didn't go poking around in the abandoned cabins. That was the kind of thing I was worried about. That they would get wrapped up in some conversation and get hit by a biker or get in trouble for going to an abandoned area," Misty says.

"So, you did expect for her to be alone at some part of the hike?" Dean asks.

"There had been a couple of occasions when Vivian's family was setting up their camp and the girls were allowed to hike a short distance on their own," John says. "It always made Misty so nervous because she didn't like the idea of the girls walking around by themselves. But I told her there wasn't anything to be worried about. They were in a park. The hiking trails are very clearly marked. And they were good, smart girls. Ashley had just turned thirteen a couple of months before and I told Misty it was time to stop treating her like a baby and really let her grow up."

He hangs his head. It shakes back and forth as he draws in a shuddering breath, as if he's trying to stop himself from crying.

"It's alright," his wife whispers, reaching over to rub his back.

It's obvious this is a conversation they've had between them several times.

"It isn't," he says. "It's my fault. If I had never said that she should be able to go, if I'd insisted she needed to stay with the adults the whole time, this wouldn't have happened. She'd be home right now. She would be the one getting ready to go to college."

"You can't blame yourself," Misty says. "You didn't know what was going to happen."

I brace myself for the next question I have to ask.

"When did you realize she was missing?"

NINE

MISTY LOOKS up at me almost as if she's forgotten we were sitting in the room with her. She keeps an arm wrapped protectively around her husband.

"The next day," Misty says. "We expected her to be staying at least one night in the park with Vivian's family. Maybe even two. But she was to call us the next day to check in, like always. But we didn't hear from her. Instead, Allison called us. She said Ashley forgot her backpack and was going to come by the house and drop it off. I was really confused. I couldn't figure out what she meant. So, when she got here I told her Ashley wasn't home. I thought maybe Allison hadn't stayed with the others. Maybe she had gone home and for some reason had Ashley's backpack."

"We weren't thinking clearly, obviously," John says. "I can't really imagine anybody would in that situation."

He's defensive now, already on edge as he waits for Dean and me to react to the story they're telling.

"That's completely understandable," I say. "A situation like that isn't something you ever expect to happen. You don't know how you would react or what it would feel like. It makes perfect sense that you were confused. What did Allison say when you told her Ashley wasn't home?"

"She was confused, too. But she wouldn't explain why. Said she would go talk to Vivian and left really abruptly. I remember she was on her bike and she rode away so fast it almost looked as if she was going to lose balance. As though she wasn't holding herself up well and was going to fall over. I actually remember standing there at the door watching her ride off until I couldn't see her anymore because I was so afraid she was going to fall and get hurt," John says.

"When John told me what was going on, I didn't know what to think. If it wasn't so horrible, I would almost say it was funny," Misty says.

"What do you mean funny?" I ask.

"My husband is the more permissive parent. He always has been. Ever since the girls were little, he has encouraged them to explore and figure out who they are. That's something we always try to instill in them. That they are individuals, and it's important for them to figure out who they are as people and live their lives to their fullest extent. I was more cautious with them, but John really encouraged them to try new things, depend on themselves, see the world as their own and take it. He wanted them to feel strong and independent.

"I was always the worrier. I wanted them to be strong, independent, capable women as they grew up, too. But I still had so much of a mama bear heart. I was protective and wanted to know both my girls were safe all the time. It terrified me to think something could happen to them. That was why I insisted on her checking in, even when I thought she was with other parents. I needed to hear her voice and know she was all right. John and I had always told both of my girls that if they were ever in a situation where they were uncomfortable, or something was going on they didn't agree with, they could call us.

"No questions asked, we would be there to pick them up and get them out of the situation. We had even come up with code words, so if they were in a situation when they needed help but didn't feel comfortable saying that, they could use their own individual code phrases, and either John or I would know they needed us.

"In every other situation, every time one of our girls was late on her curfew by five minutes, or I heard sirens going even vaguely in the direction where I thought she was, I thought something was wrong. I just automatically thought the worst. And John would reassure me everything was fine. And it always was. But that day, he was immediately upset. He was immediately worried, and I was the one who said there had to be an explanation. That it was fine."

"Why would you think that?" Dean asks.

"Because it always had been," Misty says. "Because I couldn't wrap my mind around something so terrifying as my daughter being missing in that huge park by herself. As I said, she had gone there before. Several times. It wasn't a completely new area to her. Ashley had never been an easily confused, distracted child. She wasn't one to get lost. Sometimes she got flustered or anxious about things, but when that happened, she hunkered down. She didn't wander away or run off in a fit.

"There would be no reason the three girls would deliberately separate in the park, and even if for some reason they had accidentally gone different directions, Ashley would have been able to find her way. Or she would have called for help."

"Sherando Ridge has awful cell phone reception," I point out. "I know that for a fact because I was just there and barely able to connect with anybody, even with a dedicated source. I can't imagine the reception would have been any better five years ago. Couldn't she have gotten to a place where there would be no cell phone reception, and she was unable to call for help?"

"I didn't think about that until later," Misty admits. "It wasn't until it really sank in that Vivian and Allison didn't know where she was, and that she wasn't there with Vivian's family, that what I know now was just denial faded away. I had to come to terms with what was actually happening."

"When did the girls admit they weren't with Vivian's family?" I ask.

"That day," John says. "Soon after Allison showed up at the house with Ashley's backpack, we got a call from the police. She had gone to Vivian to tell her Ashley wasn't home. They genuinely believed she was. They explained that they were all together, they went to the park by themselves to walk around, and Ashley got mad at them. According to the girls, she said she didn't want to be there with them anymore and she stomped off. They knew we would pick her up without a second thought, so they decided to give her some space and let her leave."

"What happened after your conversation with the police?" I ask.

"They started down the runaway route pretty much immediately. There was a fairly cursory search of the park and the surrounding area. They tried to call her phone. It was either off or dead, so there wasn't any way to talk to her or to use the signal to locate her. It seemed as though for the first couple days, they put some effort into finding her, then they pretty much told us that they would keep looking, but that she would probably show up on her own by the end of the week," Misty says.

"If she had no history of running away, why would they be so confident that was an option?" Dean asks.

"They said because of her age and the fact that her friends admitted to arguing with her, it put her in a prime situation to want to get away. Letting her go somewhere like the park gave her an inflated sense of independence and self-reliance, so she felt she could go off on her own and let off some steam. Or maybe even make people feel guilty and miss her. That age is impulsive and irrational a lot of times. They feel so grown up and also feel they're completely invincible. But they're still very much children. Most don't have the capacity to think their way through being out on their own. So, they spend a day or two drifting around, then they go home."

"So, they told you to wait," I say.

Both parents nod.

"That was all they said. Just to wait. It was literally all the help they would give us," John says. "Just wait and she'll show back up on her own. But she never did. We're still waiting."

"How has the investigation progressed since then?" I ask.

"They did a couple more searches in the few months after she went missing. They interviewed the girls. They found as many security cameras in the area as they could and watched them to see if they could see her leaving or catch her with anyone. We asked them to search Vivian's and Allison's homes," Misty says.

"Why would you ask them to do that?" Dean asks.

"We were desperate. We were trying to think of absolutely anything we could that might explain where she had gone or what happened. We thought maybe she was hiding out at one of their houses. I know it sounds ridiculous. Of course, their families would notice, but we were grasping at straws."

"Did they search?" he asks.

"Yes," Misty says. "Both families were completely forthcoming and let the police search every inch of their homes. Of course, there wasn't a trace of her. And there hasn't been since. As I said, when we heard about the murders at Arrow Lake, there was some hope. We thought finally there were going to be answers. They weren't the ones we were hoping for, but there would be something. We would finally know what happened and be able to move forward."

"Are you absolutely positive one of those bodies isn't Ashley?" John asks.

"Yes," I say. "The motivation and method behind the murders was based on a very strong shared delusion between mother and son. They chose their victims based on their ages, and if they thought they would be compatible with Aaron, the younger son who drowned when he was little. The ages of the victims always closely coincided with what his age would have been at the time. To within a range of about two years. In one of her interviews, Laura Mitchell explained she always encouraged Aaron to have many different kinds of people as his friends, but they stayed in the same age group, so they were on the same level."

"And there's no way they were lying? Trying to get themselves out of other charges?" John asks.

"No," I say. "First, it would be futile to try to lie about something that specific but also that easily provable. Second, they had already taken responsibility for the deaths. Laura cannot comprehend what happened. She still doesn't believe she and Rodney murdered those people. She wouldn't have the capacity to lie about it."

He nods. "Then where do we go from here?"

TEN

He called her Thirteen.

She had a name, but he didn't care. He never said it and he never let her say it.

Maybe one day she would forget it. It didn't matter anymore, anyway. She didn't need it. She hadn't for a long time.

He figured he could call her whatever he wanted. She was his, after all. Wasn't that how it worked? People named what belonged to them. As soon as she was in his hands, she was his. No one else who had ever touched her or held her or seen her face mattered anymore.

She was his.

She didn't want to respond to it. He could tell every time he said it. But that didn't matter, either. Some things took time to get used to. She was strong. A fighter from the very beginning. It might take her longer to respond, but she would. One day, she would accept it and no one would ever know her as anything else ever again.

Thirteen.

ELEVEN

USUALLY, in an investigation like this, the first step would be to collect all the available information from the media, primary sources who were involved at the time, and anything the police were willing to provide. Dean had already gathered up everything he possibly could, and Ashley's parents filled in a lot of the blanks with the information they collected over the years.

The police won't provide us with the files, citing a still-open case. That makes me angry. Clearly, they aren't doing anything to justify calling it still open. They turned off the display of concern a long time ago, and other than having her name still on their website as a missing person, there doesn't seem to be any sort of progress being made on the case. But they still wouldn'twon't hand over the information.

Which means Dean and I have that much more ground to cover.

The next day, we're back at my father's house, searching for the friends Ashley was with the day she went missing. Xavier and my father are in the backyard with two long shelves my father constructed. They've lined up various objects, and the last time I looked out the window, Xavier was running by and knocking them off with one arm, then turning around and repeating on the other side. I haven't seen a cooler or any bag ties coming into play, but this is Xavier. I've learned to never assume until all has been revealed.

"I think I found them," Dean says as I'm making a cup of coffee.

"Yeah?" I go back into the living room and sit beside him.

"Allison has a different last name now, so I guess she got married. Garrett, this has to be them."

He turns the screen toward me slightly and I see two smiling teenagers, their arms looped around each other's waists as they pose on a beach. They aren't pressed up against each other. Instead, they've left a gap between them. Ashley's absence in it is almost tangible. I nod.

"That's them. Reach out. See if they can talk in a couple days when I'm there," I say.

Dean types a message into the social media platform and it takes only seconds for it to alert him to a response.

"Allison is willing to talk," he says. "She wants to know if we want to do a video call rather than waiting until we're down there."

"Absolutely."

He sends another message. This time the wait before a response is longer. I wonder if she might be checking with Vivian to see if she will participate. Finally, another message pops up.

"She says she's at work until tonight, but will be available then," Dean says.

"Fine with me. Set it up," I say.

With that settled, I gather my files and notes from the other cases I'm working and spread them out so I can keep digging. Ashley's case has caught my attention and I want to focus on it, but there are other tangles I still need to unravel. Until those are done, I can't just put them aside.

"Did I tell you Millie's attorney finally got back to me about her will?" I ask.

Dean shakes his head. "No."

"Yeah. He was dragging his feet because he says it still hasn't been resolved. She left everything to her brother," I say. "So, it hasn't been resolved for obvious reasons."

"Her brother?" Dean asks. "Isn't that a little strange?"

I shrug. "I never heard her talk about parents. She wasn't married. I don't know of any particularly close friends she had. I guess she went with the only option she had other than choosing a charity to leave it to. But here's my question—which brother?"

"He didn't tell you that?"

"No. He said it's confidential until the matter has been resolved. But he did very specifically say 'brother' and not 'brothers'."

"That's interesting," Dean says.

"Maybe. What about Lilith Duprey's house in Saltville? Has anything come of that?" I ask.

"There's been so much red tape to get through because of Mason Goldman living in the house before he faked his death. The house belongs to Lilith, but the investigators still have it tied up," Dean says. "They know what happened. They know Mason faked his death. But they still won't release access. It's considered an ongoing investigation."

"It is, technically," I admit. "We know what happened. But Mason disappeared with the rest of The Order members. We can't prove he's alive or that he committed murder to fake his own death. Until we're able to track them down and he's among them, they still have to investigate as if that body by the side of the road was him. Noah White has petitioned the courts to compel his ex to submit DNA from his child so that they can test it against the corpse. It was pretty horrifically damaged, but they should be able to make enough of a comparison to prove it's not him. But she's not cooperating."

"But there could be so much in that house that could help us understand what happened," Dean sighs.

"Maybe," I say. "But, I don't know. Members of The Order are extremely careful about protecting the secrecy of the organization and everything that implies, especially to the rogue Harlan chapter. I don't think he would keep details of shady dealings sitting around the house."

"I'm more interested in what Lilith might have left behind. If there's an attic or a basement. Even a crawl space, I want to get in there. She's made a couple of comments that there are answers at the house, but she won't get into any more detail than that. She's still afraid of what they're capable of, even when they aren't in town."

"Like Xavier said, the walls have eyes," Dean says.

"That's true," I say. "We know there were connections with the prison and the facility Xavier was kept in during his trial. The most challenging part is that Lilith isn't just afraid for herself anymore. The last time I visited with her, she told me she is thankful I saved her. She's grateful to be alive and that she has a chance to see the men who tortured her and killed so many people brought to justice. But she's still terrified. She's afraid of what they could do to her, but she's more afraid of what they could do to me. She wants to help but is afraid. She doesn't want anyone to possibly overhear her sharing details and be able to feed that information back to The Order."

"I guess I can understand that. I just wish there was a way to circumvent the investigation. It seems as if Noah should be able to grant us access," Dean says.

"It's not his jurisdiction. He's cooperating with the Saltville department since the entire bigger picture straddles both areas, but that particular issue is up to the detectives in that department. He can't override them," I say. "For now, we have to figure out what we can from a distance."

"Xavier and I have to head back tonight after the video chat. I have to meet with a client in the morning, but after that, I might head over to Saltville and see if I can talk some sense into the police department," Dean says.

I want to discourage him, but there's no point. He's going to do it whether I think he should or not. At least they're used to us.

"Is it an interesting new case?"

"Probably not," Dean says. "Just a guy who thinks his wife might be cheating on him with her yoga instructor."

"I think I read that book," I say.

Dean nods. "In all honesty, he could figure it out for himself, but if it makes him feel better for me to follow her around and take pictures, who am I to say no? It's an easy case to pad my bank account a bit without having to put a lot of time into it. That way I can focus on Ashley without feeling as though I'm missing out on something."

We both know even if he stopped taking paying clients completely while he was investigating Ashley Stevenson's disappearance, he'd be fine. Not only would I never let my cousin struggle, but he has Xavier. We're not entirely sure why, but Xavier has more money than he knows what to do with. It's not something he talks about, which leads me to believe he either has always had that much money and is just used to it, or doesn't realize how much he actually has.

Either way, he owns the house he and Dean live in and has given Dean access to his money to help him with things like paying bills and going grocery shopping. Those are the kinds of things Xavier's best friend Andrew used to do for him before he was brutally murdered as a part of an Order initiation ritual that sent Xavier to prison for eight years.

As a contingency of his release pending his new trial, the judge required Xavier to have someone to help him reintegrate into the world he had trouble with before he was kept out of it for almost a decade. Dean had already connected with Xavier and stepped in. Since then, the two have developed a strong bond that is really amazing to see. They understand each other in a way I'm not sure anyone else does, and Xavier is fiercely protective of Dean. He knows Dean is supposed to be the one taking care of him, but as Dean once told me, they saved each other.

But that doesn't mean Dean is willing to just let Xavier support him. He wants to continue to work and contribute, even if that means squeezing in awkward reality TV-esque cases between bouts of investigations he cares more about.

TWELVE

MY FATHER and Xavier have just stalked purposefully through the living room and out the front door, my father with keys in hand. I'm not sure how I feel about whatever is going on between the two of them.

Actually, I do. Ominous. Ominous is how I feel about it. This is where things can start to go sideways. Not that I want to think two of the most important men in my life would actually go down a destructive path, but accidents happen.

My phone rings and I reach for it without checking the screen. My heart has already jumped into my throat and I'm starting to get up, expecting to hear Eric on the other end of the line.

"Hello?"

"Griffin."

That is not Eric. That would be Creagan.

"Yes," I say, dropping back down onto the couch.

"Maybe you should straighten up your attitude when you're speaking to me," he says.

"We're not in the office, Creagan. You called my personal number when I am not on duty," I point out.

It aggravates me to no end when he says things like that to me. Some of the things I've heard the guys on the team say to him and to each other would be unfit for public airwaves, but he's never called them out on it.

"That's right. You're not. Yet I hear you're poking around the disappearance of that girl," he says.

"You're going to have to narrow that down a little. Unfortunately, there are a lot of girls who go missing," I fire back, even though I know exactly what he's talking about. I just enjoy chipping away at his arrogance.

Creagan is the type of man who likes to think everybody around him is so invested in what he thinks they will scramble to anticipate his priorities.

"The girl whose family tried to say she was a part of the Arrow Lake Campground murders," he says.

"Her name is Ashley Stevenson," I say. "And it's not as if her family was trying to piggyback on those murders. They had every reason to believe there was a good chance she was one of the victims. The details of her disappearance correspond with many of the aspects of that case. She was ruled out, but she is still missing."

"Her case isn't the territory of the FBI. We're not involved in trying to find her," he says.

"I'm aware," I say. "Considering that's my case. I know the scope of the investigation. But I'm not including her in that investigation. I'm acting on a private basis. Consulting with the private investigator secured by the family."

"Your cousin?"

"Yes," I say. "As a matter of fact, Dean has been in extensive contact with the family, and they want him to take over the search for her. The local police haven't made much headway. As you can imagine, five years is a long time for them to be just sitting around waiting to find out what happened to her."

"Don't let it interfere with the Arrow Lake investigation," he says. The tone of his voice suggests he's trying to warn me about something, but I stopped being intimidated by Creagan a long time ago.

If there is one thing that gives me the occasional moment of hesitation when it comes to being in the FBI, it's Creagan. It's never been exactly a lovefest between us. There's been some friction since I joined the Bureau at twenty-three. I'll never say that I was in the shadow of my father, especially since his career is with the CIA rather than the FBI, but everybody knew who I was from the beginning.

And from the beginning, Creagan made it clear he didn't exactly have the most faith in me. So, I proceeded to prove him wrong time and time again. At this point he doesn't have much of a choice but to believe in my skill. He just doesn't like to admit to it.

"I'm more than capable of managing my career and prioritizing investigations," I say.

"Good to hear. And speaking of which, you said that you'll be going to the campground this week?" he asks.

"Yes. The day after tomorrow," I tell him. "I'm meeting with the team to discuss progress and go over new evidence."

"Perfect. You can take Agent James with you."

I sit in silence for a few seconds. "Excuse me, what?"

"Agent James. The new agent I told you about. She will be back in Harlan then and I can't imagine you would make the drive down to Sherando Ridge without going through Harlan to visit your cousin. You can meet Agent James there and she can accompany you on the investigation. It will be the perfect opportunity for her to start getting to know you, and she can shadow you while you're at the campground," Creagan says.

"Shadow me?" I ask. "Creagan, this isn't the Big Sisters program."

"No, but it is an order. Whether you want to deal with it or not, I'm still your supervisor. I will let her know you'll be there the day after tomorrow. Watch your email. I'll send her contact information."

With that, the call ends. I don't know if he hangs up first or I do, but there isn't a goodbye from either side.

When I get off the phone, I'm angry and frustrated. I have enough going on right now. I don't need to add watching over a brand-new agent to my responsibilities. And I definitely don't need anybody shadowing me. But it seems I don't have a choice. So, I do what I know will make me feel better the fastest. I pick my phone back up and call Sam.

"Hey," I say when he answers.

"Hey," he says. "Are you okay? You sound upset."

"Just aggravated. Creagan hasn't let go of wanting me to buddy up with this new agent. Now he wants me to bring her along with me when I go back to the campground so she can shadow me during my investigation," I explain.

"Has he never met you?" Sam wonders.

"You know, I'm starting to wonder," I say.

"Look, this is obviously a thing for him. And even if you don't want to consider the possibility, it seems he's asking you to do this because he trusts you. Maybe he sees potential in this new agent, but he knows you would be the one to make her the best she can be," he offers.

I head for the kitchen to make another cup of coffee.

"You manage to make it sound so optimistic," I comment. "Why are you so good? It makes me feel guilty."

"It shouldn't make you feel guilty," he says. "Trust me, I understand where you're coming from. I'm just trying to make you feel better about the whole thing. You shouldn't look at it like a punishment or a roadblock. You should see it as a chance to unleash another kick-ass FBI agent on the world."

"I'm not quite there, yet. But I'll work on it," I say.

"That's my girl. All I can ask for is progress."

"Uh-huh."

We'll see how that works for him after I meet her.

"Why don't we talk about something more pleasant?" he suggests.

"Aren't you busy?" I ask. "Shouldn't you be solving crime and helping old ladies across the street?"

"As devoted as I am to my hidden persona of Boy Scout Batman, I'm actually on my lunch break right now," he says. "Which makes this the perfect opportunity to talk about our wedding."

"Not that I'm averse to talking about our wedding, but what about your lunch break makes it the perfect time?" I ask.

"Ruby Bea's Catering brought in box lunches for us," he says. "They might be on the list for caterers if we decide to have the wedding here in Sherwood."

"That actually is a good transition," I note. "Good job."

I lean back against the counter and sip on my coffee as we bounce ideas about various details back and forth. It's hard to really nail anything down when we haven't even decided where we're getting married yet.

For a little while last year there was some ambiguity as to when our engagement actually started. I sort of asked Sam to marry me as he carried me out of a building after I had been shot. I say sort of, because I didn't actually ask so much as tell him to do it. Following that up with my almost immediately going unconscious, I'm not sure if he even answered me. Sam seems to think he did, but he's not positive about it, either.

That left us with a couple of months of uncertainty. We knew we were getting married, but weren't all the way sure if we were officially engaged. That brought us to Christmas and the official proposal and ring. We figure that makes it the perfect choice for the season when we will get married as well.

That was the easy choice. It's harder deciding what kind of wedding we want. I'm torn between different lives. Part of me always envisioned getting married in Florida. It's a place I love dearly and where my mother is buried. Where she died. Where my last memories of her are, even though I didn't realize that until just a couple of years ago.

Florida is a perfect setting for a destination wedding. A beach backdrop or something unexpected and fun, like exchanging vows on a hot air balloon. It would be small and intimate. Just our closest friends and family gathered around us.

Then there's home in Sherwood. Our home, where our lives together began. Not just when I came back to help Sam with his investigation into a string of deaths and disappearances in town, but when we were just children. For all the moving around and mystery of my childhood, Sherwood was always there. I came there often to visit my grandparents who lived in the house that's now our home. Having a wedding there would be much more traditional and let us invite far more of the people we care about.

It's a debate we've been going back and forth on for several weeks now. As of now, we don't seem to be getting any closer to a conclusion. As soon as we feel we're leaning toward the same option, one of us will change his or her mind and start leaning forward the other. And that one will catch up with the same thing only for the other to start going back the other way.

It'll come to us eventually. Hopefully fairly quickly, so we can actually plan it before the date comes.

THIRTEEN

LATER THAT EVENING, Dean and I sit close together in front of my computer and make the video call to Allison Garrett. When she answers, she looks as though she isn't sure how to feel about the situation. Gone is the bright, vibrant smile in the beach picture; in its place are tightened eyebrows and a slightly downturned mouth.

"Hello," she says.

"Hi, Allison," I start. "I'm Agent Emma Griffin. I'm with the FBI. This is my cousin, Dean Steele. He's the private investigator who got in touch with you."

I gesture toward Dean and he waves at the screen.

"Hi," she says. She gives me a bit of a strange look. "Did you say you're with the FBI?"

"Yes," I nod, then press one hand to my chest. "But I'm not talking to you now in that official capacity. This is a private investigation."

She nods, still looking hesitant.

"As I said in my messages, we just want to talk to you about Ashley," Dean adds. "We're trying to figure out what happened to her when she went missing. Her parents are ready to bring her home."

"I think they've been ready since the day she left," Allison comments.

Dean nods. "They have been. You probably heard about the deaths in Sherando Ridge, at Arrow Lake Campground."

"Yes," she says. "It's horrible. I can't believe that's somewhere I used to go all the time. I still go up there sometimes to go hiking. It's so hard to believe something like that was happening right there and nobody knew."

"Did you know that Ashley's mother and father contacted the police to find out if Ashley might be one of the victims?" I ask.

Allison swallows hard. "Yes. We still stay in touch a bit. Not as much now as we used to, but when you reached out to me, I called them. I didn't want to do anything behind their back."

"Why would talking to us be doing something behind their back?" I ask.

"If they didn't know there was an investigation going on," she explains. "A lot of people have latched onto Ashley's case over the years. And not for the best reasons."

"What do you mean?" Dean frowns.

"People want to tell stories about her. They want to come up with sensationalized explanations or spread gruesome rumors. There have been a couple of TV shows that have approached Misty and John about featuring Ashley's case and acted as if they were going to get her name out so more people would know about her. But then they just painted her as a rebellious teenager who was off getting into mischief and ended up disappearing. Almost as though it was her fault. I didn't want that to happen to them again."

"They didn't mention any of that when we spoke with them," I say.

"It isn't the most pleasant thing for them to talk about," she says. "I'd think they are probably pretty embarrassed by it."

"I can imagine," Dean sympathizes. "But that's why we're doing this. We want to make sure that whatever happened to Ashley is uncovered. And whoever is responsible, if there is anyone responsible, will be held accountable for what theyhe or she did."

"What do you mean 'if there is anyone responsible'?" Allison asks, sounding put off by the choice of phrase. "You think she did something to herself?"

I wasn't expecting her to suggest that. Up until that moment, it hadn't even occurred to me to think she might have harmed herself. The expected behaviors weren't there. At least, no one was talking about them.

"We don't know what happened," I say, trying to hold her to the conversation. She has information we need and if she gets angry and logs off, we won't be able to get it out of her. "But we want to know. That's why we're talking to you. We know you were very close."

This seems to take some of the edge off. Allison nods.

"We were. And Vivian. We were always together."

"Ashley's parents mentioned you and Vivian are a little older than Ashley," I say.

Allison nods again. "Yes. Almost two years."

"So, you weren't in the same year of school. How did you end up forming such a close bond? She was still in middle school and you were in high school."

"We met when she was in the sixth grade and Vivian and I were in eighth grade," Allison explains. "In our school, enrichment classes weren't divided by grade. None of the three of us could decide which enrichment class we wanted to take, so all three of us ended up in what they called Exploratory. Which basically just meant we rotated through different classes for each semester. That's when we became friends. We stayed friends after that, even when we went into high school. She was really looking forward to joining us in a couple of years."

Her eyes well with tears and her head drops down for a second before she looks up at us again, fighting to keep her composure.

"Would you say Ashley was mature for her age?" I ask.

Allison nods. "She never seemed younger than we were. She was so smart. If I didn't know her, I might even think she was older than we were. She had always been the one to make the good decisions."

I notice her wording but don't know if she did it on purpose, so I decide to move on.

"What do you remember about when she went missing? Was Ashley at all upset on that day or the days leading up to it? Did she talk about leaving, or problems she was having with her family or anything?"

Allison shakes her head. "No. She was in a fantastic mood. She was happy and excited to be out. The only thing that was upsetting her at all was the weather. It had been raining for so long and the temperature dropped so it didn't feel as much like a summer hike. I remember her saying her mom told her she had to bring a hoodie with her, and she thought it was so ridiculous. She didn't want to have it and had almost left it in the car, but then at the last second, she pulled it out. She ended up wearing it an hour later."

She lets out another short laugh.

"How was her relationship with her mother?" Dean asks.

"They were close," Allison says. "They argued like any mother and thirteen-year-old daughter. But it was never anything serious. I never heard her say she didn't want to be at home anymore, or anything like that. She spent a lot of time with her mom. Ashley was never one of those kids who was embarrassed to be seen with her mom. She would actually still hold her mother's hand when they were at the mall. Not because she was scared or couldn't get around by herself or anything. Just because she wanted to hold her hand."

"How about her father?"

"They were close, too. I never saw any problems between them. Maybe not as close as with her mom, but not in a bad way," Allison shrugs.

"And she had a sister," I say.

That's when I realize how easily we've slipped into referring to Ashley only in the past tense. I hate that it's the natural inclination.

No one, not even her parents, has said anything about her in the present tense. Nothing has been that she is a certain way or did certain things. Everything is about who she used to be and what she used to do.

Even if they still have hope she could be alive, they're too afraid to say it.

"Yes," Allison confirms. "Leona. She's three years older."

"So, it would have been more likely that you were friends with her than with Ashley," Dean comments.

Allison's eyes narrow. "Why are you so fixated on our ages? People can't be friends if they aren't at the exact same age?"

"It's not that," Dean says. "It's just an observation."

"We're trying to understand the dynamics," I add. "It's not that you shouldn't be friends with someone younger, it's just interesting that of the two sisters, you were friends with one with a larger age gap than another."

"Leona is really quiet. Not unpleasant or anything, just really quiet and not exactly social. When we were over at Ashley's house, she would sometimes come and hang out with us, but Ashley was much more like us than Leona, so we were friends with her," Allison explains.

"So, Ashley and Leona got along well?" I ask.

"The most part," she shrugs. "I mean, there was some tension between them sometimes. But I think that's the way it is with all sisters. It would probably be stranger if they got along perfectly all the time."

"That's true," I say. "So, what can you tell us about that day?"

I don't mention anything Ashley's parents told us. I don't want to lead Allison or dissuade her from saying anything she might have if I hadn't given her a basis for what we already know.

"The three of us, Ashley, Vivian, and I, wanted to hang out because it had been so rainy. We went to the park to do some hiking. We live so close by, going there is like going to any neighborhood playground. We'd been a million times before. It was nothing new.

We set up camp and Ashley was talking about how she hadn't told her parents we were camping out. That was a little bit strange, because we almost always camped out when we went to the park unless we were just there for a couple of hours in the morning.

"We told her we were sure they knew, and it was going to be fine. She was really anxious about it. As though she thought she was going to get in trouble. I don't know, maybe she'd had an argument with them earlier and we didn't know about it. But she was really on edge. She kept looking at her phone and checking the reception. Eventually, she said she was going up to the bathhouse and was going to try to call her parents," she says.

"Did you let her go by herself?" Dean asks.

"Yeah," Allison nods. "It wasn't all that far away. And as I said, this is a familiar area. She came back and said everything was fine, but that she was going to have to leave early. The next morning she wasn't at the campsite anymore. Her shoes, phone, and everything else was gone, so we figured her parents had come and picked her up from the parking lot next to the bathhouse. We realized she'd left her backpack and decided to take it to her house. That's when everything fell apart."

"But you were in the park that whole day?" I ask.

"All day. We got there in the early afternoon and stayed the whole time."

"And you were alone?" Dean asks.

Allison shifts uncomfortably. "Yes. Vivian's family had brought us up there a bunch of times before, so Ashley's and my parents just assumed they would be with us. Vivian's mom and stepdad thought she was with her dad. We weren't planning to do anything wrong. We just felt old enough to hang out in a place we were already comfortable with by ourselves. We didn't want adults hovering over us."

Her voice breaks a bit, and her lip starts to quiver, but she takes a deep breath and steels herself.

"I still feel guilty about it. And for not looking for her. We should have realized something was wrong."

An idea comes to my mind. "Dean and I will be up there at the lake the day after tomorrow to continue the investigation there. Would you be able to meet us at the park and show us where everything happened?"

"Sure," Allison nods without hesitation. "I'll talk to Vivian and see if she can come, too."

"That would be perfect."

When the call ends, I look over at Dean. He has the same expression on his face.

Something isn't right about her story.

FOURTEEN

"You are absolutely positive you're okay and nothing's going to happen over the next couple of days?"

I'm holding my phone between my shoulder and ear as I pack for my trip down to the park.

"Yes," Bellamy insists. "Everything is perfectly okay. I feel fine and I just went to the doctor this morning. She says as far as she can tell, I'm still not showing any signs of impending labor. Things will take their time for a little while. So, you're fine. Go do what you need to do."

"Okay. Well, I'll miss you."

"I'll miss you, too. I'll see you when you get back," she says.

"It better just be you," I warn her. "Don't you dare let that baby come without me."

"I'll give her a stern talking-to and make sure she understands Auntie Emma tells her she has to wait."

"Do I get to be there?" Eric calls out from the background.

"If you have to be," I roll my eyes.

"Great," he says. "Thanks for your flexibility."

"How are you doing?" I ask.

"Doing fine," he says. "I've got everything under control. I'm putting the car seat in today. We packed B's hospital bag. Now it's just a matter of picking out what she's going to wear on her way home, and we're ready to go."

Eric sounds completely calm and collected. Which tells me he's still freaking out. He gets very calm and steady when things are really getting to him. If he's a little bit upset or things are going wrong, then they're going to work out, so he can be loud and upset. When they are really serious, he starts to shut down. When Eric gets quiet in a crisis, that's when you know it's time to worry.

"Alright. Well, I'm not going to be gone long. A couple of days, max. Call me if anything happens or if you even think something is going to happen."

"We will," Bellamy says.

I don't feel a lot more confident about this trip when I get off the phone. But I try to tell myself I'm only going to be a few hours away. If something happens, they can call me, and I will get to her as fast as I can. But it's not just worrying about missing the birth of Bellamy's child that's giving me pause. I also know what's waiting for me in Harlan.

And it's more than Xavier and whatever complicated, potentially disturbing game he's playing with my father. Creagan made sure to go over my head and get in touch with the new agent so she knew to be waiting for me today when I go through town.

It wasn't that I was going to try to not meet with her or pretend I'd forgotten about the whole thing. I know this is inevitable. But his setting it up makes it feel like a blind date. It's uncomfortable, to say the least.

When my bags are packed and I'm prepared with the basket of road trip snacks I always keep in the car, I call my father and let him know I'm heading out. He mumbles his usual words of wisdom, which are basically the same ones he's been giving me since I was a little girl. Apparently, his advice is applicable whether I'm trying to jump rope a thousand times without missing, going to my first formal dance, starting college, or investigating serial murder.

There was a time when he would have started and I would have just let his voice go to white noise because I'd heard it a thousand times before. I might have even tried to cut him off early and hurried away. I can't do that anymore. After spending so many years without hearing those words, I treasure every time I hear them. Any chance I get to hear my father's voice, I want to take it. I know too well what it's like to not have that chance.

The drive from my father's house to Harlan is uneventful, and soon I'm in the outskirts where Xavier and Dean live to pick them up. They will ride with me down to the park, and Agent James will follow us. The guys are waiting outside when I pull into the driveway. Xavier waves enthusiastically and grabs the handles of the three duffel bags sitting at his feet.

I've gotten used to his compulsion to obsessively overpack for anything we're doing. It makes him feel more comfortable. I've actually found that sometimes he brings along things I never would have thought of, but that prove useful. As long as I have an extra corner of the trunk and the floorboards are open, he is welcome to bring whatever he wants.

Dean is much more practical with his single bag and a pillow tucked under his arm. They climb into the car and Dean searches my face.

"You look excited," he notes.

"You know how I feel about this," I say.

"About what?" Xavier asks, bouncing forward and leaning around my seat so he can look at me. A second later it seems to sink in. "Oh. The new agent. What's the problem you have with her?"

"It's not that I have a specific problem with her. She doesn't even matter. I just don't like the idea that Creagan's attaching somebody to me. Especially not during an investigation. I don't need an extra person latching on while I'm trying to solve these crimes," I say.

"That's how you got me," Xavier points out. "I attached myself to you while you were investigating Lakyn's disappearance. You briefly considered I might be a murderer, but I still latched myself onto you."

"That's kind of how you got me, too," Dean adds. "You were figuring out the escape room from hell on that train and I just kind of joined in. And come to think of it, you thought I was a murderer, too, for a little while there."

"See?" Xavier says.

"And remind me again, how did you and Sam reunite?" Dean asks, an edge of teasing on the words.

"Alright," I roll my eyes, pushing them away from me as I turn back to the road. "I got it."

"Did you ever suspect him of killing people, too?" Xavier asks. "That would give you the full collection."

"Not that I can recall," I shrug. "But my collection is still full."

"You're going to be fine," Dean says, reaching into the snack basket for a strip of beef jerky. "You'll probably just meet her, let her follow you around while we check in on the investigation, then you'll give her your card, tell her good luck, and send her off on her way. Creagan will be off your back and you can go right back to your untamed rebel ways."

I glare at him. "Eat your damn jerky."

I DIDN'T WANT TO PICK AGENT JAMES UP AT HER HOUSE. THAT just feels too familiar and uncomfortable. Instead, I asked her to meet us at the coffee shop in Harlan. I'm not sure what to expect as we pull up. I don't particularly want to go inside and do the dance of "should we sit down and have some coffee before we go, or do we just hit the road?" Is there a conversation we need to have here?

I reach for my phone so I can call her to tell her to come out. Then I realize somebody is sitting at one of the tables scattered on the small patio out front. It's difficult to see her.

"Is that her?" I ask, nodding toward the table.

Dean looks, tilting his head around as if trying to get a better view of her, then looks at me.

"How am I supposed to know that? I've never met her," he says.

"Then why would you look?" I ask.

"Because you asked about her," Dean says. "It's just instinct to look in the direction somebody is indicating."

"Hey! Are you Agent James?"

Dean and I look into the back seat and see Xavier hanging halfway out the window.

"How did he get the window open?" Dean asks.

"He pressed a button," I say. "I don't put child locks on them."

"Maybe you should consider it," Dean tells me.

"Why?" I ask. "He's an adult. He can open windows with abandon."

"Agent James?" Xavier calls out. "If you are Agent James of the FBI, please make yourself known. If you are not, disregard this comment."

Dean gestures toward me and I shrug.

The woman at the table looks over at the car and stands up. She waves and Xavier slithers backward to drop back down into his seat.

"I think that's her."

"Thank you, Xavier," I say. I let out a breath. "Let's do this thing."

We get out of the car and I realize the woman is already almost over to us, moving quickly and smiling widely enough to almost make me take a step back. Her dark hair is pulled up in a bun behind her head, dark sunglasses balanced in front of it rather than over her eyes. A black suit and crisp white shirt are cliche FBI. A cliche I've fallen right in line with plenty of times, admittedly, but still a cliche.

"Hi," she greets us, already holding out her hand toward me when she's still a few feet away. "I'm Aviva. Aviva James."

"Aviva?" I ask. "Emma Griffin. Nice to meet you." She takes my hand and shakes it firmly.

"That's a beautiful name," Dean comments. I glare over at him. He's definitely noticed her big eyes and dark hair.

"Thank you. It means 'life,'" she says.

"Actually, it means 'springtime,'" Xavier corrects.

"Xavier," I say under my breath.

"Your name," Xavier continues. "You said it means life. Which I can understand, because it has many of the same sound cues as words that do evoke the concept of life. Vitality. Verve. Vital. Vivacious. Then, of course, viva. Which means live. 'Vive la France' and what have you. But Aviva is actually a Hebrew name that means springlike or fresh."

"Xavier," I murmur again. "We don't correct people about what their names mean. If that's what she says her name means, that's what it means."

"But it's not," he protests.

"It doesn't matter," I hiss.

"Yes, it does. It's the meaning of the word. I can't just say 'hi, my name is Xavier, it means 'Lord High Lizard King,'" he says.

"Xavier," I warn.

He looks over at her and holds his hand out. "Hi. My name is Xavier Renton, it means Lord High Lizard King."

"Nice to meet you, Xavier. I actually like springtime better for the meaning of my name," she offers.

"Good. Because that's what it means," he says.

She shakes his hand. "Hi, I'm Aviva. It means 'springtime.' But my friends call me Ava."

He looks at her for a second, then at Dean, then me, then back at her. "Was that just an added bit of information, or an invitation?"

Dean gently guides Xavier to the side so he can shake Ava's hand.

"Hi, I'm Dean Steele. I'm a private investigator."

"Ava," she says, shaking his hand.

"I guess Dean is her friend," Xavier whispers. "This could get confusing."

"You're Emma's cousin," Ava says. Her eyes then snap to me. "I'm sorry. That sounds completely creepy and stalker-like." Her hand flies up to cover her mouth. "I shouldn't have said that. I'm sorry. That was really insensitive of me. I should be more careful with my words when I'm talking to someone like you."

"Someone like me?" I raise an eyebrow.

"Someone who's gone through all the things you have. I shouldn't just throw around words like that. Or at least give you a trigger warning or something before I'm careless," she explains.

"Can you warn someone you're going to do something carelessly?" Xavier wonders, still in a low voice.

I'm almost convinced he thinks she really can't hear him.

"It's fine," I tell her. "If I needed a trigger warning for everything that I've seen or been through, there would have to be one on essentially everything I encounter."

She laughs. I'm not sure why. A second later she realizes the rest of us aren't laughing and stops, looking uneasy, but still smiling.

"I'm really looking forward to today," she says.

"We're going to look through bones and teeth and pieces of people's belongings that were scattered through the woods and chained to the bottom of a lake by two serial killers," I say.

"I know," she says after a thoughtful pause. "It's just my first investigation."

"You're not investigating," I clarify. "You're shadowing. You're just there to watch me and get used to things."

Dean gives me a slow, incredulous look. A bit of guilt shoots through me.

"I'm sorry," I say. "That was..."

Ava shakes her head, holding up her hands to stop me. "No. No, it's fine. I understand. I'm too eager. I won't get in your way."

"Well, it's a campground. There's a lot of space. So that shouldn't be hard," Xavier adds.

"Speaking of which," I say, looking her up and down. "The suit might not fare terribly well out there."

Ava looks down. "Oh. Yeah, probably not." She looks up at me. "I just wanted to look my best when I met you. It's such an honor. You have no idea how long I've admired you. I've been following your career since you went to Feathered Nest. You're such an inspiration to me, and I just can't believe you're willing to be my mentor. It's amazing. I barely know what to do."

"Whatever she says," Xavier says.

Dean gives the smile he always does when it's time to step in and be a buffer.

"Just shadowing her," he says. "Emma is the best, so just pay attention to her."

Ava nods.

This is off to a splendid start.

"I'm going in to get some coffee, then we'll get going. We don't want it to be too late before we get to the campground. I need some time with the main investigation before we talk to Allison and Vivian."

I go into the coffee shop and get the biggest cup of their strongest, darkest coffee. Stepping back outside, I drop my sunglasses down over my eyes and head for the car.

FIFTEEN

"She's not going to make it a month," I say the second we get in the car and head out of the parking lot.

"Why do you say that?" Dean asks. "She seems nice."

"Exactly," I say. "She seems nice. And just a little bit unhinged."

"I think that was the coffee," Xavier shrugs. "I notice at least two cups on the table with her and I can smell it coming off her. Maybe she has a caffeine sensitivity and was feeling jittery."

"She was feeling something," I mutter. "She sounded as if she can barely keep it together."

"I think she was a little starstruck," Dean says. "Did you hear the way she was gushing over you?"

"That's ridiculous," I say.

"No, it's not," he counters. "You obviously made a big impact on her. And now she's not only getting to meet you, but see you in action and learn from you. That's a big deal. Wasn't there anybody who you would have had that kind of reaction about when you first got started?"

"No," I say. "I had my father. I didn't need to be impressed by anybody else."

"Fair enough. But not everybody has that. It was an awkward start, but give her a chance," he says.

IT'S EERIE TO BE BACK AT ARROW LAKE CAMPGROUND. THIS IS the first time I've been back since we left a couple of weeks ago. I've been checking up on the investigation and staying in touch with the people on the ground here over video and phone calls, but other cases have kept me from being here in person until now.

That brutal night wasn't long ago, but somehow it also feels surreal. Almost as though it didn't happen. I step out of the car in the makeshift parking lot set up near the campground and look around. There's far more life and activity here now than there was the last time I was here. Everywhere I look, there are cars and people and stations set up to process evidence.

The last day I was here, the team was smaller. Now it almost looks like a movie set. Part of that is simply because of the sheer unfathomable nature of the crimes that took place here. It wasn't just murder. There were so many more layers. I'm still trying to really wrap my head around all of it.

But I'm less concerned about how I feel being here than I am about Dean. I look over at him. He's still standing by the car as if it's anchoring him. His eyes move slowly around the space, sweeping over the people; flitting over the blue tarps spread out across the ground with their waterlogged mementos of horror lined up across them.

This isn't easy for him. He's the reason I came here in the first place. It started with something inconsequential. Just a TV show. Some supernatural ghost hunters. Something I thought was silly, but the rest of the group wanted to see. I had no idea what it would turn into. How it would unlock a part of my cousin's life I had no idea even existed.

I look at him differently now. Not in a bad way. Not that I'm judging him, or that I don't trust him as much. There's just more about him. I can't help but wonder sometimes if I have the whole story now.

"Agent Griffin," a voice calls up from down closer to the water.

I look and see an officer coming toward me.

"Hey, Calvin," I say.

"Good to see you back in person," he says.

I nod. "How is everything going?"

"We've found quite a few more items. If you want to take a look..."

He gestures toward the beach and I nod again. "Absolutely." I glance back over my shoulder. "Dean, I'm going down to the lake. Where's Xavier?" I realize I can't see him and I look around, searching the shadowy spots between the cabins and under the evidence tents. "He didn't bring all that equipment with him again, did he?"

"No. He went up to the cabin to say hello. Just in case there are spirits there. Because, as he said, you did not conclusively prove there aren't."

"According to him, it's impossible to prove something doesn't exist," I say.

"Exactly," he nods.

I head down to the lake and find more people. More tarps. More evidence tags. So much came up out of the water that night; it's hard to imagine so much more still existing beneath the dark surface of the lake. At the same time, the water stretches on far into the distance and the lake is deceptively deep. We know Rodney and Laura Mitchell were killing for years. There's no telling how much could have sunk to the bottom or floated further out from shore. We'll do everything possible to find as much of it as we can. We'll figure out who it belonged to and how it got there.

I spend the next several minutes going from station to station, looking at evidence on the tarps and talking with the investigators. They catch me up on the progress that's been made in identifying remains brought up from the water and found in the surrounding woods. We know of several victims who haven't yet been found among the bodies, and there are other partial skeletons we haven't been able to connect to identities yet.

So we have to keep working. We aren't done until everybody has a name, and every person we know was lost on this campground is found and brought home.

"What's this?" I ask, crouching down to pick up what looks like a ring from the closest tarp.

"We just found that today," Calvin tells me. "We divided the lake up into a grid and have been sifting through the silt trying to find any other remains or belongings. That came up just a couple of hours ago."

"Was it attached to anything?" I ask.

"No," he says. "And nothing came up with it."

I look at the ring, turning it from all angles to examine the unusual insignia in relief on the round front.

"Do you know what it is? What this represents?" I ask. "It looks like an organization or a fraternity. If we can identify what it is, it might help to narrow down the identity of who owned it."

"DeMolay."

The voice beside me makes me jump and I whip my head to the side. Ava is beside me, looking over my shoulder at the ring in my hand.

"Excuse me?" I ask.

She looks at me, then points at the ring.

"DeMolay. That ring. It's from the International Order of DeMolay."

I continue to stare at her, those words absolutely nothing to me.

"What's that?" I ask.

"It's a fraternal group. Almost like a baby version of the Freemasons."

"Is that actually an accurate assessment of what they are? If not, for the love of God, don't tell Xavier you said that," I say.

"Said what?" Xavier asks, coming down the beach toward me. "I said hello to them for you, by the way."

Now is not the time to get into another discussion about the presence of long-dead campers in and among the cabins, so I move past it. Instead, I show him the ring.

"Oh, the International Order of DeMolay," he says.

"Does everyone know about this thing but me?" I ask.

"I'm sure not everyone," Xavier says.

"I didn't," Calvin offers.

"See?" Xavier says, gesturing toward him. "He didn't."

"Great. But here's the question. How obscure is this group? Could this ring be linked to a victim?" I ask.

"Maybe," Xavier says.

"Have you checked for an engraving?" Ava asks.

I hand the ring back to Calvin. "Research the organization. Find out if there are member lists and if you can access them. Look at rings from different years; find out if there are ways to differentiate the year that particular ring was made or given to whoever owned it. That should start narrowing it down."

Calvin nods and I head back up the beach. Ava and Xavier come quickly behind me. Closer to the cabins, another tent and table are set up to hold the evidence found in the woods. It's nearly covered with fragments of clothing, tiny pieces of bone, papers, and other miscellaneous objects. These are only what's been found today or possibly the in last couple of days. It will be recorded and tagged here, then collected and sent to the lab for further investigation.

I talk to the investigator nearby. They've found some pieces of cloth that look as if they might belong to one of the boys who went missing a decade ago but who hasn't been found. They've also found items that seem to belong to people of several different ages, but they can't be absolutely sure to whom they belong, or if they even have anything to do with the cases here. This is a campground, after all.

For all we know, teenagers might have sneaked in here at night over the years and left trace evidence.

It just makes our job that much harder.

Xavier and Ava come over and I gesture toward them.

"You probably remember Xavier," I say. "And this is ..."

"Agent Aviva James," she says, sticking out her hand and shaking the officer's. "FBI"

"Good to meet you," he says. He looks back at me. "I have a few more things to process and then I'll have a more thorough report. Are you going to be around for a while?"

"I'll be here for a bit longer today. I'm staying for a couple of days before I need to go back to take care of a few things."

He nods. "Good. I'll have something for you to review tomorrow."

SIXTEEN

As we're walking away from the evidence table, Ava looks over at Xavier.

"I thought you had already talked to him," she says. "You said you told them I said hi."

"I wasn't talking about him," Xavier says. "I was talking about the ghosts."

I let out a long breath.

"Ghosts?" she asks. "Oh, my gosh. That's right. You were here doing a paranormal investigation when you uncovered the murders."

"No," I clarify. "I was distinctly not doing a paranormal investigation. I was here because a woman went missing. A real, live woman disappeared moments after appearing on camera on a live stream I was watching. That was why I was here."

"I was doing a paranormal investigation," Xavier offers.

I throw my hand up toward him. "There you go."

I'm headed up toward the cabin where a little girl named Violet Montgomery disappeared, setting off the chain of events that brought me here. And that will never leave Dean's mind. Now that we know what happened to her, I want to go over the area more carefully.

While she didn't have anything to do with the other deaths, her disappearance and the discovery of her body in a cave in an isolated part of the woods brought attention to this place.

Laura Mitchell was devastated thinking about the small child's death, a sign that told me she wasn't the one responsible for it. But Rodney didn't seem to show as much concern about it. That tells me he was more calculating than his mother. While she never considered their actions wrong, and therefore wouldn't have tried to think of ways not to get caught, Rodney did.

He might not have fully understood the magnitude of their actions, but I wouldn't put it past him to be drawn to the cabin where Violet's family was staying. It's possible some of the answers we're looking for could be connected to this space.

Ava stops a few yards from the cabin and stares at it.

"Wow," she says.

"What?" I ask.

She shakes her head. "It's just... this is Cabin Thirteen."

That makes my skin crawl a little bit, but I don't show it.

"Yes," I nod. "It is. One of them, anyway."

"Exactly," she says. "What are the chances you would have two cases that would bring you to different places with the same name?"

I immediately look over at Xavier. "That was rhetorical. She does not want you to calculate that."

He nods and I can almost see the gears that were starting to churn in his head slow and stop.

"It's so surreal to be here," she says, looking around. "I know you were an agent for a long time before your first run-in with a Cabin Thirteen, but that was the case that brought my attention to you. That was what really solidified in my mind that this is what I want to do. That I could do it."

"Weren't you already in school by then?" I ask.

"Yeah," I was. "That's the thing. I started wanting to be in the FBI when I was much younger. It was something I thought about a lot. I really thought it could be an amazing life. You know, when you're in elementary school and middle school and the teachers are asking you that whole, 'what do you want to be when you grow up' thing?" she asks. "Everybody is saying things like singer. Actor. Marine biologist."

"That's a big one," I acknowledge.

"Right? I never really understood that. I mean, I get that dolphins are cute, but there's a big jump between having sparkly ones on your notebook and wanting to study them intensively for your career. And yet, I'm the one they all looked at strangely when I said I wanted to be in the FBI. As if it was a completely ridiculous thing to consider. I can't tell you how many guys said I couldn't do that because I'm a girl," she says.

"You don't have to tell me," I commiserate. "But why? Why would you want to do this? Do you have family in law enforcement?"

She goes quiet and turns her back to the cabin to look out toward the lake. "There was a case in my hometown. I was really young, but I remember hearing about it. My parents were watching the news one night and they started talking about this disappearance. It was the first time I ever heard about somebody being missing and I was fascinated. They tried to turn the TV off before I heard much of it, but I was hooked. I watched every news report I could and tried to find the newspaper to read. I had to know what happened."

"What case was it?" I ask.

"A girl named Bethany DeAngelis. There's a camp right outside my hometown. Or, there used to be. I guess it's still there, but it hasn't operated in years. Camp Pine Trails. When Bethany was just out of high school, she went to spend her last summer there as a camper. Her best friend woke up one morning and Bethany was missing. They found her bathing suit at the edge of the lake, but that was it. They couldn't find any other trace of her. That sparked my interest in crime. I knew I wanted to find people who did terrible things to other people."

"I know the case," I tell her. "Fifteen years later her best friend went back to the camp because someone wanted to do a film adaptation of Bethany's story."

"Right," Ava nods, looking over her shoulder at me and nodding.

Before I can say anything else, I notice Dean coming toward us.

"We should get going if we're going to meet Allison Garrett on time," he says.

I glance down at my phone.

"I didn't realize how long we've been here," I say. "Do you know how to get to where we're meeting her? It shouldn't be far from here, right?"

"Actually," he says. "You might be surprised."

I'M EXPECTING TO WALK OVER TO WHERE THE GIRLS SET UP their campsite that night. Instead, Dean ushers me over to the parking lot, and we have to drive almost ten minutes to another area. He parks in a lot next to a bathhouse.

"This must be where Allison was talking about Ashley's going," he says.

"But this is nowhere near the campground," I observe. "Why would her mother warn her not to go to the abandoned cabins if they were staying all the way over here?"

"If she didn't know where they were actually staying," Dean says. "Remember, Vivian's parents weren't really here. The girls chose their own campsite."

I'm still thinking about this when I get out of the car. We hear a car door close across the parking lot. Allison Garrett tucks her phone into her back pocket and uses one hand to pull a ponytail holder out of her hair and shake it out before heading over toward us.

"Hi," I say. "Thanks for meeting us here."

"Absolutely," she says, shuddering slightly as she looks around. "I haven't been back here since then. It's kind of weird to be back."

"You haven't been here at all?" Dean asks.

"I've come to the park, but not this area. I just couldn't face it. After the police brought Vivian and me back so we could show them what happened, I left and didn't look back. I thought I'd never see it again. Not until Ashley's found," Allison says.

"Well, that's why we're here," I say. "To try to find her. Whatever happened to her started here. So it's where we're going to start."

Allison nods and looks over toward the entrance to the parking lot. "Vivian should be here soon. She left work to make sure she made it."

Almost as if her saying that ushered Vivian in, a car appears on the narrow road leading to the lot and turns in. It slides into the spot directly next to Allison's, and a girl with spiked black hair and intense makeup climbs out. It's a stark change from the picture taken of her just a few months ago, but I can still recognize her.

Allison meets her in the middle of the parking lot with a hug. It lingers, and I can see both are struggling with the emotions brought up by coming back here. At the same time, I wish Xavier hadn't stayed back at Arrow Lake with Ava to give her a tour replicating our movements from the night we were here. I'd be interested to see what he thinks of these two, and what they're telling me with what they aren't saying at all.

.

SEVENTEEN

WHEN THE HUG ENDS, Allison leads Vivian over to us.

"This is Dean Steele and Emma Griffin," she introduces. "They're the ones looking into Ashley's disappearance."

Vivian nods, sniffling back tears. "Thank you. It's been a long time."

"It has," I say. "Which is why she deserves to have her story told. And the two of you hold a really important part of that story. You were with her right before she disappeared."

"We didn't see where she went," Vivian says.

"I know," I nod. "But you were with her leading up to her disappearance. You might have some insight about it you don't even realize. Which is why we were hoping you would come out here with us, and kind of walk us through what happened. You already did it with the police, I know. But we aren't police. We investigate in a different way."

I don't explain exactly what that means. The point is to make them trust us, to be willing to give us more information.

"Where do you want to start?" Allison asks.

"Where did you start?" I ask.

They exchange glances.

"Right here," Vivian says. "This is where we parked."

"Where you parked?" Dean asks. "None of you was old enough to drive."

"My dad started to teach me to drive when I was thirteen," Vivian explains. "By the time I was fifteen, I figured I already had almost two years of experience, so I could manage to drive around a little. My sister worked a lot and was staying with her boyfriend more often than she was home, so her car pretty much just sat behind the house. Mom worked overnight, and I knew she wouldn't notice the car was missing until she woke up after getting home from work the next day. So, I took it."

"Did you tell the police that when they interviewed you?" I ask.

Vivian shakes her head. "No. They didn't ask."

"They didn't ask how you got here?" Dean asks.

She shakes her head again and Allison joins in. "All they cared about was that we were here without parents and Ashley went missing. They saw three teenage girls who lied to go do something they knew their parents wouldn't let them do, and one of them ended up a statistic."

It's a harsh evaluation, but I also know it's accurate. I've seen it happen just that way too many times before. Detectives get an initial impression of what's happening and won't budge from it. Especially if a detective has a personal sticking point or a vendetta against a specific type of person or crime. Any of them can get clouded into automatically fitting a situation into that mold based purely on what he or she first absorbs from a situation.

And unfortunately, I can see how that could happen in this story. I'm keeping quiet. I'll withhold my judgment until I know the truth. Which I have no doubt I haven't heard yet.

"Show us what you did," I tell them. "Just walk us through everything you remember from the time you got here until you realized Ashley was missing."

They venture into the woods and Dean and I follow them. As we wind along an overgrown pass, I notice the girls glancing over at each other every few seconds. There's something in that look. I can't tell if it's making sure the other one is walking in the same direction, or waiting for the other one to say something, so they know what story to tell.

We finally stop at a small, primitive campsite. There are signs that people have stayed here fairly recently, but it's definitely not one of the more popular locations.

"This is where we set up our tents," Vivian says.

"Is this the same place you would stay when your parents brought you?" I ask.

"Yes," she nods. "That's how we knew how to get here."

"Okay. So, you get here, and you set up your tent. What did you do then?"

"We started a fire," Allison chimes in. "Back then, there was a rock ring right in the corner over there. We got a fire going and started cooking the food we brought in."

"Right off the bat?" I frown. "You just got to your campsite and you're already cooking? I thought you said you were there in the early afternoon."

"We were," Allison says. "But we didn't have enough ice in the cooler and we were worried about the food. So, we went ahead and cooked it. Ashley was worried about her parents. She hadn't told them we were staying here overnight. Then she went to the bathhouse. She was gone for a while, and when she came back, she said everything was fine. She said she would be picked up in the morning. I figured she had talked to them and everything was okay."

"How about after that?" I ask. "That night and the next day."

"We hung out. Talked. Then we went to bed. The next morning, we woke up and made some coffee. Had breakfast. Then we decided to go on a hike," Vivian starts.

Allison makes a sound beside her and Vivian looks over.

"A hike?" I frown. "Was that before or after you realized Ashley wasn't with you anymore?"

Vivian looks embarrassed and startled. She opens her mouth as if she's going to say something, but she can't get it out. A few sounds creak out into the thick air before she looks back at me.

"I mean..." she starts.

"It's been a long time, Vivian. It's hard to remember exactly what you told the police, isn't it? Because according to what you told Ashley's parents, the three of you argued that day and she stormed off. You knew they would pick her up, so you didn't question it. I have to say, that makes a hell of a lot more sense than the story you just rattled off."

"Vivian," Allison whispers.

"What actually happened? Because I've known this story was a lie from the beginning. I just wanted to see how far you'd get yourself into it. So why don't we start from the beginning again? Did you actually come here the day Ashley went missing?" I ask.

Allison lets out a heavy sigh and Vivian nods.

"Yes," Vivian says. "We really did come here. That's true. It really had been raining and we really were tired of being cooped up with our families, so we decided to come out here and have some fun."

"Who brought you here?" I ask. "The story of stealing your sister's car is cute. It's too bad you didn't get to tell that one to the police. It would have given you more validity. But I know that's not how you got here."

"My boyfriend," Allison finally admits. "I told him we wanted to come out here, so he picked us up. He told us a couple of his friends were going to meet up with us later."

"Okay," I say. "Now we're getting somewhere. Is this actually where you set up your tent?"

"Yes," Vivian says. "This is the spot my family likes to camp in, so we came here."

"You set up your tent. What next? I can't see three teenage girls going to the grocery store for supplies and making a full camp meal. And you already told me the weather was still overcast and cool enough that Ashley had to wear a hoodie. If that was the case, there would be no ice emergency."

"My boyfriend told me his friends were at the park, but they wanted to meet us at Arrow Lake. They'd heard all the stories about the campground and wanted to see it for themselves. We'd never been down there, so we took the hike down there. Brady was there with two of his buddies. One of them had hung out with us a few times before and had a crush on Ashley. She'd been talking about him a little bit for the last couple of weeks, so she was happy to see him there," Allison says.

"Okay, so you go to the campground. Is there anyone there? Did you see anything? What did you do?" Dean asks.

"It really wasn't that interesting," Vivian says. "I think we were all a little bit disappointed. The whole idea of this haunted campground had been built up and when we got there, it was just like any other campground. It was just empty. It didn't look to be in the best condition; there are a lot of campgrounds in this park that look rundown and old."

"We ended up going back to the campsite. Ashley and the guy, Tegan, were flirting and getting pretty friendly with each other. It was starting to get dark."

She looks over at Allison. Their eyes plead with each other without any words being said. I look between both of them, leaning slightly towards them as I wait for something else.

"Go on," Allison says. "At this point, we might as well tell her. She knows we haven't told the truth."

Vivian's shoulders drop as she lets out a breath, then turns back to me.

"We got the fire going and were going to hang out for a while before going to sleep. But then Ashley said she and Tegan were going to be alone for a while. She said not to wait up."

"And you just let her go?" Dean asks.

"Yes," Vivian says without hesitation. "As I said, she had been talking about him for a couple weeks. It was obvious she really liked him."

"She was thirteen years old, Dean says.

"And we were fifteen," Allison counters. "You can't expect us to think like adults, even if we wanted to act like them."

"When did you realize she was missing?" I ask.

"The next day," Vivian says.

"That part was true," Allison adds. "We woke up and she wasn't in the tent with us. We just assumed she had gone off with Tegan and not come back until really late. Then her mom came and picked her up just as she'd told us. I didn't know that wasn't the truth until I took the backpack to her house and found out she wasn't there. I realized she hadn't actually talked to her mother the night before."

"Why do you think she would tell you that?" I ask.

Both girls shook their heads.

"I don't know," Vivian says.

"It could have been Tegan," Allison says. "She might have actually been unsure about staying until she talked to him and found out he was coming."

"Did you tell any of this to the police?" I ask.

They shake their heads again.

"No," Allison says. "We've never told anyone. We didn't want to get in trouble. But we also didn't want to get the guys in trouble. They were a lot older than we were."

"So, you realize your best friend is missing, you know the last time you saw her she had gone off with some guy, and you don't bother to say anything to anyone?" Dean asks.

"We talked to him," Vivian says quickly. "As soon as we found out Ashley was missing, we went and found Tegan. We asked him what happened, and he told us the two of them had gone off together, but she changed her mind."

"About having sex with him?" I ask.

They seem startled by my blunt question, as if either they didn't think I was following what they were suggesting, or they didn't think I would actually say it.

"Yes," Allison says. "Tegan said they just made out for a while and fell asleep. When they woke up, it was really early, and she was upset because she needed to leave. He brought her back to the campground and he saw her running toward the bathhouse. He thought she just needed to use the bathroom, so he didn't really hang around to watch her."

"But you just said you don't think she talked to her mother the night before. So, why would she tell him she needed to leave? If her mother wasn't coming to pick her up, where would she be going?" I ask.

"It could have been somebody else," Vivian shrugs.

"What do you mean? Like who?" Dean asks.

They exchange another one of those looks. I'm wishing this wasn't the first time I've interacted with Vivian. It would have been better if I could have gotten the full story from both of them separately. But that's not an option now; I'm going to have to work with what I have.

"Was there another guy she had been talking about?" I ask.

"Yes," Allison says. "He was older. We didn't know him."

"What do you mean, 'older'? You just said your boyfriend and Tegan were older."

"Yeah," Allison nods. "But they were still teenagers."

"And you don't think this guy was?"

"Not by the way she talked about him. I think he was an adult. She'd started talking about waiting for Prince Charming. That's what she would always say. She was waiting for Prince Charming, and one day he would show up and they would get married. She just didn't know when," Vivian explains.

"And you didn't mention that to the police, either?" I ask.

"I did," Vivian says.

"What?" Allison gasps, sounding shocked. "You did?"

"They don't know it was me," she clarifies. "I called the tip line they set up after she went missing and told them everything I knew. It never went anywhere. I figured that meant we were wrong."

"Or they just couldn't find him," Dean says.

"Are you still in contact with Tegan? I think it would be helpful to talk to him."

"No," Allison says. "He died in a motorcycle accident a couple weeks after Ashley disappeared."

DEAN AND I SIT IN THE CAR AFTER WALKING OUT OF THE WOODS, watching the girls cling to each other again. They stand beside Vivian's car, hugging and talking in voices too low for us to hear all the way across the lot.

"What are you thinking?" Dean asks.

I don't take my eyes off the girls.

"That they just fed us a load of bullshit," I say. "Again."

"You don't believe them?"

"This little thirteen-year-old girl was supposedly all wrapped up in some unknown, unnamed adult man, but she went off into the woods to have sex with a teenage guy the night she thinks the adult man might come for her?" I ask.

"They said she changed her mind," Deans points out.

"According to a guy who died right after she went missing. Don't you find that a little convenient?"

"Do you think there's something suspicious behind the motorcycle accident?" he asks.

"No. I think it was an accident. I also think it's a smokescreen. It's hard as hell to get corroborating details from a dead man."

"That's true." He looks through the windshield again as the girls finally part and get in their separate cars. "What I don't understand is why they would change their story. The one they told her parents made sense. She got mad, she left, they thought they picked her up. Why change that?"

"Five years is a long time to try to hang onto a lie. I don't doubt guys were around that day. It's just figuring out what they know."

"So, what's next? Dean asks. "Can you go back to the police and ask them for the records again?"

"Not the police," I say. "Track down that tip line. Usually, they're operated by an outside organization. See if they still have information from when Ashley first went missing. It's entirely possible to find it still active. They could have recordings of the tips that were left. See if there actually is one about this Prince Charming."

"What are you going to do?" he asks as I take out my phone.

"It's about time the public sees Ashley's parents again," I say.

EIGHTEEN

HE SAT IN THE RECLINER, *watching the televised statement.*

It was the first time in years he had seen Thirteen's mother like this. She hadn't made a statement since a year after that summer.

Now, there she was, begging for her child's return.

He knew her face. He knew her voice.

No one, not even she, knew how many times their paths had crossed.

He wondered what she knew.

And why the two people behind her were there. He'd seen them before.

The blond woman with quiet authority and eyes that cut like honed steel.

The man beside her with the imposing presence of a lion and a sharp, piercing stare.

They showed no emotion as the broken mother gripped the edge of the podium and pleaded for her daughter to come home. They were watching for something. Waiting.

What did they know?

NINETEEN

"AND NEVER FORGET what we always said to you, baby. Remember who you are. Remember where you came from. Nothing will ever matter more. We love you."

Misty steps back from the podium and takes a brief pause, almost as though she's going to say something else. But then she turns and hurries away under the frantic shouting of questions from the reporters who came to watch her statement. They can sense the building tension. It's like blood in the water for them.

Dean and I go after her and I wrap my arm around her shoulder.

"You did a great job," I say. "That was perfect."

"You really think so?" Misty asks.

"Yes," I nod. "It was everything you needed to say and nothing you didn't."

"You were so much stronger than I could have been," John says. "Thank you for being able to be the one who did that."

"I just hope it does something," Misty says. "I told you that when I heard about the murders at the campground, it gave me some hope. Just because it would be an answer, and I might finally know where Ashley has been for the last five years. But the truth is, I never wanted to really believe it. I want her to be out there. Somewhere. I know that means she could be going through something horrible, and I hate myself for even wanting that for a second."

"It's not that you want her to be going through something horrible," I assure her. "You just want her to be alive. You want her to be able to come back to you."

"It's what I wanted for five years," she says. "And maybe making this statement will make a difference to somebody."

"I know it wasn't easy to do, but you're right. It might make a difference. There have been plenty of times when a parent's making a statement about a missing child has jogged the memory of somebody who saw something and didn't realize it. Or unlocked a guilty conscience," I tell her.

"Maybe Ashley heard me," she says. "I want her to know how much I love her."

I nod and rub her back to comfort and reassure her. I want to seem as optimistic about Ashley as I can, but it's hard to with the statistics hanging over me. I know that's exactly what Allison was talking about. I hate any investigator or police officer who would immediately jump on the idea of numbers and likelihoods to dismiss a grieving mother.

But it's impossible to ignore. I can't pretend that I think this will have a happy ending. I will keep a smile on my face as much as I can for her parents, but there's a dark feeling inside me that Ashley met her end a long time ago. It's just a matter of finding out what happened to her and why.

This public statement about Ashley, reminding people about her and her case, didn't have the goal of bringing her home. That's not the point. I'm hoping hearing about her will be enough to make people talk. Someone knows something. Something more than he or she is telling. And there might be far more people involved than we think. A mother's words can be powerful. Often in ways she could never have imagined.

While Dean goes back to the campground with Xavier and Ava, I go to the Stevenson house. We sit down in the living room to talk over the statement and how we're going to move forward with the investigation. Misty brings out tea and cookies, but the tray is more or less a centerpiece. None of us reaches for either one.

"There's something somewhat sensitive I need to speak with you about," I say after a few seconds.

John and Misty look at each other and John stands up.

"I need to do some work in my office, anyway. Let me know if I can be of any help," he says.

I wasn't expecting him to leave, but I realize it does lessen some of the tension surrounding the conversation. While I would have been interested to hear what he has to say about it, just having Misty here might let her open up more than she would have if her husband was here.

"Dean and I have been talking with Allison and Vivian about the day Ashley went missing," I start. "We know Vivian's family wasn't there with them at the campground. But they revealed to us that they weren't alone, and someone else might have been involved in her disappearance."

Misty's face goes pale. She reaches for one of the cups of tea, but her fingers brush against the handle and fall rather than picking it up.

"What do you mean?" she asks, her voice soft and shallow. "What happened to her?"

"I don't know the details," I say. "But I need to ask you... was Ashley involved with any guys?"

"Boys?" Misty asks, her voice now rising in shock. "No. Absolutely not. She was only thirteen."

"I understand that," I say. "But there are plenty of girls that age who are already well on their way in that category."

"Are you suggesting something about Ashley?"

"No," I say, shaking my head for emphasis. "I'm not suggesting anything. All I'm asking is if you ever heard your daughter talking about guys, or if you think that she might have met up with one that night."

"No," she repeats. "That's ridiculous. Not Ashley. She wasn't like that. She had her rebellious moments, of course. All thirteen-year-old girls do. But not those kinds. She was still just a little girl."

"Okay," I say, pulling back before she can totally shut down. "How about her computer and her phone? Were they part of the investigation?"

"Her phone was with her. It's never been found. The police searched her computer, but said they didn't come up with anything," she says.

"Is it still here?" I ask.

She nods. "Yes. I kept her room just as it was. I suppose that's silly."

"No. It's perfectly normal."

I know I need to meet Dean and the others at the campground. There's evidence to review, and I need to do another search of the area where I found Elsie. But the lure of the computer is too strong for me to leave just yet. I have Misty's permission now, but it might not stay.

Misty takes me upstairs and down the hallway to a closed door. A small white plaque hangs on a white ribbon from a nail in the center of the door, her name painted in red script across it. Misty touches it with hesitant fingertips.

"Her favorite color," she says with a hint of a bittersweet laugh. "I always thought it was too bold. It's hard to find decorations and things for a little girl in red."

She opens the door and I step backward five years. This is certainly the room of a thirteen-year-old. The details in it show that strange place thirteen can be, straddling childhood and teendom. This is when so many girls want to be seen as grown up, but also aren't ready to let go of their teddy bears and ballerina jewelry boxes. Some never will. They'll carry those things with them throughout their lives, unafraid of what anyone thinks of them.

Others will have them forced from their hands.

"Are there passwords you can give me?" I ask as I sit down at a desk against the wall and open up the old laptop. "For her email, social media, those kinds of things?"

"What are you looking for?" she asks, opening the top drawer of the desk and pulling out a small pad of paper.

"Anything I can find," I explain. "Sometimes there are little things that are easy to miss but that tell a big part of the story. Friends you might not have known. Events she was looking forward to. Interests she might not have shared with you. You remember being that age, don't you?"

"I do," Misty nods. "It was different then. The internet wasn't like this. There wasn't so much influence."

Misty can't be much older than I am, but I know where she's coming from. It's a different world than it was when we were younger. I'm reminded of it all the time. In some ways that are fantastic, like being able to call and see Dean and Xavier, or my father, even when we can't be together. And in other ways that are horrific and sobering.

Like Lakyn's life cut so brutally short.

Like Mary Preston, killed in a horrific attack.

Like a teenager disappearing without a trace.

TWENTY

MISTY SHOWS me the list of all of Ashley's passwords and then leaves the room. As I'm signing in to the computer, my phone rings.

"Hey, babe," Sam says when I answer. "How did it go today?"

"It went as well as I could have expected it to. Misty did great. She got emotional, but she kept it together," I tell him.

"What about her friends?" Sam asks.

"I was watching them for as much of it as I could. They were doing all the right things. Crying, looking worried. I had asked Xavier to keep an eye on them, so I'm going to talk to him when I get to the campground and see if he has any impressions of them," I say.

"You aren't with him?" I ask.

"No," I say. "I'm at the Stevensons' house. They gave me permission to look through Ashley's computer to see if I can find anything."

"What about Ava?"

"She's with Dean and Xavier," I say.

"Isn't she supposed to be shadowing you?" Sam asks.

"She's supposed to be watching how I work," I say. "And this is how I work. This issue with Ashley is sensitive enough as it is. I can't just bring in another person to sit around and observe. Right now, she's at the campground, watching the evidence brought in and processed. Dean is working on the investigation and Xavier is... I'm not sure what Xavier's doing. But I'm never sure what he's doing, so that isn't really a change. I'm going to look through this and see if anything stands out to me. Then I'll meet them there. I just really hope the televised plea does something."

"I know," Sam says.

"I just wish I didn't know that the 'something' I think I might find is going to lead us to information about what happened to Ashley, not to Ashley herself. You know as well as I do that the chances of her being alive are next to nothing," I say.

"Remember Iris. Plenty of people said the same thing about her and Julia. You were the one who fought for them," he says.

"I know," I say. "But it's not the same thing. Just as it wasn't the same thing when I was first looking into the deaths at the campground. Iris didn't just disappear. I wish I could believe that Ashley is fine out there somewhere, and maybe she is, but the realistic part of me says if she was envisioning a fairy tale, it didn't have a happy ending for her."

"Do you know when you're going to be back?" he asks.

"I'm still aiming for two more days. The investigation into the campground is going well. There's a lot of evidence for me to go over there," I say.

"Okay. I miss you," he says.

"I miss you, too. I'll see you soon. I love you."

I hang up and get back to the computer. A quick glimpse at her email inbox tells me there's more to sift through than I have the time to do right now. I take a picture of her passwords with my phone so I can access the information later. Then I sign into her social media to scroll through posts from around the time she went missing.

I'm surprised to find an abundance of images with no captions and no explanation. Most people her age like to take social media as an opportunity to show off or speak their minds. Ashley might have been doing that as well, only she chose to do it silently.

I don't recognize the places she took pictures of, but they obviously hold significance. I take out my phone again and start snapping pictures of some of the images. It will be easier to share these with Dean this way rather than just showing him the feed. I'm so entrenched in digging through this girl's life, the voice coming from the door makes me jump.

"You think she's dead."

I whip around toward the door and see a young woman standing there. She looks vaguely like an older version of Ashley, but slightly heavier and with short, straight hair rather than the long curls I've seen in pictures of the missing girl.

"You must be Leona," I say.

She gives a single nod but doesn't come any further into the room.

"Do you think my sister is dead?" she asks again.

I hope she didn't hear my conversation with Sam. She's clearly upset, and I want to handle this as diplomatically as I can without lying to her.

"Right now, I don't know what happened to your sister. But I'm going to do everything I can to find out," I say.

She nods again and peers around the room.

"Do you ever come in here?" I ask.

"No," Leona says. "I don't like looking at her things."

"That's understandable," I say. "But, you do still live at home?"

Her eyes shoot to me, cutting into me as though I'd asked her something deeply offensive.

"I have to," she says. "I haven't been able to leave my mom. Not after everything she's been through."

"But you'll be going away to college," I point out. "You were up near DC looking at a campus."

"That's for Dad," she says. "He wants me to go. I want to stay and be here for Mom."

"You're an adult, Leona. You're allowed to live your own life."

"Mom needs me," she says. "I won't leave her the way Ashley did."

She walks out of the room, leaving me slightly stunned by the comment. There's almost a bitterness in her voice. As if she blames Ashley for her own disappearance. Maybe she knows more than the other people in her sister's life. Maybe there is some credence to the idea that she got swept up in something and chose to walk away.

I take a few more pictures and take notes on my phone so I don't forget the thoughts that pop into my head. Signing out of everything, I go back downstairs to thank Misty.

"Would it be alright with you if I accessed her email and social media from my own computer to look through it again later?" I ask.

"Absolutely," she says. "Anything you need."

"Thank you. I'll be in touch soon," I say.

The drive to the park is only a few minutes. I can definitely see why this area appeals to teenagers. It's a sprawling area with plenty of corners and shadowy areas where they can hide from a world telling them what to do.

As soon as I get to the campground and get out of my car, I see I might have waited just a bit too long to make it back here.

Pushing my sunglasses up onto the top of my head, I rush across the parking area to the nearest evidence table. Xavier is standing in front of it, his arms crossed tightly over his chest as he stares down Ava. Dean is beside them, seeming to try to talk both of them down.

"What is going on over here?" I ask as I approach.

Dean looks relieved to see me, but Xavier's tense expression doesn't change.

"Ava is tampering with the evidence," Xavier says.

"Excuse me?" I ask.

Ava lets out a sigh. "I'm not tampering with it. I just suggested a different organizational method. I thought it might make it easier to see everything."

I get closer to the table and look over the pieces of evidence, then look at her.

"They're organizing this evidence based on my instructions. I am the head of this investigation and they are under my command. This is how I like my evidence laid out, so it can be easily cataloged and sent to the lab," I tell her.

"I'm sorry," Ava says, taking a step back. "I just thought a streamlined approach would make things more efficient."

"Simply because you see something as streamlined doesn't make it right," I say. "You have just started in this career. I've been here for years. I know what I'm doing, and I have earned my place leading investigations. When you've gotten to the place I am, then you can determine how things are handled. Until then, please don't interfere."

I turn on my heel and stomp down toward the lake. I need to make sure she hasn't gotten her hands in anything else. The thing is, I see her ambition. I know she wasn't trying to mess anything up or cause any problems. Behind her awkward exterior is determination. But she needs to keep that determination out of my way.

For the rest of the day, she hovers in the periphery, but doesn't try to get involved. I don't interfere with that mindset.

With some promising progress on this case giving me a boost at the end of the day, I head to my car, with Xavier and Dean behind me. Ava walks slowly to hers with a sheepish look. A she's waiting for something.

"Is that it for the day?" she asks.

"Yes. Go on back to the hotel," I say. "We'll let you know what's going on tomorrow in the morning."

"Oh. Okay," she says. "Um... do you know of any good places for me to grab something for dinner?"

She's seen the same restaurants as we have the last two nights. I know it's the conversational version of climbing through a back window to get inside. She's already had the front door slammed in her face, so now she's trying to get through another way.

"There's a directory in your room. There's also room service available at the hotel. And I'm sure you could look it up on your phone," I say.

I get in the car and notice it takes a little while before Dean joins me. Xavier climbs into the backseat and we sit in silence. After several seconds, Xavier's arm appears in my peripheral vision. One finger sticks out and pokes the radio button, turning it on.

My car radio is attached to a music streaming service on my phone, so pressing that button only fills the cabin with staticky white noise. That doesn't seem to bother Xavier, but it acts as the soundtrack to the tension between Dean and me.

"What?" I finally snap, cutting a glance over to him.

"Don't you think that was a little harsh?"

Xavier's finger appears again and turns off the radio.

"What am I supposed to think was a little harsh?" I ask.

"The way you just talked to Ava. She was obviously trying to find out if we were going to dinner or hanging out," he says.

"Please, Dean. Don't start with me about that. Her puppy eyes might have gotten to you, but I'm not so easily swayed," I say.

"This isn't about her puppy eyes," he says. "It's about how hard you're being on her. For no good reason."

"No good reason?" I ask incredulously. "Did you not see what she was doing?"

"She made a suggestion for how evidence could be arranged. That's it," he says. "It's not ideal..."

"It's not her place," I cut him off. "This isn't her investigation, Dean. She doesn't get to make the decisions or determinations about anything. Especially when I'm not around to know she's doing it."

"I think maybe you're forgetting how hard it is to just get started in the Bureau," he counters.

"No, I'm not. I'm not forgetting any of it. I remember every single second of how hard it was when I first started. And I didn't get someone to hold my hand and walk me through everything. I got thrown right to the lions. It made me stronger for it. She got this far, Dean. She went through the Academy and she got through her training. Now she needs to see what it's really like to be an agent. And part of that is learning her place. That she isn't always going to be in charge or be the one people are listening to. That's how investigations get compromised," I say.

"I know that," he says. I can tell he has something else on his tongue, but he bites it back.

I nod. "Now, I have a lot to go over with you about Ashley Stevenson's case. Are you up for it tonight?"

He sighs and leans his head back against the seat cushion. "Let's do it."

TWENTY-ONE

"I MEAN, honestly, a lot of this is exactly what I would have expected. It's just full of young teenage angsty stuff. Some poetry. Pictures of her friends. Complaints about schoolwork and teachers. There isn't really anything that jumped out at me specifically," I say.

We're sitting in the hotel room around boxes of pizza. I've changed into my pajamas and washed off my makeup for the night, but I know there is still plenty of work ahead of me. Dean is going over the pictures I took on my phone, and I have my laptop open with her email inbox pulled up.

"There isn't anything that makes you think she's talking about this older guy?" Dean asks.

"Not specifically. I mean, there are a couple of references to love stories and finding the perfect guy. But I think that probably shows up on most thirteen-year-old girls' computers. It's not direct enough for us to connect it to anybody. What's really getting to me is these pictures," I say.

I gesture to my phone and then sweep across the screen to look through the locations again.

"There are no captions," Dean observes. "We don't have any idea where these places are."

"Exactly," I nod. "But they must have meant something or she would have taken pictures of them. Remember the group of teenagers thatwho disappeared from the campground right after it shut down? The mother knew where her son was. She was able to send investigators there because he took a picture of Cabin Thirteen. But she said he was a photographer. That's what he did. He chronicled his entire life by taking pictures of everything he did and everywhere he went."

"And it doesn't look as though Ashley did that," Dean says.

"No," I shake my head. "Not with that level of consistency. There are definitely things she took multiple pictures of, which tells me they were really meaningful to her. Each one was more than just another place she saw or another thing she did. It wasn't just a random moment on any given day. She took a picture of each of these places because it's significant. She was recording an important piece of her life."

"So, we need to find out where they are," Dean says. "Maybe if we can identify all of that, we can piece together what they mean."

"Exactly," I say.

"Great," he says. "I'll take these and look around the area tomorrow while you're at the campground."

"Perfect. From the looks of how everything is going there, I think everything is looking good and they can handle it without me after tomorrow. We can spend a little more time and energy on Ashley before we have to go back."

"Sounds like a plan," Dean says. "If things are working out with that case before you go back, I might stay here with Xavier. We'll just rent a car and I'll keep digging until you can get back."

With that settled, I climb in bed for the night. I don't immediately fall asleep. I can't stop thinking about what Dean said about Ava. I'm not here to coddle her, but I also don't want to come across as being unreasonably hard on her.

It's good to push her. For her to understand what she's gotten herself into. If she can't handle me, I don't understand how she thinks she's going to be able to handle the rest of the Bureau.

BY THE NEXT EVENING, IT STILL DOESN'T FEEL AS THOUGH WE'RE much closer to understanding Ashley or what might have happened to her. We are back in my hotel room and Dean is going over what he found during the day. He and Xavier spent hours driving around the entire area, comparing the images on social media with places they could locate.

They also showed the images to local business owners and even some kids they ran into, hoping somebody could point them in the right direction.

"We were able to find a few of them," Dean says. "I took pictures of what they look like now. Some of them haven't changed much at all, and other ones have been completely developed. There are some that I wasn't able to identify."

"Xavier, what do you think about Vivian and Allison? You were watching them during the statement from her mother. How did you feel about the way they were acting?" I ask.

"They were doing everything they were supposed to do," he says.

"That's exactly what I thought."

"Five years ago," he clarifies.

I pause. "What do you mean?"

"She disappeared five years ago. There hasn't really been any more development into what happened to her. No one has found any evidence that she is dead, or that she's been through torture. Nothing has really changed. But they were devastated," he says.

"It can be hard when things are brought back up," Dean offers. "Maybe they hadn't thought much about it over the last few years, and it was just fresh to them."

"They're still young," Xavier says. "This is still new in a lot of ways. And they lied about what they experienced the day she went missing. That doesn't leave you. They've been carrying that with them all these years. But only now are they showing anything."

"You think they were faking it?" I ask.

"I don't think they are faking the emotion they're showing. I only wonder what is behind that emotion. You said the two of them didn't seem particularly emotional when they were showing you around the woods," he says.

"Not overtly, no. I mean, they seemed a little sad. They teared up a bit. But they weren't crying or resisting going back to those locations," I say. "It didn't look as if they were bothered being there at all. Even though Allison specifically mentioned she hadn't been there since showing the police around."

"What questions did they ask you?" he asks.

"None," I say. "They didn't want to know what our investigation has uncovered or if there's a specific reason we were investigating her again."

"Could they feel her there?" Xavier asks. "Did it seem as if they could still see her or they knew where she would be standing?"

I shake my head. "No."

"Look at when some of these pictures were taken," Dean says. "A few of these were taken leading up to the day she went missing. Even though her parents said she hadn't been doing anything because of the rain."

"As far as I know," I said.

"Then there's nothing on the day she went missing."

"But there's one on the day after," I say, noticing the details for the first time.

"What?" Dean asks.

"Look." I point it out. "This picture has a timestamp on it. As they all do. But this one shows it was taken and automatically uploaded the day after her friends noticed she was missing."

"But what is it?" Dean asks. "You can't even see where she is or what she's taking a picture of."

I shake my head. "I don't know. But we need to try to find that out," I say.

He nods. "I can have some guys look at it. See if they can enhance any of it and maybe figure out what it shows."

"This tells me she didn't look at her social media again after she was at the campground with Allison and Vivian. She would probably have deleted this picture," I say.

"That's something," Dean says.

"Yeah," I nod. "I don't know what. But it's something."

My phone rings and I pick it up.

"Hello?"

"Emma?" Ava says.

I can't help but roll my eyes.

"Yes, Ava," I say.

"I was just wondering about the investigation. If anything significant came out? I couldn't really follow along when the investigators were talking to you," she asks.

"Ava, I am right in the middle of another investigation that is more pressing than what's going on at the campground right now. I really can't stop and go over all the details with you," I say.

"Just wait," Ava says as I start to end the call. "I'm supposed to be learning from you. I'm supposed to be involved in these investigations."

"No," I say. "You're supposed to be shadowing me on the investigation that is being handled by the FBI. This is not your first case, Ava. And the investigation I'm doing with Dean has nothing to do with the Bureau."

"I still might be able to help," she says.

I hear another call coming in on the other line.

"I'm going to have to go," I say. "I'm getting another call."

"Emma, I know we didn't get off to the best start. I'm not always great with people. And I came into this wanting to impress you."

Dean answers his phone and I see his eyes get wide.

"It's Eric," he says. "He called me when he couldn't get through to you. Bellamy is in labor."

TWENTY-TWO

I don't remember getting off the phone with Eric. It's entirely possible I didn't. Everything that happens in the next few minutes is a blur as I try to shove clothes in a bag as fast as I can and get dressed. Soon we are on the road, but the trip seems to stretch on impossibly long.

I've done this drive countless times. It's never felt quite so much as if somebody has the other end of the road and is unfurling it like a piece of ribbon under my car. It feels as though no matter how fast I think I'm driving, I'm not actually getting anywhere.

"Don't get too worked up," Dean says as I let out a spiel of expletives when a light turns red in front of me. "Eric said it's just the beginning. She's still in early labor, and her doctors don't seem to think that there's any rush. We're only about three hours away. Everything's going to be fine."

I try to take the words to heart, but all I can think about is the possibility of missing the baby's being born. Bellamy has told me over and over since she announced her pregnancy how important it is to her that I'm there. And it's important to me. Bellamy has been there for me through some of the hardest times of my adult life. She's also seen me through my happiest times.

I want to experience this with her. Bellamy is as much family as my father, just like the others. This new baby is our next generation. She'll carry on not just Bellamy's and Eric's genes, but the traditions and memories that come from the rest of us as well.

After we've been on the road for about an hour, I call Sam and let him know what's going on. He's closer to the hospital than I am, so we should be arriving close together.

"Try not to worry," Xavier says. "Send good thoughts to the baby. Good energy. She is a brand-new person getting ready to start her journey on this Earth. Make a good impression for the rest of us."

"Do you think I have some sort of cosmic connection to the baby so that it can feel my energy and know what I'm thinking?" I ask.

"I wouldn't put it past you," Xavier says. "You've talked to her a lot."

"So have you," I counter.

"Yes," he says. "But I don't feel we've truly bonded. It seems there's a barrier between us, but I feel we are working through that."

This is one of those moments with Xavier when I'm not sure if he's being serious or telling a joke. He very rarely gives any sort of emotion or signal to let us know. Now he's just staring out the window, so I don't bother to react at all.

Another hour passes and we end up stuck in traffic, bringing our progress down to a crawl. In general, I try to hold myself together. I try to be at least somewhat in control of myself when in public. This is not one of those moments when it's working out for me.

Slamming my hands against the steering wheel, I let out a growl of frustration and shout a few unflattering suggestions to the cars around me.

"They're not going to move any faster withif you scream at them," Dean tells me. "You're not going to vaporize the cars so wecan get down the road more easily."

"She might," Xavier offers.

"I just don't understand why people in this absurd town seem to completely lose their abilities to function and operate motor vehicles as soon as they are within the city limits. What is it about these streets that apparently removes driving capabilities?" I gripe.

"Their unforgiving and confusing wheel-and-spoke arrangement overlapping a classic grid layout?" Xavier suggests. "It's difficult at best, homicide-inducing at worst."

"These people have GPS systems built into their cars for the most part. They literally have little voices telling them what's coming next and what to do at essentially every given moment. All they have to do is follow little lines and do what the voices tell them to do," I say. "And yet we sit here for ever-increasing amounts of time waiting for people to figure out what the hell they're doing."

"Would it help you through if I sang a song to pass the time?" Xavier asks.

Without my answering, he bursts into a rendition of "Swing Low, Sweet Chariot".

"Xavier," Dean says.

"Not the right choice?" he asks. "How about an interactive song? Five hundred bottles of beer on the wall, five hundred bottles of beer. You take one down, pass it around," he uses the back of his hand to smack the ceiling, window, and seat behind him in tempo. "Four hundred ninety-nine bottles of beer on the wall."

I'm not even going to try to stop him. It takes all the way to three hundred bottles of beer for us to get to the hospital. My parking is haphazard at best, but I toss my keys back in so Dean can straighten it out if he wants to, and I run inside. I get on the elevator to ride up to the maternity floor, trying not to think about the last time I was here.

When the doors open, I rush to the information desk and ask for Bellamy.

"I can't send you back right now," the nurse tells me. "But I will let them know you're here."

He gestures toward a brightly lit waiting room. I can already tell that's not going to work out.

"Would you be able to lower the lights in there?" I ask. "Just a little?"

"Lower the lights?" the nurse asks.

"One of the people who's going to be waiting with me is going to be up here in just a few moments and he doesn't handle bright lights well. If we're going to be here for a couple of hours, the light in there is going to push him right to the edge."

An understanding nod and a flick of a couple of switches later, the waiting room is at a much more comfortable level of lighting for Xavier. I can't absolutely guarantee he's going to handle it well, being in a hospital for so long, but at least it will help if he's not over-whelmed by the lights, too.

I make a cursory search of the waiting area and take stock of what's in the vending machines so I can fill him and Dean in when they get inside. But all that completely loses my attention when I see Eric come in.

Running toward him, I gather him in a close hug.

"How is she?" I ask.

"Powering through," he says. "They say she is definitely in labor, but it's still pretty early in terms of how far along she's progressed. They've got her hooked up to a monitor right now to make sure every-thing's going well with the baby."

"She should be walking," Xavier announces, coming into the waiting room. "Gravity. Hi, Eric. Happy baby emergence day, assuming all body parts are fully independent of Bellamy before midnight."

"Thank you, Xavier."

"Can I go back and see her?" I ask.

"Absolutely. She's been asking when you were going to get here. Come on," he says.

"Dean, look out for Sam. He should be here any time now. Let him know I'm back with Bellamy," I say.

He nods as he tries to work a remote hanging in a plastic sheath from a cord attached to the TV. He's ready to settle in for the long haul.

Eric and I hurry out of the waiting room and through doors that lead us into the halls of the maternity ward. He opens the door to one of the rooms and I step through. A curtain separates the door from the bed, and I call out to Bellamy.

"B?"

"Emma! You're here!"

I walk around the curtain and find her propped up in bed, attached to the monitor beeping beside her. Even with her hair clipped onto her head in a messy bun and wearing a pink paisley hospital gown, she looks beautiful.

"How are you feeling?" I ask, taking her hand and leaning down to kiss her cheek.

"Doing okay right now," she tells me. "The contractions are getting stronger, but they haven't gotten regular enough yet."

I remember what Xavier said and pull the blankets off her. "You should be up out of that bed. Come on. Let's get you walking around. Gravity will get things going for you."

"I'm attached to things, Emma," she protests.

"Well, call the nurse. Get unattached. We've got to get those contractions going."

Eric laughs. "And you were just saying you wished you'd gotten a doula."

"Should have known I already had one," Bellamy chuckles.

She presses the call button on the side of her bed, and a few moments later a nurse appears at the door.

"Everything alright?" she asks.

"Can I get up and walk?" Bellamy asks.

"Absolutely," the nurse says. "You've been on that monitor long enough. Getting some laps in will help move things along."

"Told you," I say.

"Xavier told you," she counters.

"How did you know that?"

She looks at me and I just nod. The nurse disconnects the monitor and helps Bellamy up. She's wearing hospital-issued socks with grippy bottoms, so she doesn't have to put shoes on before we're on our way. Eric and I walk along with her up and down the hallways, talking about anything and everything to keep her distracted.

We've only been walking for a few minutes when she suddenly draws in a sharp breath. Turning to Eric, she wraps her arms around his neck and leans against his chest. Eric puts his hands on her hips and holds her, swaying her back and forth as he whispers into her ear.

It's surprisingly beautiful. I find myself blinking away tears.

A few moments later, we continue on our way. This process repeats several more times before the nurse catches up with us at the corner near her room.

"The doctor wants you to come back in for another check," she says.

"I'm going to go see Sam," I say. "I'll come back in a little while. Do you need anything?"

Bellamy shakes her head and I look at Eric.

"Some coffee would be amazing," he says. "I haven't been getting a lot of sleep the last few days, and I have a feeling I'm not going to be getting much in the next couple, either."

"No problem. See you in a bit," I say.

As they head into the room, I make my way back to the waiting area. Sam is standing at the vending machine just outside. He's gripping several bills in one hand and deeply contemplating the snacks and drinks inside the machine.

"Hey," I say.

He turns around, his face lighting up when he sees me. In an instant, his arms are wrapped around me, his face buried in the curve of my neck and shoulder.

"I missed you," he says.

"I've missed you, too," I say. "What are you focusing so hard on?"

"I can't decide what kind of snack to get," he says. "I already looked through all the machines in the waiting room, but I can't settle on anything."

"Well, don't ask Xavier to help you choose. That would get you into a whole conversation you are not ready for yet."

"How is Bellamy?" he asks.

"Doing well. We got up and walked around a bit. Her contractions seem to be getting more frequent. But I wouldn't expect anything to happen within the next couple of hours," I tell him.

"So, I should probably settle in with a couple of snacks?" he asks.

I nod. "I would go for the full assortment. Whatever catches your eye, grab it."

He takes that suggestion to heart and chooses several snacks and drinks before we make our way back into the waiting room. Xavier has taken up residence on a giant teddy bear and is lying on the floor staring up at the TV that Dean managed to tune to a game show channel.

"Nothing yet," I tell them. "Looks as though we've still got a ways to go. I'm going to the cafeteria to get Eric some coffee. Anybody want anything?"

"One of those clear cups with the little jiggly squares of gelatin and whipped topping," Xavier says. "They always have those at hospitals. Green. Blue if absolutely necessary. A banana if they only have red."

TWENTY-THREE

"Two hundred eighty-nine bottles of beer on the wall. Two hundred eighty-nine bottles of... oh. Maybe that's inappropriate considering our setting."

"I think it's fine, Xavier."

"No, I don't want to be perceived as a negative influence so early on in this life. It's fine. I'll change it. Two hundred eighty-nine bottles of milk on the wall. Two hundred eighty-nine bottles of milk."

He pauses.

"You okay?"

"Now I'm worried I'm mom-shaming. I've heard that phrase. Is that what I'm doing? Bottles of milk. Should it be bottles of formula? Or is that discouraging natural feeding? Two hundred eighty-nine mammary glands of milk on the wall."

"No!" Dean and Sam say simultaneously.

"Well, it's definitely not that," I say, groaning slightly as I pull myself up to a sitting position from where I was lying on the giant bear pointed in the opposite direction as Xavier.

"How about root beer, Xavier?" Dean suggests.

"I like root beer," he nods.

"There we go," Dean says.

Xavier dives back into his song and I head for the desk to call Eric. Bellamy hasn't been progressing as quickly as they would like her to, so about an hour ago they started giving her Pitocin to encourage her contractions along. They paired it with an epidural to help her get some rest and she's been trying to sleep to help her get through the rest of labor.

A few moments later, Eric comes to the door and ushers me through. Bellamy is awake and seems to be moving along a lot quicker than the last time I saw her. She's sitting on a labor ball, bouncing as she breathes through a contraction.

"I thought the epidural was supposed to take away the pain," I say.

Bellamy definitely doesn't look as if she's not in any pain.

"Sometimes they don't take full effect. It took the edge off, and she was able to rest a little bit, but then the pain came back. They don't want to give her more medication if they don't have to, so she's getting through it," Eric explains.

I go to Bellamy and run my hand over her sweaty hair. "Is there anything I can do?"

Without saying anything, she reaches up and takes my hand. Her other reaches for Eric. He and I look at each other and smile.

"XAVIER'S LOG. STARDATE... EARLY AUGUST. MAYBE LATER. I'VE lost track. Bellamy has been in labor for approximately four thousand hours. No end is in sight. Morale is dwindling. Supplies running low. God help us all."

I put my phone back in my pocket.

"It was just a message from Xavier," I say. "How are you doing? Need anything?"

"For this baby to be out of me," Bellamy says.

"I would offer to squeeze you like a tube of toothpaste to help you along, but I don't think that's considered an appropriate tactic," I say.

She nods. "I appreciate your willingness."

"I'm going to go check on the guys. I'll be back."

"Tell them I really appreciate that they're here, but they don't have to stay. They can go home and rest."

I lean down to kiss Bellamy on the top of the head, then rub Eric's back encouragingly as I walk out of the room. This time when I get to the waiting room, I find Xavier facedown on the enormous teddy bear. Dean is sitting on the floor nearby, scrolling through something on his tablet, while Sam sleeps on a bed he's crafted out of several of the waiting room chairs.

It looks a little bit like one of the vending machines exploded. One of the small tables overflows with wrappers and bottles from the various snacks and drinks they've bought since we got to the hospital. Another table has the remnants of at least a couple of trips to the cafeteria.

"Everybody hanging in there?" I ask.

"It's a little touch and go," Dean says. "How are things going with Bellamy?"

"Still working on it," I say. "She really appreciates that you guys are here, but she knows you're tired and it isn't the most fun in the world to be here waiting. She says you can go home and we will let you know when the baby gets here."

"No," Xavier says, his head popping up from the bear. "We've been here this long. This is our reality now, and it cannot change until we have seen the conclusion. We can get through this. I can start the song again. Let's do ginger ale."

"Start it on the inside, Xavier," Dean says. "I'll catch up with you in a bit."

Xavier's face ends up right back in the teddy bear, and I lower myself down to sit next to Dean.

"What are you doing?" I ask.

"Looking through the pictures from Ashley's social media again.

I've run them through a reverse image search trying to connect them to something, but they aren't coming up. Which means she took these pictures herself, rather than downloading them. So now I'm trying to isolate images in the back and on the edges to try to figure out where they might be," he explains.

"Finding these places could be really significant," I say. "Or it could mean nothing. That's the thing we have to remember. Ashley was thirteen years old when she took these. Girls at that age tend to not make a whole lot of sense all the time."

"That's true," he says.

"What about the poetry and captions she has on her page? Does any of them stand out to you? They seem to be fairly standard stuff for a young teen girl. Trying to figure out emotions, dealing with her identity. Some of them talk about having feelings for someone," I say.

"But there's nothing to indicate that might be this Prince Charming older man," Dean says.

"Not directly. She talks about its being wrong that she wants him the way she does. But honestly, that could just mean he's a friend's brother. Making it forbidden would make it more dramatic for her. Which, of course, means more romantic," I say.

"What's romantic?" Sam mumbles in a somewhat croaking voice from his pieced-together bed.

"Nothing," I say. "We're just talking about Ashley Stevenson's social media."

He nods and starts the process of unfolding himself from the chairs.

The door to the waiting area suddenly flings open and Eric appears at it.

"Emma. Come on," he says.

I jump up and rush after him to the room where Bellamy is now positioned in the bed. She reaches for us as we come in and Eric and I each take a hand on either side of her.

"You ready for this?" I ask Bellamy.

"Come on," she says with a hint of a laugh. "This is nothing."

I⊤ TURNS OUT XAVIER WAS RIGHT TO PUT THE CAVEAT IN HIS greeting to Eric. It's just before six in the morning when I go to the waiting room for the last time.

"Guys," I say, "there's someone who wants to meet you."

The three tired, grumpy men follow me to the recovery room where they moved Bellamy just a few minutes ago. She's sitting up in a fresh nightgown, cradling a little pink bundle in her arms. But as soon as they see her, the grumpiness is instantly gone.

"Hi," Bellamy says softly, looking up from the baby's face to them. "You can come closer."

They all creep ahead until they are at her bedside, gazing into the peaceful tiny face.

"Everybody," Eric says, reaching over from where he's standing next to me at Bellamy's head. "This is Emmabelle."

Bellamy and I look at each other with teary smiles and I lean forward to rest my forehead against hers. I couldn't believe it when she told me the name she gave her baby girl. It's an honor I can barely put into words.

Sam and Dean coo over the baby, asking all the expected questions you ask after a baby is born. How long? How much does she weigh? Did she cry a lot?

But I notice Xavier is standing in silence, staring at the baby with his head tilted slightly to the side as if he can't quite process something.

"You alright, Xavier?" I ask.

He doesn't look at me but steps up closer to the edge of the bed and reaches his hands out toward the baby. When Bellamy doesn't immediately move, he wiggles his fingers at her to urge her. She glances at Eric, then carefully places the newborn into Xavier's hands. He takes her gently and cradles her as he walks across the room to the window at the far side.

Adjusting her position, he leans Emmabelle against his chest while supporting the side of her head so they can look out the window together.

"You see that?" he asks softly. "That's the sunrise. I wanted you to see the very first sun on your very first day of life. I always like to watch the sun come up on my birthday and I'm honored to share it with you."

My eyes widen and snap over to Sam, then to Dean. He looks just as surprised as I feel.

"Xavier?" I say.

He turns away from the window with a serene look on his face. "Hmm?"

"Today is your birthday?"

He nods and holds the baby up slightly to display her. "Our birthday."

"Why didn't you tell us?" I ask.

He shrugs as he settles her onto his shoulder and rocks her tenderly. "Turning another year older doesn't seem like an accomplishment that needs celebrating. She was just successfully born. That's worth celebrating."

Dean crosses the room to him.

"Xavier, another year with you on this earth is definitely worth celebrating."

"Absolutely, it is. And after everything you've been through, the fact that you're here right now is even more worth celebrating."

"It is?" he asks.

"Yes," I say. "We have to do something special. Think of something you'd like to do."

He nods. "I will." He looks at Emmabelle again. "Maybe when you're a little bigger we can have a joint birthday party. How about unicorns?"

I smile. That seems appropriate.

TWENTY-FOUR

I'M on the phone with my father as we get back to the house a couple hours later. He's upset he missed the baby's birth, but work took him out of town for a few days.

"Bellamy will bring her over to meet you when you get back," I tell him.

"Good. I can't wait to see her. How's everything else?" he asks.

I let out a breath. "Still sifting through things. In all the cases."

"It will come together," he says. "You'll figure it out."

"Thank you," I say.

"You sound exhausted. Get some sleep. I'll see you in a couple days."

We get off the phone and I kick off my shoes. Without a word, Xavier heads toward the back of the house and disappears into my bedroom. He'll sleep in there while Sam and I take over my father's room and Dean crashes on the couch. I'm exhausted. I know I should be heading right to bed, but I can't make my brain quiet down.

I suddenly realize I haven't eaten anything since before we even showed up to the hospital, with the exception of a couple of chips I snagged from Sam during one of my forays into the waiting room, so I head for the kitchen. I don't have it in me to cook a whole meal. Thank goodness for the frozen burritos my father thinks are delicious, even if his doctor tells him he really shouldn't be eating them.

I microwave a stack of them and bring them into the living room. Just as I'd expected, Dean is sitting on the couch with his tablet on his lap. Sam is in the chair to the side, leaned over so he can see the screen. I set the plate on the coffee table and go back for drinks.

"What do you think?" I ask Sam, nodding toward the screen.

We don't even have to talk about not going to sleep or diving right back into the case. It's obvious we're all on the same page.

"Do you remember when we were teenagers and there was that abandoned drive-in the next town over?" he asks.

I nod as I hand him his drink. "Yeah. That's where everybody went to hang out until we got caught and they put up the fence."

"Right. These places have that same kind of feeling, though. They don't seem to be just random places or places she might have visited once," he says.

"That's what I thought, too," I say. "They feel significant. Dean, did you notice anything new about them?"

"There's definitely at least one building. This hazy coloration on the side here looks like brick. But that's all I've been able to really narrow down right now. I'm not familiar with the area, so it's harder to come up with ideas of what it might be," he says.

For the next half hour we eat our way through the burritos and talk about the case, trying to piece together anything we can. It's leaving us stumped, and that's frustrating as hell. We're getting ready to call it a night when Xavier wanders down the hallway back into the living room. He looks as if he's still most of the way asleep.

"The only way two people can keep a secret is if one of them is dead. The internet never dies," he says. "Emma, I want to ride a roller coaster for my birthday."

"Okay, Xavier," I say.

He turns and goes back to the bedroom. Dean and I look at each other.

"Holy shit," Dean says.

I nod and grab my computer. Logging into Ashley's social media, I scroll through until I find the names I'm looking for.

"Both are old accounts," I point out. "Neither Vivian or Allison has posted on these accounts in a couple of years."

"Probably moved on to newer and better things," Sam says.

"Yeah," I say. "Without Ashley."

"Let's see what kinds of secrets they're keeping," Dean says.

We go back through the accounts until we get to around the time Ashley disappeared, and we scrutinize the postings.

"Nothing," I say after going through Allison's page. "As in, literally. There are no posts for three days. That doesn't make sense. She was all over it before that. And then after."

We go through Vivian's account and see that there are a few more postings than Allison's, but nothing that seems to make any connection. I'm disappointed until I notice a comment.

"'It looks better at night,'" I read. "What does that mean? Somebody posted that on a picture of her feet."

"Not just anybody," Dean points. "Look at the name."

"Tegan Herrara," I say. "That's the guy Allison and Vivian said Ashley was with the night she disappeared."

"And who died not long after," Dean confirms.

"And he's hitting on this girl...because of her feet?" Sam asks, sounding confused.

"I mean, maybe," I say. "That's a thing. But I don't think so. I think there was another picture on this post and she deleted it."

I click on Tegan's name and scroll through the brief stretch after the disappearance. A picture immediately jumps out at me. "Look."

Dean looks at the picture on the screen, then at his tablet. "That's the same place. It's a different angle and it's obviously at night, but it's the same place."

I nod. "It's from the night Ashley went missing."

"From a time when they were supposedly at the campground," Dean says. He pulls the computer toward him and narrows his eyes at the picture, tilting his head to get a different perspective. "Looks as if they couldn't keep a secret."

We break our meeting to get some sleep with the new knowledge not only of where the mysterious spot in the picture is, but also that we need to go there. We rest for a few hours and I'm back up putting in a video call to Allison and Vivian. They both look surprised to hear from me, and to realize they're both on the call as well.

"I'm going to ask you a question that I think I know the answer to, but I need both of you to answer me honestly," I start.

"Go ahead," Vivian says.

"Is Sherando Ridge the only place the three of you girls went the night Ashley went missing?" I ask.

"Yes," both of them answer.

"You didn't go anywhere else?"

"I mean, before we went to the park we went to the store and picked up some food," Allison shrugs.

"But you didn't go anywhere after you got to the park? You went and you set up your tent, you went to Arrow Lake Campground, and back to your tent?"

"Yes," Allison says.

"Okay," I say. "So, do you want to explain to me why Tegan seemed to think all of you hung out behind the old elementary school?"

They aren't in the same place, so they can't exchange glances. That doesn't stop them from looking at each other through the screen. Both of them are waiting for the other one to just say something. I know it's because they weren't ready for this moment. They didn't have the chance to prepare anything to say.

"Behind the old elementary school?" Allison finally asks.

"Yes," I confirm. "From what I understand, it's somewhere you went pretty often."

"How could he have told you that?" Vivian asks, the edge in her voice something close to being offended, but also just startled. "He's been dead for years."

"Yes," I say. "He has. But his social media was never shut down. People love going on and leaving comments to him. They might not remember that all the posts you ever made are still there. Including the picture he posted the night Ashley went missing. A picture of the old school ground. The same place she posted pictures of, that same night."

"That could have been any time," Vivian counters. "He could have taken that picture days before."

"Maybe," I acknowledge. "But it doesn't make a lot of sense. He commented on a picture of the school Ashley posted that day, saying it looked better at night. And then he posted a picture of that place at night. All of this posted the day she went missing. Meaning this activity was going on at the same time you were supposedly at the park."

They hesitate again.

"Maybe we went there earlier in the day," Allison says. "I really can't remember. It was a long time ago."

"Five years isn't that long," I say. "Not long enough for you to forget something like that on a day that affected you so much. And, again, the picture he posted is at night. And if you look closely enough, there are shadows in the picture. Now, we can't prove who those shadows are, of course. But we can make a pretty good guess. This would be the time when both of you need to stop lying and start telling me what actually happened. Because both of you look incredibly suspicious right now. I don't know what you're trying to hide, but it's getting worse the more I look into this."

"We are not trying to hide anything," Vivian protests. "He posted a picture of a place we hung out sometimes. That's it. You can't prove when he took the picture or if we were even there. We told you we were at Sherando Ridge. And that's where we were."

"What are you thinking?" Dean asks when we close the computer screen.

"That they are nowhere near as innocent as they want people to think," I say.

I lean back on the couch, the image of the three girls from a picture hung in Ashley's room stuck in my mind.

Could her two best friends know more about what happened to her than they're saying?

And could they be the reason she's gone?

TWENTY-FIVE

THE NEXT MORNING, we get to the hospital just as Eric is finishing getting the baby dressed. He settles her into Bellamy's arms and comes to give us hugs.

"How was the first night?" I ask.

"Not too bad, actually," Bellamy says. "She woke up for feedings pretty much on the hour, like clockwork. Eric is already a diaper changing champion."

"That's great," I smile. "When do you get to go home?"

"Well, the doctor says we'll probably have to stay for at least another day. She's doing really well, except her bilirubin is higher than they like to see. Nothing dangerous at this point, but they just want to monitor it and see if she's going to need any other intervention."

"Maybe she'll get to be a glow-worm," Xavier says. "That would be fun."

Bellamy laughs and shakes her head. "I'll remember to tell her that when she gets older."

I settle on the side of the mattress and give the baby a nuzzle with my nose. When I look up, I notice Xavier watching us. He has that same look on his face that says something is turning around in his brain.

"What, Xavier?" I ask.

"Oh, I was just noticing something," he says.

"What?" Eric asks.

He sounds a little nervous, which I can't really blame him for, but Xavier doesn't look worried. There's a hint of an amused smile on his lips.

"When they sit like that," Xavier explains, pointing to each of us in turn. "B - EB - E. Bellamy, Emmabelle, Emma. Bebe. Like 'baby' in French."

Bellamy grins and kisses the tiny head snuggled up in the curve of her neck.

"Bebe," she says. "I like it."

And just like that, Xavier has given Emmabelle her nickname.

We tell Bellamy and Eric about our plans to go explore the location we finally identified and then take Xavier for his birthday celebration at a local theme park we found. I feel bad about leaving again, but Bellamy shakes her head.

"Don't worry about it," she says. "We're going to be here in the hospital for at least another day, and then my mom's coming into town to help when we first get home. Everything's going to be fine. Take advantage of time away while you have it. I'm absolutely going to be milking the Auntie Emma card as much as humanly possible when you get back."

I laugh and lean down to hug her. "Deal."

We leave the hospital and head out for Sherando Ridge and Ashley's former stomping grounds. Now that we know what we're looking for, it doesn't take long for us to find the abandoned old elementary school. Sam and Dean did some research and found out that this school shut down decades ago. It was meant to be repurposed, but the community never got around to it.

That left the building and the schoolyard around it empty and unattended. The perfect place for teenagers wanting to get away from the watchful eyes of adults. We park out in front of the building and walk around to the back.

"Can you see it?" I ask Sam.

More specifically, I ask Sam's face on the screen of my phone. He headed back to Sherwood this morning after we visited Bellamy in the hospital. But he's curious about this location and what it has to do with Ashley's disappearance. I agreed to do a video call with him while we were here, but now I'm realizing how difficult it is to try to show him what I'm seeing just by moving the phone around.

"Sort of," he says. "Tilt me down a little bit."

The three of us split up and each head out in our own directions to roam around the old playground. What I can imagine used to be a grassy field with playground equipment and tall trees is now dry and brown. The frame of a metal swing set stands a few yards away from me. The swings are long gone, but a single chain hangs down from the top of the metal frame.

A rusted merry-go-round is off to the other side. I can't even imagine how many children were hurt trying to push that thing around in circles, then jump onto it without losing their balance. And how many more ended up getting slung off by the force of the spinning.

I orient myself and look around.

"This is definitely the same place," I observe. "And by the looks of some of this trash, it hasn't been forgotten as a hangout. I wonder if the local police even have this place on their radar."

"I would hope they would," Sam says. "I know I keep an eye out on any abandoned buildings. Before the old high school was turned into the community center, I used to send guys down there to check it out regularly."

"I remember," I say.

I also remember the single running shoe sitting in the middle of the track, and the woman waiting for me inside the abandoned building with a knife.

"So they came here to hang out without any adults knowing what they were up to. How is that any different from going to Sherando Ridge?" Dean wonders.

"Going to the park is legal," I tell him. "They aren't trespassing. And it's a good story to tell parents."

"Alright," he nods. "But they came clean. They told us they were there with guys when they actually last saw Ashley. Why bother lying about that? Why didn't they just stick to what they said originally?"

"They knew Emma was getting suspicious," Sam pipes up from the phone speaker. "They could tell she wasn't believing their story. Maybe they wanted to seem as though they were opening up and telling the truth, even if it made them look bad."

"Because the actual truth might make them look even worse," I add.

"Dean?" Xavier calls from across the yard.

"Yeah, buddy?" Dean calls back.

"What exactly are we looking for?"

"We don't really know. Maybe we'll know it when we see it," Dean says.

"I see a tombstone," Xavier says.

Dean and I look at each other, then over at Xavier. He's near a tree that looks half-ravaged by weather and neglect but still has a few scraggly leaves hanging on. He's leaned over and looking at the ground, hands hanging down by his sides as if he's trying not to touch anything around him.

We take off toward him. Dean gets to his side first, and the expression on his face changes when he sees what Xavier is looking at. I get there a second later and my stomach drops.

The rock nestled up against the base of the tree is large enough to stand out from the grass grown up around it, but not so large that it's obvious from the other side of the tree. Tombstone isn't exactly how I would describe it. But it's not so far off.

"Show me," Sam says.

I turn my phone so he can see the rock and the faint etching just barely still visible in the rough gray surface.

RIP

Ten minutes later red and blue lights sweep over the yard and then go still. We hear the unmistakable crackling and garbled voices of police radio transmitters coming around the side of the building. Three stern-faced officers meet us in the middle of the yard.

"Agent Griffin," one of the officers says, extending his hand to me.

I recognize him as one of the officers who responded the night everything went down at Arrow Lake Campground.

"Officer Perkins," I say. "Good to see you again."

"I wish I could say the same, but your being at the site of an emergency call probably doesn't mean something good is happening," he replies. "What's going on here?"

"You remember Dean," I say, gesturing to my cousin behind me.

The officer nods and reaches out to shake Dean's hand. "Of course. How are you feeling?"

"Almost as good as new," Dean says. "Thanks."

It's an oversimplification of his actual condition, considering just a few weeks ago an arrow shot from a compound bow tore through his shoulder and out of his back. But he recovered well in the hospital and has barely been showing any signs of lingering pain. Occasionally I notice him favoring that side, but he wouldn't want anyone to mention it. Acknowledging any lasting effects of the injury would be continuing to acknowledge Rodney Mitchell, something he's just not willing to do.

"Dean and I are investigating a missing persons case that came up during the initial investigation of the campground. Ashley Stevenson."

Perkins nods. "I know the name. That's that girl who ran off when she was with her friends, right? Why are you looking into her? I thought she was a runaway."

"Why do you think that?" I ask.

He looks confused. "That's what the detectives said. She was a teenager who got rebellious and ran off."

"She was thirteen," I say. "Barely. She'd just turned thirteen a month before. I don't know about you, but I've never known a thirteen-year-old who would be capable of starting a new life and staying invisible for five years. Her parents don't think she ran away, and we've gotten some information that suggests there's a lot more to her going missing than just her running off. That's why we're here."

The officer's face goes dark. "Did you find something?"

"I don't know. It might be absolutely nothing. But considering the gravity of the case we're investigating, I can't make that assumption. It needs to be thoroughly looked into," I say.

"What have you got for me?"

WHEN THE OFFICERS FIRST SEE THE STONE, I CAN TELL IT doesn't have much impact on them. But they aren't going to tell me they won't look into it. They call it into the station and a detective arrives. I introduce myself and make my statement.

"Thank you," he says. "I appreciate the call. I'm going to need to ask you to leave so we can evaluate the scene."

I can already tell he thinks being here is completely ridiculous. He sees nothing more than a stone with a few letters scratched into it. Getting us to leave is just his way of getting us off his back.

"I'm going to put a call into the detective handling Ashley Stevenson's case and let him know what's going on," I say. "I suggest you put effort into the search. He wants to put this case to bed. If you need anything from me, call. I won't be available tomorrow. I'm traveling. But I'll be available the next day."

"Should be fine, Agent Griffin. You go and enjoy your trip. We'll be in touch."

TWENTY-SIX

"IF YOU DON'T RIDE the rollercoaster first, then you risk being stuck in line when they close. No one wants the last thing they do to be 'Tiny Tim's Terrible Tuesday'," Dean says.

"I said what I said," Xavier responds, stuffing his hands into his pockets and leaning back on his heels.

It feels as if I have interrupted a deep and long argument, and when Dean sees me over Xavier's shoulder, he rolls his eyes. Xavier turns to look at me and raises his eyebrows in a similar exasperated expression.

"Emma," Xavier says. "Dean seems to be under the impression that rollercoasters go before bumper cars. He has no appreciation for the slow increase of H.P.A. and the inherent connection to the perception of fun."

"H.P.A.?" I frown.

"Heartbeats Per Attraction," Dean explains. "It's a system he made up to rank the scariness of rides."

"Not scariness," Xavier says. "Otherwise 'Tiny Tim' would be dead last." He shudders. "The clown out front gives me the willies."

"Dean," I say, touching his arm, "it's Xavier's birthday."

"Celebration," Xavier corrects.

"Birthday celebration," I say.

"Because my birthday already happened."

"Right," I say.

"I guess, technically, I could always say that. I have had birthdays before," Xavier says. "My birthday has happened multiple times over. I am referring to my most recent birthday." He stands taller and clears his throat as if to make an announcement. "I am celebrating my most recent birthday, not the many birthdays of my past, nor birthdays of my future, should I have any."

I stare at him for a moment, and when he nods, I assume he is done.

"Right," I say.

"Which I hope to," he blurts out before I can continue my thought. I stay silent, waiting for him to say something else, but he doesn't.

"Right. So," I say. "Whatever Xavier wants to do, we do."

"Fine," Dean admits, "but I am going to chase you around that track until your H.P.A. is at rollercoaster level."

"I look forward to it," Xavier grins. "Prepare to be bumpered."

"They're called bumper cars because of the bumpers that surround them," I say. "It's not a verb."

Am I correcting Xavier? Willingly opening the floodgates for one of his explanations? What the hell kind of nonsense is going on in my head?

He looks at me and I prepare to chase around his words and try to make them make sense.

"Emma. I was being whimsical."

"Oh," I say after a pause. "Well, whimsical away."

"Dean," Xavier says. "Prepare to be bumpered. You, too, Emma."

"I'm well prepared. Let's go."

"Not yet," Dean says.

"We don't need to wait for Sam," I say. "He's just run to the help desk to get us the picture pass. He'll call me when he's done."

Sam insisted on coming down to celebrate Xavier's birthday with us. He got here early this morning and will head back to Sherwood tonight. It's an exhausting jaunt for him, but he didn't want to miss this. He's so sweet and cares so much about other people. It's one of the reasons I love him.

"No, not Sam," Dean says.

"Then who?" I ask, completely confused.

Dean nods behind me. I turn to see Ava making her way toward us, holding a lanyard with a clear plastic cardholder on it to her chest with one hand and the other raised in a wave. She's jogging toward us in an awkward gait somewhere between hurrying and trying to look as if she's not hurrying.

Oh, you have got to be freaking kidding me.

I turn back to Dean, heat rising up the sides of my face.

"What is she doing here?" I whisper, trying to keep my voice calm.

"I invited her," Dean shrugs. "She's actually a very nice person if you give her a chance. I thought it would be nice to have her with us at the park. Especially considering you kind of abandoned her when you found out Bellamy was in labor." Those last words spill out of him fast to make sure they're all out before Ava gets to us. His face brightens in a smile. "Hi!"

I look over at Xavier. His head is tilted to the side as he watches Dean and Ava greet each other. He's trying to figure it out, to process that she's there and that he's going to have to integrate her into his plans. He doesn't push back, so I take a breath and force myself to get some perspective.

It's awkward for sure, but I want to make the best of it. The day is about Xavier after all, and as long as he isn't going to be too upset, I really don't have a reason to be, either. Dean is right. I did just peace out and go to the hospital without telling Ava we were leaving or that we wouldn't be there to investigate the next day. I barely even remembered she was a thing until I saw her coming toward us just now.

But this is precisely why I had misgivings about this whole situation. There's a reason I don't have pets or houseplants. In a lot of ways, she fits into that category. No pets, no houseplants, no extra people on the periphery of a case.

Sam joins us as we make our way to one side of the park where the games that most closely resemble midway games are. It's an interesting park, different from any I've been to before. But Xavier wanted a roller coaster for his birthday, and this is the closest one we could find. While Xavier frets about raising his H.P.A., I am wondering if there's even enough to do to make it until nightfall. The park is tiny and unless he's going to be sampling the kiddie land after the bumper cars, there won't be much progression to be had.

We stand in line for the bumper cars, and Sam joins us, coming up behind me and wrapping an arm around my waist.

"Bumper cars?" Sam raises an eyebrow.

"Starting slow," Xavier calls back.

"He has to raise his H.P.A. carefully," I explain.

"Is that something I need to be concerned about?" he asks. "I won't give up the cinnamon rolls."

I shake my head with a laugh.

When we get in our cars and wait for the electricity to jolt them to life, Dean doesn't go immediately for Xavier. Instead, he veers off to the side and bumps Ava. Not hard, but enough to get her attention before zooming off.

Interesting. Maybe his inviting her here didn't really have anything to do with my abandoning her after all.

But I'm not going to dwell on that right now. There are other things to think about, and while I'm trying to enjoy my time at the park with everyone, I can't stop my thoughts from wandering back to the case. It feels as if I'm staring at a locked door. Just beyond is whatever is tugging at the corner of my consciousness. If I could only get inside, I could probably figure it out in a flash. But I can't seem to get it open, no matter how hard I try.

That gets harder and harder with each new thing Xavier guides us to. Dean stops pouting about the roller coaster after getting a few licks in on the bumper cars and then getting Xavier to challenge him in a couple of skill games. It's impressive how good Xavier gets after one or two tries at each one, and Dean seems to know it's coming, not spending more than three rounds at any of them.

"I'd like to try this one," Ava says as the boys move on from a game where the object is to shoot water at a target in a duck's mouth to get a little duck above to move. "Emma, will you play?"

It sounds so innocent that it's almost cute. I nod, not even realizing I am doing it. Sam sits down between us and pays for the three of us to go with tickets he has balled up in his shirt pocket.

Ava wins the first round, which sets off my competitive streak. I pull the tickets out of Sam's shirt and we go again. This time, I win. Sam seems to notice the tension and stands up before I can reach in and go for the tiebreaker.

"Come on," he says. "I think Xavier wants to get food."

"Fine," I say, standing reluctantly. "Where?"

"There." Ava points to a little building made up to look like a giant cupcake.

Xavier is already walking back toward us, a giant cone of cotton candy in one hand and a drink in the other. Dean follows him with his own.

"What in the world?" Sam asks. "That has to be two feet of cotton candy."

"Good eye," Xavier says. "They advertise it as two feet, but I had to get them to re-spin it. The first time only came out to a foot and eight inches."

"Clearly, Xavier wasn't going to get one pulled over on him," Dean laughs. His cotton candy, baby blue compared with Xavier's hot pink, is already partially eaten. Dean seems to take the method of filling his entire mouth with it on each bite.

"Want some?" Xavier asks, holding the sugary treat close to my face.

I pull a chunk of the spun sugar off and put it in my mouth. It's been years since I've had cotton candy. I've forgotten how delightful it is to just let it melt in all its nutritionally useless glory on my tongue.

"Are your heartbeats up enough to head for the coasters?" Dean asks.

Xavier nods, too invested in his cotton candy to engage in any conversation. We make our way to the corner of the park containing a handful of large roller coasters and stop in the middle so Xavier can consider all of them.

"Which one would choose you, Emma?" he asks.

It reminds me of our first encounter; when he asked me which snack in the vending machine would choose me to describe itself.

I glance at all the names and find one that fits perfectly.

"The Skeleton Key."

I'm thinking about the skeletons, but Xavier knows better.

"Ahh," he nods. "Yes. Capable of unlocking anything from the right angle."

TWENTY-SEVEN

THE ADRENALINE of the coasters gets to me. I find myself relaxing and having fun after the first ride, running from line to line with the rest of them. Watching Xavier on the rides is a wonder in and of itself. As excited as he is, he makes no show of it. He sits down, patiently waits for the safety harness to be secured over him, then stays completely silent for the duration of the ride.

There's no screaming. No cheering. Not even laughter. He sits there and looks around as if he's on a leisurely train ride, either hanging on to the bar in front of him or throwing his hands up into the air. But when he gets off the ride at the end, he's bubbling over about how much fun it was.

I look forward to seeing the on-ride pictures.

After a long day, we've ridden everything, and an evening crowd is starting to trickle in, so it's time to head out. We stop at a cluster of old animatronic mushrooms that stands without explanation in a flower patch between two sections of the park. We discovered earlier that they burst into song like a barbershop quartet at seemingly random intervals. It requires at least a video and a commemorative picture.

I'm admiring the snap we just took when the picture disappears and a phone number appears on the screen. I don't recognize it, but the area code is for this area, so I pick it up. My blood runs cold when I hear the voice on the other end of the line.

"What's wrong?" Sam asks when I end the call and shove my phone back in my pocket.

"That was the police department. They say I need to come in immediately."

We rush out of the park and head directly for the police station. I'm barely inside the building when Misty Stevenson descends on me. Her face is red, her eyes wild.

"What the hell were you doing?" she demands.

"Misty, what's wrong? What are you talking about?" I ask.

"How could you be so dismissive? I thought you actually cared about what happened. I thought you were really coming here to help us," she says.

"I am," I tell her.

"Then what the hell were you doing while the police were pulling my daughter's body out of the ground?" she asks through gritted teeth.

"What?" I ask, feeling the color drain from my face.

An officer appears behind Misty and takes hold of her shoulders, pulling her away from me as she tries to force herself closer.

"Calm down, Mrs. Stevenson," he says. "This isn't going to do you any good."

"Wait, what is she talking about?" I ask.

"Agent Griffin."

A familiar voice from behind me makes me turn around. I see one of the detectives I interacted with at the campground standing at the door to the back of the station and walk up to him.

"You want to tell me what the hell is happening here?" I demand.

"Come on back with me," he says.

Misty is still fighting behind me and I gesture toward her.

"You're just going to ignore her? She's clearly distraught," I say.

"We're having transport take her to the hospital for sedation. She says she hasn't slept in the last few days. Clearly, it's starting to affect her," he says.

He ushers me through the door and into an office where we sit down.

"What is she talking about? You found Ashley Stevenson's remains?" I ask.

"Not exactly. I can't go so far as to say that right at this moment. The team alerted us to your call yesterday. The responding officers didn't seem to think there was much to the stone against the tree, but it struck my interest. This case has been hanging over this department for years now, and even though the general belief is that she ran away, there are still questions. It's not settled until we know exactly what happened," he explains.

"She didn't run away," I tell him. "And the more you repeat that, the less likely it's going to be that you ever find her."

"Which is exactly why I decided the schoolyard needed more investigation. We sent a team out there and they brought cadaver dogs with them. Both dogs alerted in the area around the tree. That suggests there is evidence of human remains in the area of the rock marked RIP. Now, you know as well as I do that a cadaver dog alerting to a spot is not conclusive. It doesn't necessarily mean there was a body, and even that doesn't prove that the person was killed," he says.

"I know. There are a lot of things a dog can alert to without its being a corpse, but two dogs alerting to an area that has a marker on it seems compelling," I say.

"It is," the detective agrees. "So, we are excavating the area."

"If you are only excavating, how did Misty Stevenson find out?" I ask. "She's out there on the brink of snapping. Who told her what was going on?"

"The media caught wind of the cadaver dogs out there. Mrs. Stevenson showed up at the station saying she knew the dogs had to do with Ashley because your name was mentioned in the news report."

I roll my eyes, then close them and rub the lids with my fingers. "Shit. People have got to stop thinking that freedom of the press means the right to blow up investigations."

"We've tried to reassure her, but as you saw, the news is hitting her hard," he says.

"Do you think it's possible Ashley is buried there?" I ask.

"I don't have an answer for that. Right now, all we have is the response from the dogs and the rock. The excavation is underway and we should have more answers tomorrow," he says.

"Thank you for letting me know," I say.

He looks me up and down and a strange hint of a smile tugs at the corner of his lips.

"I have to say, I'm used to seeing you so put together. It's interesting to see you a little messy."

I look down at my jeans and old t-shirt. I'm sweaty and not wearing any makeup. My hair is tied behind my head but a good portion of it has slithered its way out of the elastic band over the course of the day.

"I was celebrating a very dear friend's birthday today. He wanted to go to a theme park," I tell him.

"A theme park?"

"He loves roller coasters."

"Don't you have enough adrenaline in your life, Agent Griffin?"

MISTY IS NO LONGER IN THE LOBBY WHEN I LEAVE THE STATION. I call Dean on speakerphone as I pull out of the parking lot.

"Everything alright?" he asks.

"I'm not sure. They sent cadaver dogs to the schoolyard and they hit on something near the tree," I explain.

"Do they think it's Ashley?" he asks.

"They don't have any real details yet. They're excavating the area. I'm headed over there now to see what I can find out."

"Alright. Keep me posted."

"I will. How is everybody?"

"Xavier fell asleep. Sam says he's going to stay here until you're back," he says.

"Tell him I'll be there as soon as I can," I say.

I end the call and drive another few miles to end up on the empty road leading to the abandoned elementary school. Seeing how far out of town this place is makes it easy to understand the decision to close it down. There's an isolated, unnerving feeling about the area. The fact that it's empty and overgrown definitely contributes to that, but I don't think even bright green grass and hallways full of students could take away all of the disconnected feeling.

The cars parked in front of the building and floodlights illuminating the entire yard are a stark contrast to the still quiet from the day before. I park and jog up to the nearest officer.

"Agent Emma Griffin, FBI," I say. "I need to speak with the supervising officer."

The woman gives a single nod. "Wait here."

She leaves and I take the few steps over to the chain-link fence surrounding the yard. Threading the fingers of one hand through the gaps, I grip the warm metal and watch the methodical process in front of me.

Officers filter around the yard, which glows in the light of the bright lamps. Despite its being called an excavation, no large machines are waiting to dig out massive chunks of the land. Contrary to what TV crime shows would have you believe, those are rarely used to recover bodies at potential crime scenes. The use of a tool like that can lead to damage and loss of evidence if the investigators don't know how deep to dig.

Instead, the process is slow and painstaking. Layers of the dirt are removed slowly and carefully. That's what's happening now. I can see the tarps spread on the ground around the tree and two officers with spades digging down into the dirt.

An officer comes toward me and I let go of the fence to shake his hand.

"Detective Billings," he says. "You're Emma Griffin."

"Yes," I say. "Have you found anything?"

"Not conclusively. But we're still early in the process," he says.

I nod and look over at the dig again. "What do you think?"

"I don't know yet. I've found that dogs are generally accurate when it comes to identifying places of interest. Does that mean a body was buried out here? That's still yet to be seen."

"Please keep me updated," I tell him.

He nods and shakes my hand again. "Will do."

TWENTY-EIGHT

"Cadaver dogs were brought to the area behind the old elementary school today in what we're told is the ongoing investigation of the disappearance of Ashley Stevenson, a local girl who went missing five years ago. Law enforcement declines to comment on the exact nature of the investigation or what, if anything, has been found. You might remember Ashley's name came up during the recent horrific discovery of a series of murders uncovered at Arrow Lake Campground that rocked the local community.

"Though officials can confirm Ashley was not one of the victims of those alleged serial killers, the appeal by her mother has generated renewed interest in the case. While the FBI has been brought in to investigate the deaths at the campground, sources confirm Agent Emma Griffin, who has been involved in several high-profile cases in the last few years, is involved in both investigations.

"We'll bring you any updates on this developing story as soon as they are available."

He sat in his recliner, leaned back with one leg propped in front of him, watching the news. Archival footage of Thirteen's mother making her plea to the public played in the upper corner of the screen. Occa-

sionally pictures broke in. A big smile. A sleepy, bewildered look from beneath a red and white checked comforter. Three friends playing together in the sand.

They were the kinds of pictures meant to humanize a name said so many times across the airwaves it started to become white noise. It was the same thing that had happened five years before. The news was saturated with the desperate, dramatic story of a bright-eyed young teenager who seemed to vaporize into thin air. But only for a short time. Then it faded.

Now the story was back; they were pushing as hard as they could to force that name into people's thoughts and conversations, as if that would make a difference. As if talking about her would make her reappear.

He looked over at his girlfriend where she sat on the couch, mindlessly crocheting a baby blanket. She was staring at the screen, too, and he wondered what thoughts were going through her mind. He turned back to the TV and the image of bright lights flooding a neglected schoolyard.

"Looks like you lost your buried treasure," he muttered. "Keep looking. Keep looking."

TWENTY-NINE

WHEN MISTY OPENS her front door the next morning, she looks as if she hasn't slept. Tugging a long, thin cardigan tighter around her body and dabbing at her nose with a tissue that has seen far better days, she steps back and gestures me inside.

The house smells like many layers of coffee. Cup after cup, brewed throughout the night. There's something sweet among the bitter notes. On the table are two bowls of partially-eaten oatmeal heavily laden with milk and brown sugar. They've tried to eat breakfast.

Tried.

"Why haven't we heard anything?" she asks.

"The investigation team wanted to take their time and make sure to search the area thoroughly. I don't want to make any premature conclusions. They worked through the night searching the entire area. They asked that I be the one to tell you what they found," I say.

John reaches out and grasps his wife's hand, squeezing it tightly as he prepares himself to hear what I have to say.

"They did find evidence of human remains. But it's not Ashley. The team found fetal remains. Most likely a stillbirth prior to viability. But the medical examiner is going to have to make a final conclusion about that," I say.

I'm expecting Misty to seem relieved. Instead, she's overcome. Her face goes pale and she lets out a sob before her knees buckle under her. John swoops in to grab her before she hits the floor and brings her over to sit on the couch.

"I'm sorry," she whispers, pressing one hand to her chest while covering her eyes with the other.

"Don't apologize," I tell her. "Are you alright?"

John watches his wife for a few seconds before looking up at me with sadness in his eyes.

"Misty lost a baby years ago," he explains. "It's still very difficult for her. Anytime she hears that a woman lost a child, it really gets to her. It's been especially difficult since Ashley went missing."

"I'm so sorry to hear that," I say. "I know this isn't easy for you. Everything that's happened over the last couple of weeks must be extremely difficult. But we're doing everything we can to find out what happened to Ashley. This isn't going to be easy to hear, but I do need to ask both of you for a DNA sample."

I didn't relish the idea of making that request when I headed over here this morning, but now I feel particularly uncomfortable about it. The whole idea of the baby is clearly overwhelming for Misty. But there's never going to be a good moment to ask Ashley's parents for DNA, so there's no point in hesitating.

Misty looks up at me with wide, reddened eyes. Her mouth is open as if she's so shocked by the request she can't even bring herself to make any sound. Finally, she lets out a sound that's somewhere between a breath and a gasp.

"They think it was Ashley's?" she asks.

"Right now, no one is coming to any conclusions. They just have to cover all the bases. That location was obviously of significance to Ashley, so it's important any evidence found there is treated as though it could be a part of her disappearance," I say.

"She was only thirteen years old," John points out. "She was just a baby herself."

"I know," I nod. "And I'm sorry. I can't even imagine how upsetting this must be for you. But it's important that the investigation is as thorough as possible, even when it's uncomfortable. We need to identify the mother of that baby and find out how it came to be under that rock. You can submit samples at the police station. It's a very easy process."

John shifts in his seat for a second. "I won't need to take a test."

That straightens my spine and makes my skin sting as I instinctively prepare myself for what might be coming.

"Why not?"

"It won't prove anything. I'm not Ashley's biological father."

That's not what I was expecting to hear. The tension that came into me while my mind readied to hear something horrible drains out of me, but leaves questions. They aren't ones I'm going to ask. It's up to Misty and John to tell me what they think I need to know.

"Alright," I say.

Misty's shoulders sag under the weight of a long exhale.

"I married John after Ashley was born," she tells me. "He isn't either girl's biological father. But he's been the most incredible father either of them could have."

I nod. "I don't doubt that. But in that case, yes, Misty will be the only one who needs to be tested. Then we'll go from there."

I WENT WITH MISTY TO SUBMIT HER SAMPLE, THEN MADE SURE she didn't need anything before heading back to the hotel to meet up with Xavier and Dean and update them on everything that's developing. Xavier is on a video chat when I walk into the room; I'm surprised to see my father's face on the screen.

"Hey, sweetie," he calls over.

"Dad?" I frown, taking a seat on the couch beside Xavier. "What are you two talking about?"

"Clandestine soup can concealers. The ever-present risk of unintentional clue discovery and its solutions," Xavier rattles off.

I have two options here. I can ask him what the hell he's talking about and open myself up for that conversation. Or I can pretend I fully understand and move forward. At this particular juncture in my life, I'm going to opt for the latter.

"How's everything?" I ask my father. "Where are you?"

"Iowa," he says. "I had a few things I needed to take care of here."

I know better than to ask what he means by that. Iowa carries a lot of meaning for me and for my family. Even though my memories of the place are limited to brief snippets I'm not even sure are completely real, I know the value of the place to my parents. I visited a few years ago when I was still trying to understand what happened to my mother. I didn't find much. But I know there are still secrets hidden there that I don't need to know about.

"How is your case going?" I ask.

"It's kind of at a standstill right now. There are some unexpected turns I need to research before I can move forward. But that's actually working in my favor. One of the men I was telling you about reached out to me," he says.

"From The Order?" I ask.

My father nods.

"Emma," Xavier says in a low tone, leaning slightly toward me.

"I told you I thought he might. He said there's an event coming up he thought I might be interested in. It's for long-standing members, and they needed to further verify my status within the organization before inviting me," Dad goes on.

"Emma," Xavier repeats.

I pat his arm to acknowledge I hear him, but don't look away from the screen.

"Isn't that exactly what you said wasn't happening in the other chapters, though?" I ask.

"It is," Dad confirms. "Which makes it particularly interesting. And the idea of verifying my status within The Order stood out to me. I'm not sure what he meant by that."

"You mentioned there were two men who you thought might know more than they were letting on," I say.

"Yes," Dad acknowledges. "But one had to take leave for a while. Apparently, he sent a message to the others saying he needed to go care for his sick grandmother."

That strikes me in a strange way, but I'm not sure exactly why. Beside me, Xavier starts scooting across the cushions, pushing me to the side. I'm trying to respond, but his jostling me is distracting.

"Xavier, what are you doing?" I finally ask when he's managed to nudge me almost off the corner of the couch.

"You stole my phone call," he says matter-of-factly.

"I'm sorry. Dad, I'll talk to you soon."

"Bye, sweetie."

They get back to their conversation and I go over to talk to Dean. He's leaned back against the headboard of one of the beds, his long legs crossed in front of him. I get on the other bed and flop onto my stomach. The angle lets me stare through the sliding glass doors of the balcony into the blue sky.

"How do you think they got Greg out on that beach?" I ask after a few long moments.

Dean lifts the remote, pointedly mutes the TV, and swings his head to the side to look at me.

"What?" he asks.

"The day he died. How do you think he got lured out onto the beach? He hated water," I say.

"I know, Emma. But we've been over this. He had just gone through a really traumatic two years and was finally free. He had a new lease on life and wanted to try all the things he'd avoided for so long," Dean says.

"Yeah, I remember that's what we said, but it's not sitting right with me," I say.

"Why not?"

I pull myself up, swinging my legs around to fold them under me so I can lean toward him and talk without interrupting Xavier and my father.

"He and Lydia were hitting it off. They had gotten to be friends. She was definitely under the impression it could turn out to be more. There was enough there that he was willing to leave the hospital with her rather than waiting for me or one of the guys from the team the way he was supposed to. So he goes against safety protocols to get discharged and leave with this woman no one knows and who he has been speaking closely with about a huge, very dangerous case in his career, and then he just walks away from her?"

"It doesn't make sense. Why would he leave with her if he was just going to part ways with her pretty much immediately, so he could go off and stand on a beach to confront his hatred of water? Do you see how that doesn't fit?"

Dean nods. "I mean, yes, that makes sense. I would think if he had this girl he really liked, and he was willing to leave the hospital with her, he would take her with him to the beach."

"That would be the logical step. Greg tended to in his own head a lot of the time, but even he could be romantic. He wouldn't be so dedicated to the concept of facing off against the great power of the ocean gods or some shit like that, that he would leave behind a woman he was interested in. Which means he didn't go out onto that beach just because he wanted to see the water and prove he could deal with it."

"Someone wanted him out there," Dean completes my thought.

I nod. "He knew he was supposed to be meeting someone and couldn't let Lydia be a part of it. But here's another question—how did nobody notice?"

"What do you mean?" Dean asks.

"DC isn't exactly a sleepy, quiet town. There are people all over the place, all the time. So, how could he get shot in broad daylight, then lie on the beach for three days without anyone's noticing?

People would have been out on that beach. Someone would have seen it happen, or at least heard the gunshot. And even if no one heard or saw anything in that exact moment, even if we could suspend our disbelief enough to say there was no one anywhere around who witnessed the murder, how did no one find his body in those three days?" I ask.

"Maybe he was kept for that time?" Dean suggests. "Somebody got Greg and held him until he killed him?"

"After everything Greg had just gone through, I really don't think he would let anyone else grab him like that. And if someone tried, he would put up a fight. There were no defensive wounds on his body. Nothing to show there was a struggle of any kind. Besides, if someone did have him for those three days, why would he or she then bring him out onto the beach to kill him? Greg would have run. It just doesn't make sense. None of it does."

"What about the case files?" Dean asks. "You said you wanted to see them because you think there's something in them that might help you figure it out. Have you made any progress with getting them?"

"No. The last time I spoke with Creagan, he wouldn't budge. He says I'm not on that task force and he still thinks I'm too close to the whole situation," I say.

"The way he was too close to the situation with your mother?" Dean asks.

It's less a question than it is pointing something out to me, and it instantly brings the anger back. I get out my phone and call Creagan.

This time, he relents. I hang up, knowing soon I'll have the full files and be able to dig deeper to find out what really happened to Greg.

THIRTY

"There's no familial link at all?" I ask Detective Billings.

"No," he shakes his head. "The DNA provided by Misty does not match the mitochondrial DNA of the fetus, meaning it could not be the child of Misty's child."

"Have you informed Misty?" I ask.

"No. I wanted to discuss it with you first," he says.

"Is that because you are hoping I'll be the one to tell her?" I ask.

He doesn't look as though he's going to come right out and admit that, but he doesn't dispute it, either.

"You are the one who talked to her about the fetal remains. It seems you have developed a rapport with her, so it might be easier coming from you," he attempts.

It might seem that telling Misty and John that the stillborn baby found at the elementary school wasn't genetically connected to Ashley would be easy, welcome news. But it's not that simple. I'm sure the Stevensons will be relieved to have absolute confirmation Ashley did not give birth. This news, however, means they are still exactly where they have been for the last five years. There's nothing new, nothing to hang their hopes on.

"I'll go see them," I tell him. "In the meantime, I have a suggestion."

"What is it?" he asks.

"Ask Ashley's friends Vivian McLemore and Allison Garrett for their DNA to compare with the fetus," I say.

***

Misty still cringes when she hears another mention of the remains, but she takes the news with the relief I hoped she would feel. She nods and wipes an errant tear from where it rests on her cheek.

"We're going to keep searching," I tell her. "We'll keep looking for leads. We're not giving up on Ashley."

She nods, staring into the middle distance as though she's seeing something I'm not.

"I want to do something for her," she says.

"For Ashley?" I ask.

She nods, straightening up and lifting her chin slightly, trying to put on a brave face and get through this.

"Her eighteenth birthday was in June. We had a little family celebration for her, as we do every year, but there should have been more. I want to do a vigil for her. The date she went missing is coming up soon. August thirteenth," she says.

"Okay. Do you want to do the vigil on that day?" I ask.

She shook her head. "No. I don't want to honor that day. This needs to be about Ashley. I want to have the people who cared about her come together at her school and we'll just share memories and talk about any progress in the case that can be shared. Just remind everybody that we still love Ashley and she hasn't left our minds."

"That's a great idea. It's a way to keep the community involved in the case, but it may also shake up anyone who might know more about what happened to her," I say.

"So you'll be there?" she asks.

I nod. "I'll be there. And I'll keep an eye out for anything that seems off."

IT SEEMED EVERY TIME HE TURNED ON THE TV, THERE WAS *another mention of the case. Another opportunity to see Thirteen's mother. She really was doing everything she could to force her daughter's face into the thoughts of anyone watching. She wanted them to say her daughter's name, to think like her. There was a strange, almost-deification happening.*

This time, the news wasn't just bringing flat, still images of her. This time it was another video.

"We've spent almost five years without our Ashley. We don't want to hit that milestone without knowing what happened to her. That's why we are asking all those who cared for Ashley to come to a belated celebration of her birthday and a vigil for her return. Please wear her favorite color, red, and come with memories to share."

She continued to talk, but he wasn't focused on what she was saying. He was watching her mouth move. Watching the sweep of her hair over her shoulder. She certainly looked different now. She looked as if she had gotten herself together.

It fascinated him.

MISTY'S INSISTENCE THAT THE VIGIL MUST HAPPEN BEFORE THE fifth anniversary of Ashley's going missing means it has to be put together quickly. Fortunately, the community has opened its heart to her since the reemergence of Ashley's story; they are willing to do what they can to help her. For the three days leading up to the vigil, it seemed every news outlet was streaming constant reminders, pictures of Ashley from around the time of her disappearance, and video clips of her parents pleading for any information about what happened to her.

It's not a surprise when we drive in as the vigil is getting underway to find a sea of red balloons and t-shirts spread across the soccer field outside Ashley's former middle school. For the last couple of days, I've been trying to press Creagan into giving me the files related to Greg's death that he'd promised. He's had plenty of excuses for not giving them over, but he's still saying he'll send them to me. While at the same time checking in with me about how Ava is doing.

It feels as if we're playing a game of chess.

Even without the files in hand, I knew I needed to get back into town for the vigil. I need to see if the public display proves too appealing to someone wanting to relive his own handiwork. I've requested that all of the evidence found at the lake having to do with Ashley be set aside so I can go through it. I need to understand how those items ended up submerged with the victims of Laura and Rodney when they had nothing to do with her disappearance.

I'll go over those things later this afternoon. Right now, my focus has to be on the people swarmed into the field and how they are reacting to the event. For some of them, it's the spectacle. That's inevitable for an event like this. People are going to come out just to witness the emotion unfolding around them. Some want to feel as if they're a part of something, some just want to see it happening.

For others, this is a time for them to remember the young teenager, so close to still being a little girl, who was taken from their lives in a way none understands yet.

My hope is that there will be another person there. Someone who doesn't fit into either category. I watch the people listening to Misty up on the podium, talking about Ashley and everything she would be doing with her life now if she was still there with them.

A person's going missing, especially when it's a child, is like a dropped stone in the middle of a pond. It doesn't just affect the people closest to that center point. The impact drifts out all the way to the far edges.

Somewhere among them, there could be that one person who was drawn here to watch the ripples.

Among the group crowded closest to the stage with the podium, I see Allison and Vivian. They see me looking at them and turn away as fast as they can. So far, neither of them has submitted DNA. According to the detective, both were disgusted and offended when he asked.

I told him to get warrants.

Misty finishes her speech and steps aside to let John come up and take a turn. He laughs and cries his way through memories of Ashley, who he calls his daughter with every drop of love and sincerity anyone could ask of him. I don't see anyone unusual in the crowd. No one stands out. No one seems to be there alone or to be particularly uncomfortable.

My focus drifts back to Vivian and Allison. They're nodding along with some of the stories, smiling at times and wiping away tears. Their emotion seems genuine, but I'm still on guard with them. I won't come to any conclusions yet. There is still too much that isn't known for me to zero in and not remain open to other possibilities.

But I also don't intend to let them off the hook easily. There's something they're hiding. They haven't told the whole story yet.

I'm going to make sure it gets told. Either they will tell it to me or I'll force it out of them.

THIRTEEN. THIRTEEN. THIRTEEN.

It was all she heard. No one was allowed to call her anything else.

They knew her name. She knew they did. But it was only ever Thirteen.

Now she closed her eyes, gripping the metal of the fence in front of her, and listened to the voices in the field.

There was hope in them and there was fear. Laughter and sadness. But above all, there was one thing. One thing she had been waiting to hear. She had been waiting to know that they saw her, that they knew her.

She gathered her strength and stepped through the gate.

"ASHLEY."

THIRTY-ONE

MISTY HAD GONE BACK UP to the podium for another speech when I saw her face go pale. Her eyes widened and her mouth fell open slightly for just an instant before she said it.

"Ashley."

She's said the name dozens of times in the last half an hour we've been standing in the field, but it sounds different this time. Her eyes are locked not on the crowd gathered in front of her, or on the sky she's glanced up to several times already, but across the field toward the gate leading in from the parking lot.

A few people have already turned around to see what she's looking at. Gasps and whispers roll through the crowd. Misty pushes away from the podium so hard she nearly knocks it over. Behind her, Leona's hands have fallen from where she clasped them hard in front of her as she listened to her mother talk, fighting emotion to keep her face still and blank.

I turn and see what caused the reaction.

A girl is walking across the field, her dark hair clinging to the sides of her face, and her neck with sweat from the already-hot

August air. Her clothes hang on a thin body and her face is hollow. But it's unmistakable. It's Ashley Stevenson.

An instant later, there's chaos.

Misty scrambles down from the stage with John close behind her. People from the crowd have started to head toward Ashley and I can already see the look of panic rising in her face. I take off running toward her, needing to stop the crowd before they can swarm around her.

I stop a few feet from her and hold my arms out to create a block-ade, screaming for the people to stop. I push them back with the sheer force of my stance and the volume of my voice. They comply, backing up a few steps and leaving space for Misty and John to surge in front of them.

Dean and Xavier rush to my side, following my instructions to form as much of a barrier as they can between the people and the parents gripping their daughter in their arms. I want them blocking the phones snapping images and recording these fragile, sensitive moments. Dean shouts at them, commanding them to put their phones away.

As some people do as they're told, I stalk away from the group and pull my phone out to call 911.

AN HOUR LATER I'M ON THE PHONE AGAIN, THIS TIME AS I PACE back and forth through another waiting room. This one isn't like the large, bright room where the guys waited for Bellamy's baby to be born. There's no giant teddy bear draped on the ground or TV hanging from the ceiling. It's a small, square room with chairs lining the walls and the table in the middle holding two boxes of tissues.

This isn't the type of room where people wait for joyous news.

Right now, I'm using it to talk with Creagan.

"This is now part of the investigation," he says.

"This doesn't have anything to do with Arrow Lake. She wasn't kidnapped by the Mitchells. Her disappearance can't be included in the investigation of those murders," I say.

"Then it is a different investigation. However you want to describe it, it is now the territory of the FBI. This is a Bureau case and I'm expecting you to resolve it."

"I was already investigating it," I reply, not even bothering to try to hide the edge of aggravation and anger in my voice.

"You've taken on a lot and have tremendous possibilities right now. Agent James will be on this team."

"I don't need her. Dean and I are already investigating Ashley Stevenson's disappearance," I say.

"Dean doesn't have the type of clearance she does. He might have a few tricks up his sleeve as a private investigator, but he's not going to be as valuable as another FBI agent."

"I beg to differ on that," I counter. "He has more skill and insight than the vast majority of the agents I've worked with."

"What he doesn't have is training and authorization. Agent James has those things. She's part of this investigation, Griffin."

There's nothing I can say. He's already talked to the detective heading up Ashley's case, who requested the Bureau formally step in. If he's going to assign Ava to the case, that's what he's going to do. Frankly, right now I don't have the space in my mind to push back against it. I'm too busy wrangling people and knocking down questions and pressure from the media that have already taken up residence outside the hospital.

This situation needs to get under control and that's not going to happen if I'm thinking about anything else.

I don't even know if I say goodbye to Creagan. I stuff the phone in my pocket and stalk back down the hall to the room flanked by police officers. They step aside when they see me coming.

I open the door and find Ashley in a hospital gown in the bed. She's sitting up, but the bed is adjusted to support her back so she's leaned against it as it holds her up. The gown, clouds of white pillows, and the blanket over her make her look even smaller than she did when she was walking across the field. Misty is sitting beside the bed, holding one of her daughter's hands. The other arm has a needle in it, pumping fluids into her clearly malnourished, dehydrated body.

Her head is leaned to one side, looking at her mother as if she's trying to avoid the stares of the three police officers crowded on the other side of the bed.

"We need as much information as you can give us," one of the officers says.

"The longer you wait, the harder it's going to be for us to find who did this to you," another adds.

"You need to tell us what you remember."

"Stop," Misty says, her voice trembling. "Can't you see how much you're upsetting her? This is ridiculous."

"Time is of the essence when it comes to a situation like this, ma'am," the first officer says. "If we don't get the information quickly, she might not remember details or not be willing to share them."

"What's that supposed to mean? Are you suggesting she would try to protect the monsters who did this to her?" Misty asks.

"It wouldn't be the first time a victim was unwilling to say something because he or she was defending a captor."

"Get out of here," Misty snaps, her voice low and angry.

"We need to interview her."

"Not right now."

"She's been through something very serious..."

"Obviously she has, and yet you're here trying to climb down her throat. I'm her mother and I'm telling you she's not ready to talk right now," Misty says.

"With all due respect, ma'am, Ashley is eighteen. She's not a child anymore and you can't determine if she undergoes an interview or what she says."

"Enough," I cut in, stepping further into the room. The officers turn to look at me and I take out my badge. "Emma Griffin, FBI. I'm handling this case now. You can leave."

"But..." one of the officers starts.

"I said, enough. This girl has been through hell and you're not going to speak to her that way. Go back to the station."

I stand at the foot of the bed, staring down the men until they leave the room. Once they're gone, I turn back to Misty and Ashley.

"Thank you," Misty says. "I appreciate that. I can't believe they were treating her like that."

"I'm sorry for that," I tell her. "Their behavior was unacceptable. But they're gone now and I'll make sure they don't come back here. How does that sound?"

Misty nods. "Thank you."

"Hi, Ashley," I say. "My name is Emma. I work for the FBI."

Dark eyes slide over to me. "Hi."

"I'm really happy to see you. When you're ready, I'd like to talk to you about what happened," I say.

I'm about to turn away and leave them alone again when Ashley nods.

"I'm ," she says.

"What?" I ask.

"I'm ," she says. "It's fine. I can talk to you."

"Are you sure? You don't have to right now," I say. "You can take some time to rest."

"No." She shakes her head. "I want to talk."

THIRTY-TWO

I NOD. "Alright. Go ahead. Take your time."

"Where should I start?"

"How did you get to the vigil today?" I ask.

"I walked most of it," she says. "Someone drove me part of it."

"Is that someone the person who's had you?" I ask.

She shakes her head. "No. I left. I got away and just started walking. I heard about the vigil and thought it would be the best place to go."

"Where were you?" I ask.

"Maybe that's enough for now," Misty says. "She should get some rest."

"It's alright," Ashley says again. "I can talk."

"Okay," Misty says, reaching over to smooth hair away from Ashley's forehead.

"I was in a big old farmhouse. I got out and I started walking. I walked until I got to the road, then I kept walking until someone picked me up."

"How did you know about the vigil today?" I ask.

"The news," she says. "He forced me to watch it any time they talked about..."

She goes quiet and I push forward to get her past the block.

"If you're ready, can you tell me about what happened five years ago?"

She pulls back against the pillows slightly and her eyes drop down to focus on the blanket draped over her. As though she's looking into the past. She shakes her head.

"See?" Misty says. "She's not ready. We need to give her a break."

"No," Ashley says. "I just don't remember. Not much of it, anyway."

"That's understandable," I say. "You went through something extremely traumatic. It's not unusual for the brain to lock out memories of things like that. They might come back. Just tell me anything you can remember."

She draws in a breath and lets it out slowly.

"I was hanging out with my friends. We'd gone to the park."

"Do you remember what you were doing at the park?" I ask.

She shakes her head. "No. I don't remember anything else until I woke up in the house. I was chained to a bed. Then I met Wolf."

Misty's spine straightens and an uncomfortable expression flickers across her face. She glances at me.

"Wolf?" I ask.

Ashley nods. "That's what he told me to call him."

"And what did Wolf look like? Was he young? Old?"

"I was thirteen, so he seemed old."

"Okay," I say, trying to sound encouraging. "But how about the last time you saw him? Before you came to the vigil? How old would you say he was? My age? Your mom's age? Older?"

"Older," she says. "His hair used to be dark, but then it had gray in it."

"Good. How about his eyes?"

"Green."

A knock on the door stops me from continuing. Misty goes to it and opens it just enough for her to stick her head out and look into the hallway.

"Oh," she says. "I'm so happy you came."

"Do you think we can see her?" a voice asks so softly I almost don't hear it.

But I recognize it. Vivian.

"I think she'd love to see you," Misty says.

Misty opens the door the rest of the way and Vivian steps in, with Allison right behind her. I step back away from the bed to give the girls room to get closer, but also so I can watch Ashley's reaction to them. For a brief moment, there isn't one. She just looks at the two girls, her eyes searching their faces. Then something seems to click and recognition seeps into the stare.

"Hi," she says.

"Hi, Ashley," Allison says through tears, getting closer to the bed. "I'm so happy to see you."

Ashley's mouth curves into a hesitant smile. The girls go on either side of the bed and lean down to hug her.

"We were just talking about what happened the night she went missing," I tell them.

Vivian looks into Ashley's face.

"What did happen? Where did you go?" she asks.

"I don't remember," Ashley tells her.

"There are big chunks of her memory missing," Misty says.

"That's normal, right?" Allison asks, turning to me. "I mean, after what she went through, she can't be expected to remember everything."

"Yes, that is normal. There's a chance the memories will come back. We'll work with a therapist to safely draw the memories forward," I say.

"A therapist?" Ashley frowns.

"We don't really need to do that, do we?" Misty asks. "If she doesn't remember, that's better, isn't it? She doesn't have to relive everything that happened to her."

"Wouldn't it be harder on her if you made her go through that?" Vivian asks.

"An experience like this can be deeply traumatizing in ways that aren't immediately obvious. Even if she doesn't remember right now, it could deeply damage her quality of life if trauma like this isn't addressed in a safe way. And also, frankly, for all we know, whoever this man is who took her might have other girls kidnapped. Other girls we need to reunite with their families. Any information we can get could be valuable."

Misty, Allison, and Vivian all give each other a quick, nervous look, but they seem to understand.

"It won't be something we need to do immediately," I say, bringing the attention back to Ashley rather than talking about her as if she's not even in the room. As if she's just a concept. "We'll give you some time to recover. But as soon as you think you might be ready, it could be very valuable. You could remember something that will lead us to who did this."

The door opens and Detective Parrish, one of the officers working on Ashley's case, sticks his head inside.

"Agent Griffin, can I have a word with you for a second?" he asks.

I look at Ashley. "I'm just going to step out with the officer. I'll be right back. Do you need anything?"

She shakes her head.

"It will be good for her to spend some time with Allison and Vivian, won't it, honey?" Misty asks, running her hand over Ashley's dirty, matted hair.

Soon, after they've finished the initial tests and make sure she is completely stable, they'll let her take a shower. I can't even imagine how good it will feel to be clean. But the tests and examinations she's going to have to go through first are unfathomable for someone who's already been through what I can only imagine she has.

But the state of her hair isn't what has my attention right now. I'm interested in the way she's looking at her friends. There's something there behind her eyes.

"Ashley?" I ask. "Are you okay?"

She straightens as though she didn't realize she was staring that way, and nods.

"They just look different," she says. "They've grown up."

Allison laughs through her tears. "So have you."

She reaches out and takes Ashley's hand, earning a tender, cautious closing of bruised fingers around hers. They look at each other through years and experiences Allison couldn't begin to understand.

I walk out into the hallway to join Detective Parrish and another officer waiting for me a few feet away from the door. As I'm walking toward them, I hear muffled voices and sobbing. Looking down to the end of the hall, I see Leona pacing back and forth in front of a window. She's a wreck, shaking her head and gripping her arms tightly around herself. Someone's leaning against the wall around the corner talking to her, but I can't see who it is.

"Have you found something?" I ask.

"No," Parrish tells me. "The opposite. We need to find something. Ashley's friends still haven't submitted to the DNA testing."

"Did you issue warrants?" I ask.

"No. I thought it would be a more effective approach to ask them to voluntarily submit to testing so that it doesn't come off as aggressive. I was hoping you would try to convince them," he says.

I let out a sigh. No wonder they haven't gotten the DNA yet. As much as people would like to think others care about the people around them enough to cooperate with investigations if asked, it rarely happens that way. There's an intense sense of control and freedom that tells people they don't have to do what anyone asks. They should only help if they are forced.

I've seen it time and again when it comes to law enforcement. Something as silly as not providing identification when asked, or thinking if they are being pulled over close to home, it's perfectly fine to just keep going until they get to their driveways. All the way to refusing to submit to searches, testing, or interviews that could be invaluable to bringing killers or kidnappers to justice.

"Fine," I sigh. "I'll talk to them. But be ready for a fight. The way these two are looking at her in there, they think this is over."

THIRTY-THREE

THE OFFICERS LEAVE, but instead of going back into the room with Ashley, I make my way down to the end of the hall where Leona is now leaned against the wall beside the window. Her face is in her hands; she's drawing in ragged, uneven breaths as though she can't get herself under control. Stepping up beside her, I rest a hand on her shoulder. She jumps and pulls away, her eyes wild when her hands fall from her face.

"It's alright, Leona," I say softly. "It's just me. It's Emma."

Leona looks at me for a second as if she doesn't know who I am, but then the terror drains from her eyes and recognition replaces it. She exhales as if the breath has been held inside her since the moment her sister walked out onto that soccer field.

"What's going on?" she asks.

"What do you mean?"

"What happened to her?" she asks.

I rest my hands on her upper arms, trying to steady her as I look into her eyes to keep her focused.

"We don't know yet. But we're trying to figure it out. Have you seen her yet? Talked to her?" I ask.

Leona shakes her head almost frantically. "No. No, I can't."

"Why not? I'm sure she would be so happy to see you."

"I can't," she repeats, prying herself out of my grasp and running down the hall toward the stairs.

I turn around and find the man she was talking to watching me with hollow, sunken eyes. He doesn't say anything before walking slowly after her.

As much as I want to follow them and find out who that man is, I need to talk to Allison and Vivian. They're chatting when I walk back into the room. It isn't the smooth, easy banter I'm sure used to exist among them. There's an obvious tension and awkwardness, but that's to be expected. It's been five years since they were in the same space together. They were barely out of being children then, and now they're all technically adults.

"Hey," I start, stepping into the room. "Allison and Vivian, could I steal you guys away? I just need a quick word with you."

There's that glance. The question they toss back and forth between them before realizing they really don't have a choice. They're cornered in the hospital room with Ashley and her mother. There's no way for them to say they won't talk to me without its sounding strange.

"Sure," Vivian says. She looks at Ashley again. "We'll be right back and we'll talk about your birthday. Do you remember your thirteenth? Your party was so much fun."

Ashley smiles and the two girls follow me out of the room into the hallway. We pause a little way down, away from the door.

"What did you do?" I ask.

Their faces go blank.

"W-what do you mean?" Allison stammers.

"For Ashley's thirteenth birthday," I say. "You said her party was so much fun. I was just curious what you did for it. I can't even remember my thirteenth birthday."

"Oh," Vivian sighs, her shoulders relaxing. "We went ice skating."

A brief laugh bubbles up out of Allison. "Ashley loved Christmas. She always wanted to do the whole Christmas in July thing, even though her birthday is in June. She decided since it was her thirteenth birthday, she could do whatever she wanted. If she wanted Christmas in June, that's what she could have. So, we did a whole winter-themed party with ice skating and an ice cream cake that looked as if it was covered in snow. We all wore Christmas sweaters while we skated and then went to her house and watched Christmas movies while we drank chocolate milk. We put whipped cream on so it looked like hot chocolate."

Vivian laughs at the memory and I notice tears spring up fresh in her eyes.

"It's obvious how close you guys were," I observe. They nod and I mimic the gesture back to them to show I'm listening, that I'm engaged with what they are saying to me. "Which is why I'm confused about why you don't want to help with the investigation."

Vivian's eyebrows tighten in, the laughter gone from her lips.

"What do you mean? We've answered all your questions. We went with you to the park and showed you what we did. We even told you we lied to the police and gave you the real story," she says.

"Well, you told me a story. But you haven't been upfront with me about the school. And you have refused to submit your DNA for testing," I say.

"Because we don't have anything to do with that. We already told you we weren't there that night. It's a coincidence that Tegan posted that picture," Vivian says.

"Or maybe that's where he brought Ashley," Allison chimes in, her eyes darting over to Vivian. "Remember, the two of them went off on their own together. We never knew where they went. We assumed they stayed in the park and the guys had tents somewhere. But maybe they actually went out to the school."

"That would make sense," Vivian adds. "Ashley loved that place."

"That's interesting, because when I talked to you about it to begin with, you seemed to barely even know what I was talking about. Not as if it was a favorite place to visit."

"She liked it. We went there with her sometimes," Vivian shrugs. "But we weren't there that night. We were at the park. If she was there, it was because Tegan took her."

"So, the only two people who would know what actually happened if that is the case are either traumatized with no memory of what happened or dead. Which brings us back to square one. We still need as much evidence as we possibly can to trace through what went on that night," I say.

"Why would taking our DNA do that?" Vivian asks. "And why are you bothering chasing after such a stupid detail? You're just distracting from Ashley. If you haven't noticed yet, she isn't missing anymore. She's right there. Right there in that hospital room. And instead of being in there with her, enjoying spending time with her and being happy that she's back and she's safe, we're out here with you, dealing with this bullshit about some baby in a field."

"You know what? You're right. Ashley is there in that hospital room. She came back and is alive, which is a miracle. But nobody knows what happened to her, or how she ended up being missing for five years. Those years matter. What she went through during those years matters. And whoever did it is going to get away with it, if we don't do everything we can to track down where she was and what happened the last night anyone saw her. You're talking about distraction? Refusing to have your DNA tested is a distraction. You're taking time away from the investigation by forcing these leads to stay open. If you continue to refuse, we can get a court order to compel you to comply," I say.

"When you do, let us know," Vivian snaps.

She takes Allison's hand and guides her back to Ashley's room.

"Hey, Vivian," I say as she walks away, making her turn back around.

"What?" she asks.

"I never told you what was buried behind the school."

Her jaw sets and a bright red flush streaks across her cheeks and down the sides of her neck. All the color seems to have drained out of Allison, who goes pale as her mouth falls open. Neither says anything, but they quickly disappear into the room. The door's closing firmly behind them is a message: I'm on the outside. I'm not a part of this welcome-home reunion anymore.

"Hey," Dean calls over, jogging down the hallway toward me. "There you are. Do you know how hard it was to get them to let me come up here?"

"I would think so, considering they're taking care of a kidnap victim," I reply.

My eyes move over to the door and my lips twist as thoughts turn and spin around in my head.

"What is it?" he asks. "What's going on?"

"The police kept the detail about the fetal remains out of the media, right?" I ask.

He nods. "Yes. Ashley's parents are the only ones who know that's what was found behind the school. Other than the investigators."

"That's what I thought."

"Why?"

I look back at him and realize he's alone. "Where's Xavier?"

"Security wouldn't let him through. So, he's downstairs with them. I got him going on root beer again, so he should be good for a while," Dean says.

"The drink?"

"The song."

I nod. "Well, he'll either be fine staying down there or they'll crack and let him come up."

"Why did you ask about the fetal remains?" Dean asks.

"Oh. Because Vivian just mentioned them," I explain. "She and Allison still haven't given their DNA, and the detective asked me to try to convince them to do it. They still refuse, and she was getting angry. She said that we were wasting time testing a baby found in a field."

"Maybe Ashley's mother mentioned it to them," he suggests. "They've stayed in touch. And she's seen both of them since the remains were found."

"That's possible. We told Misty not to discuss the details with anyone, but that doesn't actually mean she went along with that. But it's the way that Vivian reacted when I pointed it out to her. I said I never mentioned to her what was behind the school and she just glared at me. She didn't defend herself or try to say that Misty told her."

"Have they run a DNA test on her?" Ava's voice coming at me from behind Dean makes my jaw clench. "I'm sorry, I didn't mean to intrude on your conversation. I just got here, so I'm catching up. What have you found out?"

"Who told you to come here?" I ask.

She gives me a quizzical look. "Creagan. He told me he already spoke with you."

"He did. And I would have gotten in touch with you if I needed you," I reply.

"He told me I'm investigating this case," she says.

Tension builds through my spine and I fight to keep down my reaction to her.

"I am investigating this case," I say carefully. "You are part of it to help. I will let you know when there is something I need done. For right now, this is a very delicate situation. Everything needs to be done in a specific way to make sure other elements aren't compromised."

She nods. "I understand."

"As for the DNA, testing takes time. It's not like on TV when someone can start flashing around results in a matter of minutes. They have to do mitochondrial testing because her biological father is not part of the equation. Just as when they tested the remains, it will take a little bit of time. Likely longer, because this isn't considered as pressing an issue. Results will come in a couple of days. But for now, everyone is satisfied this is Ashley. It's only been five years and her appearance hasn't changed much."

"What do you think?" Dean asks.

I pause from where I'd started toward the steps and look at him.

"I think she looks like an older version of the picture I saw of Ashley Stevenson," I admit.

"Her growth patterns would likely be stunted by the conditions she was kept in, but the shape of her ears and the symmetry of her facial features suggests this is the same girl," Xavier says.

"Xavier?"

"Xavier, where in the hell did you come from?" Dean asks, whipping around to face him.

Glancing around as if he's not sure why everyone is so surprised to see him, Xavier points behind him.

"The stairs," he shrugs. "All the root beer had been taken down and passed around."

"What about the security guard?" I ask.

"He stopped checking on me around fifty bottles," he says.

"But how did you get up here? Guards are supposed to be positioned at every entrance," I say.

"Not at that one," he says. "I found the door in the vending machine area. No peanuts. Sunflower seeds. No baseball, no seeds. The door didn't have any words on it, but there was part of a sticker from an alarm warning."

"And you opened it anyway?" Dean asks.

"If there was an alarm on that door, it should have been properly marked, now shouldn't it have been? I was doing my duty to ensure the hospital is properly secured," he offers.

"And proved it sure as shit isn't," Dean says.

THIRTY-FOUR

"WE NEED to speak with every security guard on duty here and the police and make sure they know about that door," I say.

The door to Ashley's room opens just as I'm saying this and Misty steps out. I wonder if she heard me, and the quizzical expression on her face tells me she did.

"What door?" she asks. "What are you talking about?"

"You remember Xavier," I say, gesturing toward him. "He identified a breach in the perimeter security of the area."

Her eyes grow wide. "What does that mean? Is Ashley safe?"

"Everything's fine," I tell her. "We found it and are going to make sure everyone who is responsible for keeping guard over Ashley and securing the hospital knows about it. It will be under continuous surveillance just like every other entrance and exit. I can promise you no one is going to be able to get to her."

"How much longer is she going to have to stay?" Misty asks.

"I don't know," I say. "That's up to her doctor. Do you want me to go talk to him?"

"Yes," she nods. "I don't want to leave her."

"I'll be right back," I say.

I go out to the nurse's station and have the head nurse page the doctor to come speak with me.

I hold my hand out to the silver-haired doctor as he approaches. "Agent Emma Griffin. We spoke briefly when Ashley Stevenson was brought in."

He nods. "Of course, Agent Griffin. What can I do for you?"

"Misty Stevenson asked me to find out how much longer Ashley might need to be here," I say.

"I really can't make that determination right at this moment," he tells me. "We're still waiting for results from her tests; what those results tell us will be critical in determining how much longer she needs to stay here or if there's any further treatment necessary. She seems in fairly good condition, considering everything. Of course, we don't know exactly what she went through the last five years, but we can make pretty good assumptions."

"I can," I say, not wanting to dwell on it. "I'm guessing you're going to do a full physical exam on her?"

"Yes," he says. "As soon as I think she's ready, we will do a thorough exam and as much testing as we can. I don't want to wait too long because the evidence is degrading even as we speak. But I felt she needed some time just to be back here. To know people are thinking about her and taking care of her."

"Absolutely," I say. "Is it safe to assume she'll be here for at least another day or so?"

"I would say that is a conservative estimate," the doctor says.

"I will let them know. Thank you."

I go back to Ashley's room and find that Vivian and Allison have left. Misty is leaned close to Ashley and is talking to her in a whispered tone. She straightens up as I come back in the room.

"What did he say?" she asks when she notices me.

"He isn't able to give you an exact length of time yet. There are further tests and examinations he needs to do, then he needs to wait for the results to determine when Ashley will be healthy enough to leave. He does say she looks as though she's in good condition, so that's definitely a positive. But she will definitely need to be here for at least another day or two," I say.

Misty nods, looking saddened by the news, but also forcing a small smile as she pats Ashley's leg.

"We can do another couple of days," she says. "And I will be here every moment they let me." She turns to look at me. "What about when I can't be?"

"What do you mean?" I ask.

"If the hospital makes me leave, what's going to happen to Ashley? Now that we know there's a way for someone to access this floor without authorization, how do we know she's safe? What if the person who did this to her comes after her again?" she asks.

"You have my word, she will be safe. I'll be back to see you soon. And while I'm not here, the officers will be. I'm going to talk to the detectives and make sure that they know the security guards aren't enough. I'll have them place officers around and they will be there for as long as they need to be. No one who isn't on an approved list for one of the people on this floor will be able to get up here," I say. "You decide who you want to be able to come see Ashley, and then give the list to the officers downstairs."

"Do you have to go?" Ashley asks.

"I do," I tell her. "But I'll be back. And if there's anything that you need before I come back, your mother has my phone number; she can get to me any time. Okay?"

She nods and I say goodbye before heading for the door. Before I step out into the hallway, I hear Misty.

"Honey, I'm going to be right back. I'm just going to walk Agent Griffin out." She follows after me, pulling the door most of the way closed behind her. "Agent Griffin?"

"Call me Emma," I say, walking back toward her. "What do you need?"

"Do you really think she's safe here?" she asks.

"Yes," I say without hesitation, because I have to. "She will have people watching over her all the time. And she won't be here for long. They just need to get through the tests and make sure there's nothing seriously wrong with her that needs immediate treatment or intervention."

"She's healthy," Misty says. "Hungry and worn out. But there's nothing wrong with her that needs to be treated by a hospital."

"Nothing that we can see yet," I point out. "Sometimes there can be damage or problems beneath the surface. We still don't know what Ashley has been through over the last five years. It's not something you want to think about, I know. But the doctors have to do everything they can to make sure there isn't any lingering effect of the conditions she was living in, or the way she was treated. As soon as they know she's healthy and stable, they'll send her home and you'll be able to take care of her."

"I can't wait," she says. "I want to have my babies home with me again."

"I know," I say. "I noticed Leona seems to be taking this pretty hard."

"She is," Misty says. "She and Ashley were close. It was traumatic for her when Ashley went missing. It took a lot of time, but finally, she was able to emerge from that darkness and confusion. She was really coming to terms with what happened and finding ways to move ahead with her life. I always told her she didn't have to put her sister behind her, that she shouldn't put her sister behind her, but that she could put the hurt behind her. I think Leona was really getting there, and then Ashley showed back up. It's just hard for her to process. I think part of her feels as though she betrayed her little sister by not only no longer looking for her but coming to terms with her loss and being willing to move forward with her life without her."

"How about your husband?" I ask. "How is he taking this?"

John Stevenson was at the vigil when Ashley first reemerged, and

I know he was at the hospital in the beginning, but I haven't seen him since.

"Not well, as I'm sure you can imagine. He's struggling with the feeling that he should have been there. He should have protected her," Misty says.

"He can't do that to himself. He didn't know she was lying to the two of you about where she was going that day. She was thirteen years old. It's still so young, but at the same time, most people expect their children to have some independence by then. Where is he now?" I ask.

"He couldn't take the chaos," Misty says. "Especially with all the media. It's just too much for him. He doesn't handle stress well and this was going to push him over the edge. He wants to see Ashley when it isn't someone else's spectacle."

I meet Dean, Xavier, and Ava downstairs, where they're talking to the police about the door Xavier found.

"Dean," I say, "I need you to look into a few things for me. I'm going to email them to you."

"Where are you going?" Xavier asks.

"I need to go trace some steps. Meet me at the hotel later. Call me if you find anything," I say.

"What about me?" Ava asks.

"Go with Dean," I say.

I get in my car and attach my phone to the cradle on the dashboard. As I pull on my seatbelt and start the car, I call Sam.

"Hey, babe," he says. "The news is blowing up over this thing with Ashley Stevenson. What have you found out? Does she remember anything?"

"Not really," I say. "She says she remembers hanging out with her friends and then waking up tied to a bed."

"I guess it's really not that unusual for her to have memory lapses after everything she went through," Sam notes.

"No, it's not," I say.

"Then why does it sound as if you don't believe her?" he asks.

"It's not that I don't believe her. Obviously, she went through something. She's been missing for five years. That's not arguable," I say.

"But?" Sam leads.

"But it feels as if everyone in her life is hiding something. The only question is whether they're all hiding the same thing."

THIRTY-FIVE

KEEPING track of the passage of time in the hospital was impossible. All around, there was chaos. Everyone was trying to figure out what was happening at the same time, but nobody was listening to each other. I hadn't been able to tell if I was there for an hour or a day. Now that I'm out of the middle of it, I realize it must have been several hours.

The vigil was at noon and had been going on for less than an hour when Ashley reappeared on the soccer field. Now the sun is sliding down the opposite side of the sky and the air around me is getting that heady feeling of a summer night. I drive away from the hospital and out through the neighborhoods to the outskirts of town. An area that had been dominated by bright light and people scurrying around just a couple of days ago, examining the scene, is now silent and deserted.

I park close to the gate of the elementary school and get out. For a second, I just stand by the side of my car and let the feelings of the area come over me. I'm still not sure what Xavier meant when he told me to feel the place where I was. I know that means something to him. He lives his life interpreting the world around him in a completely different way than I do. So I try. I try to see it through his perception, to experience a place or an event on a level that goes beyond just the five senses I've always relied on.

I can't help but notice the distinctly eerie feeling that comes over me here. I know something traumatic happened here, and I'm not convinced it doesn't have anything to do with Ashley and her disappearance. The DNA proved the remains of the stillborn baby weren't related to her, but I keep getting drawn back to that rock sitting next to the tree and the picture Ashley shared before her disappearance.

Some traces of the investigation are still in the schoolyard. A couple of the pieces of bright yellow police line haven't been removed from the fence, and wooden markers stick up from the ground where the investigators divided up the area in a grid to organize the search. They instantly remind me of the bright pink pieces of plastic dotting the gravel and grass alongside the train tracks near Feathered Nest.

Those markers were there for so long after the tragic and gruesome death of a young woman who briefly thought she'd escaped the clutches of a serial killer. And in a way, she had. She managed to get away from him, to not die while he watched. She just didn't know that while she was running through those woods, the marks from the dog chain around her neck, that she was already dead. Even if the train hadn't come, she wouldn't have survived her injuries.

It makes me wonder how long these markers will stay in place. This is a much more heavily visited spot than the land beside the train track weaving through woods and open farmland. The police may not come back for them, but I can't imagine they'll simply be left alone. Someone who comes here out of morbid curiosity will take them. For now, they are lingering evidence of the sharp turn this case has taken, and all the questions still left to be answered.

I walk through the gate and across the abandoned playground to the tree. The stone is gone, inevitably brought in as evidence. It's sitting in a cardboard box in a locker somewhere now, waiting for someone to figure out who left it there. In its place is a gaping hole in the ground. It's much larger than I would have expected it to be. But the investigators likely started the dig anticipating, like many did, that they would be digging up the body of a thirteen-year-old girl. Not one of a preterm fetus.

Trying to put myself into the position of a teenager wanting to come to this place to be away from adults and enjoy myself, I walk over to the rusted old merry-go-round and lower myself down onto it. The heat of the August sun has soaked into the metal throughout the day, making it warm as I sit down.

I left the hospital during that tenuous time of day when the sun is still out, but it's clinging to those last few moments. Now it's given up and evening has taken over quickly. Around me, long shadows stretch out from the old equipment and tall trees.

This would be very much like how it was the day Ashley went missing. It wasn't as overcast today as it was then. There hasn't been any recent rain, but a chill still starts to build in the air. It reminds me of Allison's mention of Ashley's sweatshirt.

Curiosity makes me take out my phone and scroll through a search until I find a list of the weather from that week five years ago. It was raining and unseasonably chilly in the days leading up to her going missing. Though the continuous rain had stopped by that day, the temperature was still low and there were some showers in the late evening and overnight.

I can't imagine Allison and Vivian camping in the rain. The area they showed me wasn't big enough to accommodate a large tent, which means if they were there, they had just put up something small. A type of tent that would likely leak in the rain. Yet neither one of them mentioned rain overnight.

A sound off to one side breaks me out of my thoughts and I'm instantly sharply aware of my surroundings. My senses intensify and my muscles tighten, preparing for whatever might be waiting for me. I hear another sound; this time it's unmistakable. Footsteps. They are muffled by the grass and the layer of fallen leaves from seasons of neglect, but they are definitely there.

Someone else is in the schoolyard. The shadows conceal whoever

It is, leaving me at a disadvantage. Standing up slowly, I place my hand on my gun.

"Who's there?" I demand. "This is Emma Griffin of the FBI. I'm armed. Come out slowly."

This time when I hear the footsteps, they're accompanied by a sound that blends with the rustling leaves, but comes out higher. Crying.

I walk toward the sound and see a figure in the darkness near the tree. It steps out into the moonlight. The faint haze of an old streetlight in the alley behind the schoolyard illuminates her face.

"Allison," I say, both relieved and aggravated. "What are you doing here?"

"I'm sorry," she starts. "I didn't mean to startle you. I didn't know you were here."

"You've been here the whole time?" I ask.

She nods and looks back toward the alley. "I parked back there. That's how we always used to get in here. That way if the police did drive by, they didn't see our cars or catch us sneaking in or out."

"So, you did come here a lot," I say.

She nods, her face starting to clench as a new wave of tears comes over her. She wipes them away, but there's nothing that will stop them.

"All the time. Any time we could get out without our parents, this is where we came," she says.

"Including the night Ashley disappeared," I say.

She nods again and draws in a shuddering breath. "Yes."

"Allison, why are you here tonight? Is Vivian with you? Someone else?"

"No. I'm here alone. I don't come here with anyone anymore. Just alone."

"Why?"

She looks at the tree and dissolves in sobs. I put my gun back in the holster and walk over to her, wrapping my arms around her shoulders.

"I'm sorry," she whispers through her tears. "I'm so sorry."

"Allison, what happened? I need you to tell me the truth now," I say.

She gets herself together and nods, stepping out of my hands to walk over to the tree. Kneeling down beside the hole in the ground, she rests one of her hands gently inside. Her fingers clench in, digging down into the dirt slightly as her hand shakes.

"What we told you about the rain and wanting to get out of the house was all true. It was August, which meant of course we were thinking about having to go back to school. Ashley was going into the eighth grade. She was already talking about how it was her last year in middle school before she was going to get to join us in high school. She was so excited. She never felt like the other kids her age," Allison says.

"Why is that?" I ask.

Allison shrugs slightly. "She just had a different mindset, I guess. We went to the park and we were going to camp. My boyfriend and Tegan got there. It was just like we said. We went to the abandoned campground. We hiked around some. But then my boyfriend and I got in an argument. I wasn't feeling well and he wanted some... alone time with me."

"You wouldn't give him sex and he got mad at you," I say.

I need her to stop being vague, to stop with the delicate way she's presenting things and be straight up with me. There have been enough secrets and enough misconceptions at this point.

"Yes," she admits. "He got mad and left. I was upset and it was starting to rain a little, so we decided to go hang out at the elementary school for a while to see if it would stop. We were planning on coming back, because we didn't really have anywhere else to go for the night. All the different parents thought we were with another family. Tegan brought us, but he dropped us off. He went to find my boyfriend, so he could talk to him.

"Vivian had managed to sneak some liquor from her father's collection and brought it with us. We didn't really drink all that often. It wasn't as if it was all we did. But that night I was upset and stressed and feeling sick. I just didn't want to think about anything. So, I drank a little. Then Vivian drank some and convinced Ashley to as well. Then everything happened."

"You gave birth," I say.

She nods. "When you hear about women having babies, you always hear how long it takes. That it's this long, drawn-out process and takes hours. For me, it was like everything inside me ripped apart. The pain was horrible. It started like a cramp, then it got so bad I couldn't even stand up. Vivian and Ashley were scared. Ashley wanted me to go to the hospital, but I said no. I knew what was happening and I didn't want anyone else to find out. I wasn't thinking straight. She ended up taking my phone and calling my boyfriend. I guess she thought he would come and force me to go to the hospital."

"But he didn't."

"No," she says. "By the time he got there, the baby had already come. I couldn't believe it had actually happened."

"Did you know you were pregnant?"

"I didn't know for sure. I hadn't gone to a doctor or taken a test or anything. I had missed some periods and was having a few minor symptoms, but I pushed it out of my mind. It wasn't something I wanted to think about or even consider a possibility. My boyfriend and I had only started having sex a few months before, so I knew the baby couldn't possibly be ready to be born."

"You lost your virginity to him," I say.

"Yes. And like they say, it only takes one time. I was only four months along. Almost five. Not far enough for the baby to survive."

"So, it was a stillbirth," I say. "The baby wasn't alive when it was born."

"No," she mutters, shaking her head and staring back down into the hole as if she was seeing it all unfold in front of her again.

"Did you have a boy or a girl?" I ask.

I want to humanize the moment for her, to bring her into the full reality of it. She's been hiding this for five years; in that time, I can only imagine she's found so many ways to convince herself it didn't really happen. To justify what she did that night. But it's been eating at her. Chipping away at everything inside her.

She lets out a sob but also smiles. "A boy. He was so beautiful. He looked like a tiny little doll. So perfect. I tried so hard to save him. All I wanted to do was wake him up. I didn't know what I was going to do, but I wanted him to breathe. I wanted to hear him cry. I would have done anything."

Allison collapses in tears, leaning over so they fall into the grave she dug for her son five years ago. Her hands grip at the ground as though she's trying to find something to anchor her, to hold her in place.

"What happened?" I ask softly.

"I didn't want to admit he was gone, but Vivian and my boyfriend looked at him. They told me he wasn't breathing, that his heart wasn't beating. He was blue. Nothing was going to save him. I didn't want anyone to take him from me, so I wrapped him in my shirt and I buried him. We made him a gravestone and said a prayer over him. It was all I could do for him."

Her voice has fallen low and she looks lost in her thoughts.

"Did you name him?" I ask.

That makes her look up at me with a wistful, agonized smile on her dripping lips. "Charlie."

"I like that."

"He would be five years old next week. He'd be starting kindergarten in September," she says. "He should have been born in December. A Christmas baby. I've gotten him a Christmas present every year. I keep them in my closet in a box I made for him. I never want him to be forgotten."

Her head drops and her shoulders shake with renewed sobs. "I should have gone to the hospital. I should have listened to Ashley. If I had, none of this would ever have happened. Nothing would have happened."

THIRTY-SIX

"You said Ashley was upset," I say. "She wanted you to go to the hospital before the baby came."

"Yes," Allison says.

"Is that when you argued? Did you get mad at her and she left?" I ask.

It makes sense. I can understand Ashley arguing with her friend as she tried to convince her the best thing to do would be to call for help. She might not have wanted to be a part of what was happening and walked away. This was a familiar area to her. She had come here many times before, and likely thought it would be no problem to make her way home, even without the others.

They had all been clear with me that Ashley's parents would pick her up without question from anywhere if she called them. Maybe that was what happened. She wanted to remain loyal to her friends and not admit the truth to the adults, so she walked a distance away from the abandoned school, intending to call her parents and get a ride home.

What happened after that remained a mystery to everyone.

Except, Allison isn't telling that story. She's still staring down into the grave and I can see she's holding onto something.

"She didn't leave. She was here the whole time. But she was so upset. Vivian told her to drink more. She said it would help her get through it. That maybe she wouldn't remember. I had never seen Ashley drink that much, but I couldn't think about anything but Charlie. By the time I was even aware of anything else, Tegan was trying to wake her up. She was sick, but also unconscious. He finally got her awake and said we had to get her to a doctor. She could die of alcohol poisoning. I couldn't watch my best friend die out here. We had to do something."

"But you didn't call an ambulance," I guess.

"No. We didn't want anyone to know we'd been out here. We thought it would be faster to just take her ourselves. My boyfriend and Tegan got her in the car, and I sat in the back with her and Tegan. We'd already been driving for a while before I realized my boyfriend wasn't going in the right direction. He wasn't heading for the hospital. I asked what he was doing and he said he was getting her to someone who would help her. Somewhere that no one would know we had anything to do with."

"Did you argue with him?" I ask.

"I couldn't. It wouldn't have done any good. He was the one driving and he was so adamant. All the emotion left him. I'd never seen him that way. I didn't know what to do but go along with what he was saying. The whole drive he was telling me that this was the only option. It was the only thing that made sense. We couldn't let anyone know what actually happened. We would take her to the emergency room and they would find her. "

"What did he think was going to happen when she woke up? Did he think she was just going to say everything was fine and not talk about what happened?" I ask.

"Yes," she says without hesitation. "The group of us were tight. We promised to protect each other in any way we could. If she did wake up remembering what happened, she would make something up to cover for us. But my boyfriend really believed she had so much to drink she wasn't going to remember."

"Where did you take her?" I ask.

"The hospital in Acadia. It's far enough away we didn't think anyone would recognize us. We took her into the hospital, put her in a chair in the emergency room waiting room, and left. She wasn't passed out when we got there. She was only partly awake and incredibly drunk, but she had enough control to sit in the chair when we put her there."

"Did you get seen by anyone?" I ask. "You must not have been feeling great by that point."

"Not there. I was feeling dizzy and weak, but my boyfriend didn't want to stay at the same hospital as Ashley. He thought people might make the connection. So, he took me to another hospital. In the next town over. You can check. I'll authorize you to look at my medical records," Allison says.

"What did they do for you there?" I ask. "Didn't they check you and find out about the baby?"

"I told them I thought I had a miscarriage. That I went to the bathroom and there was a lot of blood and clots, and that I felt really sick and weak. They gave me fluids and discharged me. They said they didn't have to contact my parents if I didn't want them to, which I obviously didn't. I threw my discharge papers away before leaving the hospital.

"After that, we went back to Sherando Ridge. We pretended that everything was fine. We figured the next day Ashley would be at home and would call to find out what had happened the night before. We worked out the story of her getting mad at us and leaving, and that we assumed she had just called her parents to come pick her up. It seemed as if it was going to be so easy," Allison says.

"Until it wasn't," I say.

"Until it wasn't. We realized Ashley didn't have her backpack. It hadn't even crossed our minds. So, we decided the next day I would take it to her house and drop it off. I was really expecting that I would show up and her mom would be upset, but say she was inside, sick. Or that maybe even she would come to the door and ask me what happened. When she didn't, and her mom told me she hadn't even come back the night before, I panicked. I didn't know what to do. So I went to Vivian's house."

"Misty said you looked as if you were in such a hurry, you were wobbling on your bike. But it was because you were still weak and sore, wasn't it?"

Allison nods. "Vivian and I talked about it and we decided the best thing to do would be to stick with the same story we'd told to begin with. That we were at the park to go camping, she got mad at us and left. We'd figured she'd called her parents to pick her up because that was always an option for her. Obviously, the police wanted to talk to us and that was what both of us told them. They believed us and that was it."

"Why didn't you say anything?" I ask.

"I was fourteen years old and got pregnant by a nineteen-year-old I wasn't even supposed to be seeing. The baby was dead and buried in a field where we were trespassing. And our best friend who witnessed it all was missing after we left her drunk out of her mind and sick in a hospital waiting room. I was terrified. I had no idea what to do or if they would even believe me. Maybe they would think I did something to her because Vivian, Tegan, and my boyfriend would turn against me to save themselves."

"Why do you never say your boyfriend's name?" I finally ask, after having taken note of it for the last several minutes. "You've been talking about him all this time and haven't once said his name."

She shakes her head. "I don't like talking about him. And I don't want anybody to be able to track him down and ask him about what happened."

"Do you think he might hurt you?" I ask. She draws in a breath and looks at the grave again. Realization trickles down my spine like ice water. "Did you think he might have hurt Ashley?"

"I thought about it," she admits. "I didn't want to think that was possible. For a fourteen-year-old, dating someone for six months feels like forever. I thought he was my everything. We were going to grow up and get married. We'd have babies I would get to keep and raise. Everything was going to be perfect. I didn't want to think for a single second that he could have done something to her."

"But you did."

"He took me to the hospital and left. He said he didn't want to be there and possibly get in trouble. They would arrest him and put him in jail and I'd never see him again. Of course, I believed him. I was fifteen. I didn't know better than to believe him. I wanted to protect him. In my heart, he loved me. So,I sat there with Vivian and went through everything without him. He was back by the time I was discharged and ready to take me back to the campsite. But I didn't know what he was doing during that time. After I found out Ashley was missing, there was a part of me that wondered if he could have gone back to the hospital and done something to her so she wouldn't be able to tell what happened."

"Right now, we don't know for sure that he didn't," I point out.

Her face drops and she shakes her head adamantly. "No. He couldn't have. Ashley's back. She's there in the hospital. He wouldn't have kept her like that. He couldn't have."

"You know I'm going to have to tell the investigators what you've told me. And they're going to bring you in for questioning. You'll have to tell them who your boyfriend was and every detail you can think of. Don't try to lie anymore. They're going to be even more suspicious of you now," I tell her.

She swallows hard. "Am I going to be in trouble?"

"I don't know. I can't tell you for sure that they won't bring you up on charges. But if you are upfront with them and tell them everything, they are more likely to be lenient," I say.

"Will you go with me?" she asks.

"Of course."

THIRTY-SEVEN

THE NEXT DAY I'm still at the police station with Allison when I get a phone call from Misty. I ignore it, intending to call her back when the interview is done. I don't want to leave the girl's side. She doesn't want her parents here with her. She isn't yet ready for them to know what happened, but she also doesn't want to be alone.

She's also twenty years old. That means the investigator could refuse to allow her parents in the room with her during questioning. This is part of my investigation, so professional courtesy has the detective let me in the room to listen to her statement and participate in the questioning.

Allison doesn't hesitate. This time, she's ready to tell everything. It's difficult for her. I can see the pain in her eyes and the fear of what might come because of it. But I can also see how much of a relief it is to finally have the story out in the open rather than carrying it around as she has been for five years. This has been tormenting her. She wants to be able to mourn for her child and not try to keep up with the lies.

"I never wanted anything to happen to Ashley," she says. "I never wanted her to get hurt. I hate myself for what happened to her."

This is the moment in movies when a kindhearted investigator would offer her coffee and tell her what happened isn't her fault, but this isn't the movies. The truth is, Allison is at least partly to blame for whatever happened to Ashley that night after they left her in the hospital. Along with Vivian, Tegan, and Allison's boyfriend, who I just now learned is a man named Sean Melrose. They contributed to this. It was their decision not to call for an ambulance or the police. It was their decision to leave Ashley in the emergency room without anyone to watch over her. And it was their decision not to come clean when they realized everything wasn't fine.

What she went through after the last moment Allison laid eyes on her in the emergency room is still hazy. But no matter what it was, it sits partly on the shoulders of her friends.

They can't be blamed fully. Someone else is involved. The mystery of the last five years has another player. But it started with them.

My phone rings again, and again I ignore it. The questioning is getting intense, but there's a balance that has to be kept. Every detail needs to come out. Allison needs to tell us everything she remembers from the very beginning. But if the interrogator pushes too hard, she might shut down. It could compromise the investigation to come. Which is going to have to include Vivian and Sean, when we track him down.

Allison is sobbing over Charlie, begging for the return of his remains when the investigation is over, when my phone rings for a third time. Seconds after I ignore the call, it rings again. I ignore it, and it rings again.

"Give me a second," I say, standing up from the table. I rest a hand on Allison's shoulder. "I'll be right back."

I look over at the attorney who has been sitting silently next to Allison and he nods, a silent acknowledgment that I'm passing over to him the responsibility of both protecting her and making sure the truth comes out.

My phone is already to my ear when I step out into the hallway.

"I'm at the police station," I tell Misty as she answers. "There's been a development."

"Emma, they're trying to take her," she says.

"What?" I ask. "Who? What's going on?"

Misty sounds frantic, right on the edge of losing control.

"Someone put in a request to have her transferred to another hospital, to a secured ward," she says.

"I'll be right there. Do not let them take her," I say.

"I'm trying."

"Just hang on. I'll be there." I hang up and rush back into the room with Allison and the investigator. "I need to leave. Is Allison free to go?"

The detective looks at me in shock, but I need to get out of here, and I'm not leaving without knowing the direction this is moving forward.

"I don't think we're finished here," he says.

"Unless you plan to put her under arrest, you are," the attorney adds.

The detective knows he's stuck. He only has a couple of options at this point. He could technically hold Allison for twenty-four hours before bringing any charges on her. He could also put her under arrest right now. Neither of those options is ideal in his situation. They could greatly compromise the future of the case and create a number of issues. Which leaves him with the final option. Letting her go.

He glares for a few more seconds, then stands. "Don't leave the area."

Allison looks at me and I nod. "You can go. Just make sure you stay accessible."

She nods and I head out of the station to my car. I don't know for sure the direction things will go with Allison and the others. There are definitely charges that could be brought against all of them. Whether there actually will be, and if said charges will be brought to trial, is yet to be seen.

I get to the hospital and flash my identification as I run past the security guard. Misty is standing in the hallway in front of Ashley's room, wringing her hands. A doctor is standing in front of her and a police officer is at his side.

"It will be easier for everyone if we get her moved and settled into the other unit, then we can figure out where to go from there," the doctor says.

"How is that easier?" Misty demands. "After everything she's gone through, you want to disrupt her again, transport her to another hospital, and make her get used to another set of people? Without even knowing why they want to move her?"

"They want to move her into a secure unit that will be easier to monitor," the officer says. "She'll get better care and the family won't be as exposed to the media."

I stalk up to them.

"What's going on here?"

Misty looks relieved to see me. She gestures at the men in front of her.

"They want to take Ashley to the hospital across town," Misty says.

"You said the secure ward. Are you referring to the psychiatric floor?" I ask.

The doctor looks slightly uncomfortable but holds his ground. "Yes. The request states the patient would be more comfortable and better served in that environment."

"Her name is Ashley," Misty says angrily. "Not the patient."

"Ma'am, I need to ask you to calm down," the officer says. "It isn't going to do anyone any good for you to react like this."

I hold up a hand. "That's enough. There's no reason for you to talk to her like that. This is her daughter. She isn't some nameless, faceless case file. She's been missing for five years and has just come back to her family. Both of you need to show some more respect."

"I'm sorry," the doctor says. "That was insensitive of me. But I have to admit, I'm surprised by your reaction, Miss Griffin."

"It's Agent Griffin," I snap to the doctor I haven't met yet. "And you are?"

"Dr. Floriani. I'm one of the team handling Ashley's case."

"Alright, Dr. Floriani. Why would you be surprised by my reaction? You might be working on her medical needs right now, but I'm handling the case of what happened to her five years ago. It's my job to protect her and her family, and to ensure her best interests are upheld," I say.

"Which is precisely why I'm surprised," he says. "Considering you are the one who put in the request for the transfer."

THIRTY-EIGHT

Misty gasps beside me, but I hold up a hand.

"Excuse me?" I ask.

"The request was put into the hospital administrator's office this morning. It stated you wanted Ashley Stevenson moved to Gunter Memorial for admission into the secure mental health ward for observation and monitoring. It stated she would be better protected there, and it is your professional opinion that she has been through such a horrific experience she is not in a mentally sound enough state to face the investigation and the potential of a trial," Dr. Floriani says.

"Emma, how could you do this?" Misty asks.

"I didn't," I frown, then turn back to the doctor. "Why are you just saying this now? Why didn't you mention before that I'm supposedly the one who put in this request?"

"I thought it was of such sensitive nature and could be part of the criminal investigation, so it was better if I left the details out of it," he says. "It seems that might not have been the best choice."

"That is a tremendous understatement," I say. "Considering that I had nothing to do with this."

"You didn't put in the request?" Misty asks.

"No." I shake my head. "Why would I go to the extent I have to ensure there is so much security around here if I was just going to have her moved somewhere else? How did this request come in?"

"It was a phone message," the doctor explains. "The hospital administrator called Gunter Memorial and they say they received a similar message asking that space be prepared for her arrival."

"You listened to a phone message claiming to be from an FBI agent handling a kidnapping case and you just took it for face value?" I ask incredulously.

"It wasn't my decision," the doctor protests. "The administrator..."

"I need to speak with the administrator," I cut him off. "Right now."

"I'll show you to his office."

Misty looks confused and afraid when I make eye contact with her again. "Don't worry. I'm going to get this straightened out. You stay with Ashley and don't let anyone move her. No matter what anyone says, don't let anyone into the room unless it's a doctor or nurse you already know. I'll be back." I look at the officer and point at the door. "No one in. No one out." He nods, gulping, and I walk away.

The wait outside the administrator's office only gets me more frustrated. It's as if this place is designed to irritate me. Finally, after what feels like forever, the secretary lets me in. The hospital administrator stands and extends his hand to me from behind his desk.

"Hello," he says with the kind of smile that comes only from thinking he can do no wrong and defies anyone to think otherwise. "Elton McCarthy."

"Agent Emma Griffin," I say.

"Of course," he says. "I got your message earlier and I have ensured the process is underway. Ashley Stevenson will be safely transferred to the unit this afternoon."

The smile becomes even more self-satisfied. As though he's positive I'm here to thank him and praise him for the smooth, swift action
of his administration. Hopefully, the look on my face is giving him a
hint that's not the case.

"That would be great news, if it wasn't for the tiny detail that I'm
not the one who left that message," I say.

The smile falters. "Your name was very clearly stated. Along with
your credentials and an explanation of your involvement in the case.
I'd seen you on the news making statements about the case before
Ashley resurfaced, so I was comfortable with its authenticity."

"Play me the message," I say.

I'd like to think I have it in me somewhere to be patient and toler-
ant, but this is not a moment to try out that theory. I need to find out
what the hell is going on, and that takes precedence.

He plays back the message for me and I'm stunned at what I'm
hearing. When it's done, I point at the phone.

"Do you think that message sounds anything like my voice?" I
deadpan him.

"To be fair, Agent Griffin, this is the first time I'm speaking to you
in person," he says.

"Yes, but you just said yourself you saw me on the news talking
about the case. Which means you have heard me speak before. When
you heard that message, did you think it sounded like me?" I ask.

"I can't say."

"What you're telling me is you got a phone message stating it was
me, essentially demanding the relocation of a patient who has been
missing for five years, who has clearly been through some very serious
abuse, and you took it as gospel. No warrant. No documentation. No
court order. A phone message that could easily be snuggled right in
there between an invitation to lunch and someone calling out sick for
tomorrow. You didn't think it needed any form of verification? That
perhaps you should speak to the investigators, or at the very least, to
the person who supposedly left the message?" I ask.

"I didn't know the proper protocol for a situation such as this," Elton says. "It isn't something I've encountered in my career. I've never received a phone call from an FBI agent about one of my patients before."

"You still haven't," I point out, my voice rising in pitch.

"I apologize," he says, finally looking less smug, as though the gravity of what he almost allowed to happen is sinking in. "It was a mistake."

"Yes," I nod. "It was. And it could have had serious consequences if it went through. Ashley is still in very real danger. I don't know how to emphasize that enough. Yes, she is here now. She got away from wherever she's been for these past five years. But there's someone who wanted her five years ago and who wants her now. Nobody let her go. She escaped. And until we find out who that person is and have him in custody, she is at risk. It's things like this that could hand her right back over to someone waiting to keep torturing her—or kill her—to ensure she stays quiet."

"I sincerely apologize," he says. "Is there anything I can do to assist you in finding out who did this?"

"No," I say. "I will do my job. You figure out how to do yours."

Stalking out of the office, I get on the phone with Eric.

"How's everything going?" he asks.

I can hear Bebe in the background fussing. "I could ask you the same question. Everything okay over there?"

"Just time for a snack. She's gotten very good at letting us know when she's hungry," he says.

"Sounds like her mama."

"I'm not going to say anything to confirm that about the woman I love, and who has only just given me a beautiful child, but we both know I'm nodding right now," he says.

"I miss you guys. Can't wait to see all of you soon. I'm not going to keep you and I know you're not working right now…"

"What do you need?" he asks.

"I don't want to take up any of your time. You should be with B and the baby."

"She has her mother here, and she's been saying I should take a break. Let me help you," I say.

"I'm not sure working counts as a break, but I'll take the help."

I explain what happened, and Eric says he will work on tracking the call and figuring out where it originated. From there, it should be easier to narrow down who actually made it. Thanking him, I end the call and tuck my phone away in my pocket just as I'm getting to Ashley's room. I knock on the door and wait for Misty to open it.

"Did you talk to the administrator?" Misty asks.

"Yes," I nod. "And he played the message for me. There definitely was a call. But obviously, it wasn't me."

"Then who was it?" Misty asks.

"I don't know yet. But I have the best guy I know in the Bureau working on it," I tell her.

"Do I have to go?" Ashley asks nervously. "Are they going to move me to that other hospital?"

"No," I say adamantly.

"Thank goodness," Misty sighs in relief.

"The important thing to remember is that we don't know exactly why that call was made. It could very well be a hoax. Maybe someone found out the contact information for the administrator and put in the request to see if she could make something happen. It's sick and ridiculous, but people do things like that. They like to feel powerful and manipulate situations."

I perhaps know that better than anyone.

"What about the media out there?" Misty asks, flinging her hand up in the direction of the front of the hospital in her exasperation. "Could it have been one of them trying to get Ashley outside so they can take pictures of her and try to get some sort of statement?"

"It's possible. Right now, we don't know. But we're going to find out. What matters is that everyone knows that call was not authentic. There was no legitimate request. Ashley isn't going anywhere," I say.

"But I want to," Ashley says.

"What?" Misty asks, her voice almost powdery. "Honey, you don't have to do anything just because someone said you need to. You're safe here. You don't have to go to another hospital."

"I don't want to go to another hospital," she says. "I want to go home."

THIRTY-NINE

MISTY'S EYES overflow with tears that slide down her cheeks and pool in the deep lines made by her wide smile. She walks up to the side of the bed and takes Ashley's hand, leaning down to kiss it.

"Oh, baby. You have no idea how happy it makes me to hear you say that," she says softly.

"Can I?" Ashley asks. "I'm fine. They've done the examinations. They've done tests. I'm fine."

She emphasizes the statement the second time she says it.

"Has the doctor spoken to you about the possibility of leaving?" I ask.

Misty and Ashley both shake their heads.

"Not since you spoke with the head doctor on the team," Misty says.

"Alright. Let me see if I can get some answers for you."

This is a delicate situation. I notice Ashley isn't hooked up to the IV for fluids anymore, and the few days in the hospital have left her looking stronger. Right now, she is safer because of the security team and the monitored building, but if there is no physical health reason for her to remain here under the doctor's care, security isn't enough justification to keep her in the hospital.

Being home with her family, away from the constant prodding of the medical team, would give her a better chance to rest, recover, and start trying to piece life back together. The family will need time to heal as much as she does; that can't really start until they are back in the same space.

It takes another couple of hours to work out Ashley's discharge. Now is the challenge of getting her out of the hospital without turning it into a media circus. The story of a missing person who returns after five years whips up the media and acts as fodder for stories for weeks, even in big cities. Make it a town on the smaller side, and the recovery of the person as dramatic as this one was, and it's enough to create nothing short of a frenzy.

Media outlets from all over the country have camped out in front of the hospital, waiting for any sighting of Ashley or any chance to interview her family. The police have moved them a couple of times, and the hospital staff is constantly doing everything they can to shoo them along, but they haven't relented. Freedom of the press is a battle cry among this type. They will push that to the very edge of decency and legality in hopes of getting that perfect picture or that juicy story.

I have no intention of Ashley's being a part of either one. Which is going to take some coordination.

Or misdirection.

"COVER YOUR FACE WITH THIS," I SAY, HANDING AVA A PINK sweatshirt that would look very much at home on an eighteen-year-old. "Put your hair up in a messy bun."

"What do you think?" Xavier asks, coming back into the room.

He's wearing dark blue scrubs and has a lanyard around his neck with a freshly made identification card tucked into the clear plastic.

"Perfect," I grin.

"Do you think I need to wrinkle my scrubs? Make it look like I've been working a long shift and possibly slept the night in one of the cots in the doctor's lounge?" he asks.

"If that will make you feel better, go for it," I offer.

"I think it will seem more authentic."

I nod. "Go ahead." He starts for the door. "Where are you going?"

"The doctor's lounge. I need genuine cot wrinkles."

"I'll go with him," Dean says. "I might as well wrinkle it up, too."

"Alright," I say, looking back at Ava, already tucked under a sheet on a gurney. "You're just going to lie there with your face covered. They'll get you out of the hospital and into the ambulance as fast as they can. Then take your hair down, take off the sweatshirt, and get up so that if one of them follows, when you get out, you won't look like the same person."

She nods. "I can handle that."

"Good."

The guys come back to the downstairs room after sufficiently wrinkling themselves up. This is where we've been staging the diversion I hope will get Ashley out of the hospital and safely to her parents' house without the media's descending on her. Ashley and her parents are waiting in another room on the other side of the hospital. I make sure Xavier, Dean, and Ava are ready for their portion of the plan, then head down the back hallways, away from the glass windows at the front of the lobby, to Ashley and Misty.

When I get there and reassure them that the plan is underway, John will make his way outside and to the van rented for this specific purpose. As he hasn't been at the hospital before now and he's in sunglasses and a hat, he's harder to spot. The look is a cliche, but it's enough for what we need. The reporters are waiting to see Ashley and they're looking out for the people they've seen before.

John is well-enough concealed in the disguise, it won't be as easy for them to spot him, especially in this area of the hospital. They're focused on the front entrance and the emergency room. Which is exactly where they'll think they see her. Because at the same time nurses-for-the-day Xavier and Dean are wheeling their fake Ashley out to a waiting ambulance, John and Misty will slip out the back door with the real one.

It's a lot of theater, but hopefully, it will result in Ashley's being able to get out of the hospital and home without any more interference.

"Are you ready, Ashley?" I ask.

She takes a deep breath. "Yeah. I'm ready."

I give her and Misty both a solid nod, then turn to the orderly assigned to escort them out. "Keep your walkies close."

I make my way back to Xavier and Dean, who are putting the finishing touches on their wrinkles and settling Ava into position.

"Testing," I speak into the walkie. "Misty, do you read me?"

"Loud and clear," comes her response.

"Remember, there's no need to rush," I tell her. "You're just taking a casual stroll. No need to draw any attention."

Xavier looks back at me with a grin. "Emma, this is exactly why we start low with our H.P.A."

"I'm not sure I'd qualify this as an attraction," I reply, then turn my focus back to the emergency room doors a few feet ahead of us.

I lift my walkie and key the speech button.

"Everyone in position?"

"In position," Misty answers.

Dean takes hold of the gurney and begins wheeling Ava forward.

"Alright, we are go, in five, four, three, two..."

The automatic sliding doors open.

"One! Go, go, go!"

The instant we exit the door, we're caught in a swirling maelstrom of shouted questions and blinding lights.

It worked. Believe it or not, it worked. Twenty minutes later, we're all back in the driveway to the Stevenson house. The ambulance is on its way back to the hospital with an empty stretcher and discarded scrubs and sweatshirt in the back.

I watch as Ashley takes her first steps inside. She glances around, a look of wonder in her eyes.

"We've changed a few things," Misty tells her, noticing the expression on her daughter's face. "I'm sorry."

Ashley shakes her head. "There's nothing to be sorry about. It's beautiful."

"We couldn't have been expected to keep everything exactly the same way," Leona says from where she's standing on the opposite side of the living room.

She hasn't approached her sister. I'm watching the way she looks at her, gauging her reaction to having her home. What she said to me when I was going through Ashley's computer is still with me. She couldn't leave her mother. She has a huge sense of responsibility when it comes to her mother. It's obvious she's spent the last five years watching out for her and trying to help her through the torment and never-ending questions of having a missing child.

Now Ashley is back.

That sudden reality leaves something massive in its wake. I can feel it in the room around us. It's as if the air has been burned.

"Do you need anything, sweetheart?" Misty asks, ignoring Leona's comment. "Are you thirsty? Hungry?"

Ashley shakes her head.

"Why don't we sit down for a few minutes and talk?" I suggest.

The group distributes across the collection of carefully coordinated furniture in the living room, and I sort through the questions in my mind, trying to figure out which ones to ask her and how.

"Does anyone need anything?" Misty asks as we all settle into place. "Water? Coffee?"

"Coffee actually sounds wonderful, if you don't mind," I say.

"How do you take it?" Misty asks.

"Black," I tell her.

"Alright." She looks to everyone else, they all their heads, and she goes into the kitchen.

"Ashley, now that it's been a couple of days, I wanted to see if you might remember more about what happened," I start.

"I still don't know," she says, starting to shift around in her seat.

"Do we really have to do this?" John asks. "She just got home."

"I know," I acknowledge. "But it's important not to let too much time pass. The longer we wait, the harder it's going to be to get any resolution for this."

"There's been resolution," he says. "Ashley's home. She's here. She's safe."

"She might not be," I say. "I'm not trying to scare you or to make this any more difficult than it already is, but I believe in being honest. For all we know, this man who held her captive might still be looking for her. For all we know, this man might still have other young girls kidnapped. We need as much information as we possibly can to bring this man to justice."

"Justice," John scoffs. "You think there's such a thing as justice for what happened to her? My daughter was stolen when she was barely thirteen years old and held captive for five years while someone put her through God knows what. What's the justice for that? What makes that okay?"

"Nothing," I say without hesitation. "There is nothing that can make what happened okay. There's nothing that will make it go away, or take away the effect it's had on your daughter or your family. That isn't the point of the criminal justice system. It doesn't make it okay. That's not what justice is about.

"Justice is an ideal, intended to give people what they deserve. And using that definition strictly, I don't believe there can be justice for Ashley's case, either. There is no such thing as fair treatment for someone who could do what he did to your daughter. There is nothing equitable that could be done to him, and what might be considered fair isn't an option.

"That's what sets us apart. It's what maintains our humanity and ensures that our fight for Ashley's safety isn't tainted. This man deserves treatment we can't possibly dole out, because if we did, we would not only be no better than him, we would be worse. We would be choosing to mete out that kind of treatment after already declaring it barbaric and inappropriate. There's a tremendous difference between retribution and vengeance."

FORTY

"I'M RIGHT HERE," Ashley suddenly says.

John looks at her as if he's startled to hear her speak.

"Of course, you are," he says.

"Then you need to speak to her, not about her," Dean says.

I realize I've fallen right into the trap that I usually do everything I can to avoid. Rather than including her in the conversation, I've just talked around her. Pulling back from the conflict with her father, I look right at Ashley.

"I'm sorry," I say. "Are you ready to talk about what happened?"

"It needs to be done," she says.

"Tell me again about what you remember from that day," I say.

"I already told you I don't really remember much at all. My memory is gone," she says.

"I know you have a hard time with some of it, but you were able to tell me part of it. Tell me that part again. Just tell me again, as if I haven't heard it before. More details might come up that you don't even realize you remember yet," I say.

Ashley nods and sits back. "It had been raining for a few days and the weather had finally gotten better, so I decided to hang out with my friends. Allison and Vivian, the ones who came to the hospital to see me. We went to the national park to camp. Mom made me bring my sweatshirt even though I didn't want to, but I ended up wearing it."

She hesitates and Xavier eases toward the edge of his seat, leaning toward her.

"Close your eyes," he says. "You're not talking to anybody right now. You're not telling a story. You're there. Experience your senses. What do they remember?"

"The ground is hard and cold. I can't sleep. I walk around trying to find something."

"Find what?" I ask.

She shakes her head. "I don't know."

"Where's everybody else?" I ask.

"Vivian and Allison?"

"Everyone you were with that night."

"I was with them," she says.

I nod. "Where are they? When you can't sleep?"

"They stayed."

"Then what?"

"That's all I can remember," she says. "I don't know what happened between that and when I woke up at the house on Wolf's bed."

"What time was it?" I ask. "Use your senses again. Is there sunlight coming through the window? Do you hear birds?"

"The window was boarded up," she says, distancing herself from it rather than staying in the sensory moment where I'm trying to keep her. "I couldn't see outside. But my muscles hurt, as though I'd been there a while."

"Your muscles hurt. Can you remember feeling anything else?" I ask.

I'm tiptoeing around all the details I already know, waiting for something to fall into place. But Ashley shakes her head.

"No. It just felt as if I had been tied up there for a while."

"Okay," I nod. "That's good. You did a great job."

I stand up from the couch just as Misty is coming back into the living room with my coffee.

"Oh," she says. "Are you leaving?"

"I'm sorry," I say. "There's something we have to look into. I appreciate the coffee." I reach for the mug and down a few sips. "It's delicious. I'll be back soon. Ashley, if you remember anything else, anything at all, even if you don't feel that it makes sense, call me. Remember, you aren't the one in trouble here. Anything you remember, anything you have to tell me, it's not going to make anyone mad at you or cause any problems for you."

She nods, but doesn't change emotion. Misty walks us to the door and waits on the porch while we go to the car. No sooner have I gotten behind the wheel and pulled my sunglasses on when Ava leans forward from her seat in the back.

"Why didn't you ask her more? Why didn't you push her?" she asks.

"Excuse me?" I ask.

"You know what she's telling you isn't the truth. So, why did you let her get away with it? You could have pushed her and asked her harder questions and she might have cracked."

"First of all, Ashley isn't the perpetrator here. She's the victim. She's been shattered already. You don't need to crack her. Second, let me remind you that this is my investigation. You are helping. That's it. That doesn't mean you're in charge, and it definitely doesn't mean I'm open to suggestions on how to do my job. You did a fine job being the fake Ashley to make sure she got home without the media attention. There will be images of you splashed all over the news tonight along with confused headlines. Be glad you contributed," I tell her, trying my best not to snap.

"I'm an FBI agent too, Emma," Ava replies. "I got the education. I went through the training. I know what I'm doing."

"In theory. That's all it is right now. Theory. You've never done any of this before. You have no experience, no first-hand knowledge to fall back on," I say.

"That's what I'm trying to get now," she points out. "I'm trying to be a part of this investigation, so I'll be better equipped to handle my own. But even without experience, I know that she wasn't telling you everything. You just didn't dig deep enough. You could have told her what Allison told you. That might have triggered something."

"I didn't lead her," I say. "I didn't offer her information or feed her details that would influence what she's able to tell me. Giving her the story could have stopped her from being able to remember the details. And she obviously told me a hell of a lot more than she told you. I know what I'm doing, Ava. Don't ever forget that. It might not be what you think you would do, but I'm handling this exactly the way I intend to. Don't try to get in my way. Maybe you'll have your own investigation at some point and you can do whatever you want to. But this is mine."

Ava falls silent, and I head away from the Stevenson house back toward the business area of town. I pull up in front of the entrance to the hotel.

"What's going on?" Dean asks.

"I need you to contact the doctors and see if they have any more results from the tests they did on Ashley. Misty and Ashley granted permission for them to share anything that may be pertinent with the investigation team, so you shouldn't have a problem getting the information. If you do, call me. Then I need you to start hunting down Allison's ex-boyfriend Sean Melrose. See what he's been up to for the last five years."

"Where are you going?" Xavier asks.

"To the hospital where they left Ashley," I say. "That's the last place anyone can concretely say they saw her. That's where the trail starts."

They start to get out of the car and Xavier pauses. "She can't remember."

"I know, Xavier."

He starts to get out of the car, then looks at me again.

"It's your sandbox, Emma. Ava just wants to borrow a shovel."

FORTY-ONE

"It was five years ago?" asks the frazzled-looking woman I'm following down a hallway as she distributes manila folders to offices.

"Yes. Five years ago. August thirteenth, so almost exactly five years," I clarify.

She nods. "I can speak with security. They have cameras that cover the entrances and the parking lots. I believe there are also some in the emergency room waiting area. I can't be sure."

"Virtually all hospitals have security coverage for any non-private area where there will be patients," I say.

I resist the urge to point out to her that as a patient liaison, perhaps she wasn't the best choice for me to deal with. But she's who I have to work with right this second, so I'll do what I can.

"As you said, it's been five years. I can't guarantee they will have any information for you."

She finally finishes tucking the folders into the plastic holders attached to the fronts of the office doors and leads me to another part of the hospital. We go up a shadowy back staircase that doesn't seem like a good idea for anyone, and she gestures at another office door.

"Thank you," I say.

She stays behind me as I walk up to the door and knock on it. A tall woman with broad shoulders and an intense look in her eyes opens the door and stares out at me.

"Yes?" she asks.

"I'm Agent Emma Griffin. I'm with the FBI. This hospital might be involved in a case I'm working on and I'd like to ask you some questions," I introduce myself.

She looks over at the woman behind me but doesn't say anything. Apparently, she didn't need to, because the liaison turns and walks away, leaving me there in the hallway.

"Come in," the woman waves me in. "I'm Sandra."

"Hello," I say and follow her into the office.

"This is Shane," Sandra says, gesturing at a man leaned back in one of the gray office chairs at a long table functioning as a desk.

He's almost the antithesis of her: tall, but willowy. He's the kind of person who's as if he isn't going to have full control over his arms and legs when he tries to move.

"Hi, Shane," I call over. "Agent Griffin."

"FBI," Sandra says.

This instantly makes Shane sit up straighter, a nervous look crossing his face. I smile.

"Don't worry. I'm not here for you," I say.

"Oh," he says, letting out a breath of relief. "Okay. Good."

That kind of reaction is always a bit of a concern for me.

"If you've been watching the news the last week, you probably heard about Ashley Stevenson," I say.

"That girl who went missing a few years back," Sandra says. "She showed back up."

I nod. "Yes. That's her."

"She's not at this hospital," Shane tells me.

"I know," I say. "But she was. The night she went missing, she was here. At least, that's what I've been told. That's why I'm here. I want to know if there's any chance you still have the security footage from that night. August thirteenth. I know it was five years ago."

"Fortunately, our security system automatically uploads to the cloud," Shane says, turning to a computer on the other side of him. "Everything is supposed to be kept there for five years. So, it looks as if you came in right under the wire. You said August thirteenth?"

"Yes," I confirm.

"Kind of an appropriate date," he remarks.

"She was also born on the thirteenth, but of June," I say. "Superstitious people are having a field day with it."

"I can imagine," Sandra says.

"What timeframe do you want to see?" Shane asks.

"I'm not sure exactly. If you could just give me from around six until midnight, that would be great."

"Give me just a minute."

I watch as he isolates the portion of the security footage from those hours and cuts them from the rest so he can give me a copy of just the footage from that period. I give him my email address and he sends it through.

"Thank you," I tell him. "This could make a really big difference in the case."

"You have a long night of watching footage ahead of you," Sandra says.

"Maybe. But I know exactly what I'm looking for. Hopefully, it won't be hard to spot."

I leave the security office and make my way back through the hospital. It's getting on toward evening, so I order dinner to pick up at a restaurant close to the hotel. I send a text to Dean to let him know, but he doesn't respond immediately. After picking up the food, I go straight to my room and change into comfortable clothes to settle in for my cyber stakeout.

Opening the email Shane sent, I realize there is more footage than I expected. He didn't just send the perspective of the camera inside the waiting room. The same several hours were captured on other cameras positioned outside the entrance and in the parking lot.

I start with the camera at the entrance.

Almost an hour later, I'm deep in my dinner and still scrolling through footage when the electronic lock on my door clicks and Dean, Xavier, and Ava come in. I gesture toward the table near the window.

"There's food," I tell them. "I just kind of ordered everything. Did you find out anything?"

Dean goes to the table and starts filling a paper plate with a roast beef sandwich, seasoned fries, and mozzarella sticks. This is the kind of meal that's going to earn him several hours in the gym. I'll be right there alongside him, so I know what he's thinking as he pops one of the deliciously orange coils of potato in his mouth and adds a drizzle of barbecue sauce to the edge of the plate.

Worth it.

"There wasn't a huge amount to find out," he sighs, carrying the food over to the couch where I'm sitting. "They did get the results of the DNA test. It is definitely Ashley. The rest of the test results were fairly predictable. Malnutrition. Some lingering effects of abuse and what you would expect to see in a long-term captivity situation."

"Signs of sexual abuse?" I ask.

Dean nods. "Evidence of repeated rapes. No sign of her ever having been pregnant, though."

"That's interesting."

"Why?" Ava asks.

"Most predators don't think to use birth control methods with their victims," I explain. "Unless there is a physiological reason Ashley can't get pregnant, the chances of her not getting pregnant over the course of five years of abuse are very slim. That means birth control was done intentionally. That sets her apart from other kidnappings that are similar in other ways."

"Jaycee Dugard. Elizabeth Smart," Dean says.

I nod. "Exactly. Those girls were taken by men who considered them as extensions of their families. Wives, in a way. They were thought of as a way to expand the family. In situations like that, pregnancies are welcome, if not directly intentional. The children are even brought out into the world and treated well by the men who hold their mothers captive. But that's not what happened with Ashley.

"She wasn't brought in as a wife figure or a way to grow a family. That takes away a lot of the religious or cult undertones as well. The evidence of the sexual abuse isn't surprising, but from what I've seen of her, it didn't look as if she was tortured. Mistreated, yes, but this wasn't sadism."

"No," Dean says. "There isn't evidence of that kind of treatment. One thing they did note was there aren't any deep scars on her wrists or ankles. Which means she wasn't chained up for the majority of the time she was there."

"Or they used soft restraints that wouldn't cut into her skin," I counter. "Which would mean they didn't want to leave marks. Combined with the use of birth control, that tells me she wasn't just being kept by this man she calls Wolf. He was using her as a commodity."

"Trafficking?" Dean asks.

I give an unconvinced shrug. "It's possible, but it doesn't seem as if she was taken from place to place much. She would have mentioned that. And she didn't mention any other girls, so she wasn't in a brothel. This is a more focused situation. Just about her."

"Boutique exploitation," Dean mutters.

"We just need to figure out what kind, and by who," I say.

"What did you find out at the hospital?" Xavier asks, settling onto the floor with his own plate.

"They had the security footage from five years ago," I tell him. "I'm still going through it."

"Let's see it," Dean says.

"Movie night!" Xavier says.

He scoots closer to the table and I turn the computer around so everyone can see the screen.

"I haven't seen anything yet that has anything to do with Ashley.

But I still have several hours of footage to go through, so it might be a little while," I say.

We eat as I continue to scroll through the footage. The angle of the camera allows us to see everyone who was going inside, which makes it easy to spot the people who weren't Ashley. It's a small hospital; the waiting room was quiet in the early evening. But as the sun went down, more and more people started showing up.

Some were visibly injured, others seemed to be ill. Some wandered in on their own and others came with groups. As it gets more chaotic at the entrance, I slow the pace I'm scrolling to make sure we don't miss anyone going inside. Suddenly I see a familiar face glance up toward the camera.

"That's Vivian," I point to the screen.

The slightly younger version of Vivian looks the way she did in the pictures, her hair longer and her face less stern and intense. She's on one side of a figure in a sweatshirt, a man on the other, and another girl behind them. The hood on the sweatshirt conceals the figure's face, but I know it's Ashley.

"Are you sure?" Dean asks.

"Yes. What's the timestamp?" He notes the time on the camera and I go to the other set of footage. "This is the camera inside the waiting room."

We cue the footage to the seconds just before we saw the group walking through the emergency room door and wait.

"There they are," Dean says. "Ashley is in really bad shape."

That's an understatement. Ashley is barely on her own feet. The people on either side of her are holding her up as they go through the entrance toward the chairs clustered to the side of the reception desk. The woman behind the desk is already talking to someone else, so they move right past her. They bring Ashley to the far side of the seating area and lower her down into a chair tucked in the corner.

She slumps in it, looking as though she's no longer conscious as she's sitting there. She starts to slide down the edge of the chair, heading for the floor. Allison steps forward and catches her, starting to pull her up. She says something, and Vivian steps up to help her. I can only imagine how weak Allison is feeling, knowing what she has gone through not long before this moment.

The male figure who is with them starts to walk away, then pauses and looks back at them. He seems to be trying to hurry them along. No one around them is paying any attention to what's happening. The girls look at Ashley one more time, then walk away.

As they're headed toward the entrance again, the man with them looks up. The camera catches an image of his face. Dean reaches forward to stop the playback.

"That's Sean Melrose," he says. "Allison's ex-boyfriend."

I stare at the image. I've seen that face before.

It was staring at me in the hospital hallway after I talked to Leona.

FORTY-TWO

"THAT'S ALLISON'S EX-BOYFRIEND?" I ask.

Dean nods. "I looked into him as you asked me to. That's definitely him. Didn't she tell you he was the one who helped get her into the hospital?"

"She did," I say.

"Then what is it?" Dean asks.

"I'm not sure yet. Hold on," I say. "Let's see what happened to Ashley."

We continue as the people in the waiting room got called back to the doctor and others came to take their place in the chairs. No one looked Ashley's way. No one seemed to notice she was there. Suddenly, she stirred. Her head dropped back, then lifted. She looked around. A few seconds later, she stood up and made her way toward the door, walking out of the emergency room.

As quickly as I can, I cue up the footage from the other camera to the right time, so we can watch her leave. She was still shaky on her feet as she stumbled out of the sliding glass doors and onto the sidewalk. It was getting close to midnight, which means the footage will end soon. The back of my neck tingles as I watch her fall sideways and catch herself with one hand against the brick wall of the hospital.

She used it to guide her as she made her way down toward the corner of the building. Leaning against it, she slid down to sit and rested her head back. The minutes tick by. No one checked on her or even looked at her.

She sat there for almost twenty minutes. Silent. Alone. Abandoned by the people she trusted.

My heart breaks for her.

Finally, she used the wall to stand back up, and walked around the corner, disappearing from the frame.

"Is that it?" Dean asks. "Did they give you anything else?"

"No. Those are the only cameras they gave me. They didn't mention any others on the outside of the hospital. I'm guessing they only have them in the parking areas and at the entrances. That side of the building is just a narrow driveway," I say.

"So another dead end. We have her right up until she disappears. No idea what happened to her after that," Dean says, sounding frustrated and angry.

"You looked into Sean Melrose," I say.

"Yes," he said. "I sifted through his old social media and traced some of his new stuff, but most of it is private. I can crack it, but it's going to take some time. I was able to do a quick background check on him, though."

"What did you find out about him?"

"Not much. He got in some trouble before Ashley went missing. Nothing really serious. Drinking. Some traffic stuff. Trespassing. Fighting. After this, he pretty much went off the radar. It seems as though he and Allison kept things going for a while, but then he skipped town. I didn't see anything about his being back around town. He might not have been."

"He has. I saw him at the hospital."

"When you were getting the footage?"

"No," I say. "The other hospital."

"With Allison?" Dean frowns.

"No." I shake my head. "With Leona."

"Ashley's sister?" Ava asks, sounding as shocked as I was to see it.

"Yep," I confirm. "The day Ashley came back, I noticed Leona down the hall from her room. She seemed really upset and I went to talk to her. She pretty much brushed me off, but when she was walking away, I noticed the man she had been talking to. It was him. It was Sean Melrose."

"What were they talking about?" Dean asks.

I shake my head. "I don't know. I didn't hear them. But he seemed less than thrilled that I came to talk to Leona. He didn't say anything to me, but the look in his eyes was unmistakable."

"What does that mean, though?" Dean asks. "They could know each other from school. Their ages would have been closer than Ashley's."

"That's definitely possible," I admit. "We don't really know anything about that right now. It just seems odd to me that nobody mentions the connection. If they were friends back then, it would seem to me that Allison would have said that. We talked about how Leona didn't really socialize. They sometimes spent time together, but weren't exactly friends. That would have been the time for her to mention that her boyfriend and Leona were apparently on good terms."

"Maybe they've gotten closer in the time since?"

"No," Ava says. I look over at her and see her shaking her head. "He went through all this, leaving her in the emergency room, encouraging the girls to lie, so he could separate himself from this situation. He knew how bad it would look for him if anyone could connect him to Ashley that night. That's not the kind of person who would then strike up a friendship with her sister."

She looks at me. Xavier leans closer to me.

"Give her the shovel, Emma," he whispers.

"That might be true," I say.

"Might?" Ava raises an eyebrow.

My eyes slide over to her. She looks stunned I'm not jumping down her throat to dismiss her theory. I have to admit, it's a solid theory. But I don't buy it. If this was just about Ashley's being left in the hospital, if she'd died there, then I would agree with Ava. But it's not. Just seeing them leave her in the emergency room isn't enough to separate Sean from the situation.

"Something happened after they left her in the emergency room. She didn't just stay there. If Sean had something to do with that, it could explain his interest in getting close to Leona," I say.

"You think he wants to relive what he did? Or the pain it caused the family?" she asks. "That's sick."

"That would be the behavior of a thrill killer. Someone who not only kills for fun, but also gets enjoyment out of watching how it affects people. This is the type of person who will be a part of the search party and go to the funeral. He'll visit with the family and may even put on massive displays of grief or honoring the victim, even if he apparently didn't know the victim very well. It's purely for show; out of a desire to be wrapped up in the emotion and turmoil of the whole situation.

"But people who kill on the spur of the moment, or accidentally, may also be drawn to the family. Especially when the case is getting attention. They want to know what's going on in the investigation and if law enforcement is on their trail. It keeps them a step ahead. But it can also create anxiety and make them act out," I say. "That's often how they get caught. They get so wrapped up in their determination to look innocent they actually end up showing that they are guilty."

"Didn't Allison say Sean took her to the hospital after leaving Ashley? One in another town?" Dean asks. "And then they went back to the camp?"

I check the timestamps we recorded from the moment the three left Ashley until she got up and left, and then until she stood and walked out of the frame of the security video outside.

"He left Allison at the hospital," I say. "He didn't stay with her.

He didn't want anybody to know he had anything to do with her or the baby, so he left her there. He came back later to pick her up, but there was enough time for him to get her there, leave her, come back to this hospital for Ashley, get her out of the way, and then go back for Allison."

"But what would he have done with her?" Dean asks. "Why would he have kept her for five years?"

"Obsession," I offer. "He was obviously into younger girls. Allison was only fifteen and pregnant with his baby. He could have been fixated on Ashley and have seen this as an opportunity. It's interesting to me that he resurfaced at the same time she did."

"Do you really think he could be the one to have done this?" Ava asks.

"I don't know. We have to cover all the bases. Eliminate all the possibilities," I say, a yawn suddenly creeping up on me. "It's getting late. I'm going to try to get some sleep."

We clean up from dinner and the rest of them head out of the room. Ava and Dean are in the hallway when Xavier steps back inside and comes to me where I'm still sitting, staring at the computer.

"You're clicking your fingernails," he says.

I look up at him. "Hmmm?"

"Your fingernails," he repeats. "You click them when you're stuck on thinking about something. What are you thinking about?"

I look at my hand and realize he's right. As my thoughts churn through my mind, my fingers systematically flick against the pad of my thumb, clicking the nails against each other as they move up and down.

"When we were talking to Ashley about the night she went missing, she said she remembered the ground being cold and hard," I say.

"She was sitting on a sidewalk," he points out.

"But it wouldn't be cold," I say. "It was August. Even with the rain and the cooler weather, the concrete would have retained the heat. She also didn't mention either of the guys who were there. Just

Vivian and Allison. I can understand her not remembering much. The combination of the alcohol and the trauma of being abducted could make it extremely difficult to recall anything from that time."

"But she remembers the park," Xavier says.

I nod. "She remembers going to the park to camp, and what it was like walking around there. But she doesn't remember that it was Vivian's boyfriend who drove them? Or that the guy she had a thing for was there?"

"You think she really doesn't remember?"

"Maybe it's time we refresh her memory a little."

FORTY-THREE

"Do you really think this is necessary?" Misty asks, wrapping her arms wrapped around her chest as we talk in hushed tones in the hallway just outside the living room.

"Yes," I say. "It's been several days since Ashley got home. We still don't know exactly what happened that night or where she's been for the past five years. I know I've said this to you a few times before, but I feel it bears repeating. The longer it takes for us to identify the person who has been holding your daughter, the less likely it is we'll ever be able to find him. Not only does that mean that there will be no accountability for what he did to Ashley, but he will be free to do it to someone else. And I assure you, if he did it to her, the chances are extraordinarily high he will do it to someone else, if he hasn't already. I don't think I need to go into detail about the types of things she could have gone through, but..."

Misty shakes her head, closing her eyes as if so stop the words from getting to her.

"I get it," she finally says. "I understand. I just don't want to hurt her any more than she already has been. I wish there was some other way."

"I know you do. But there isn't another way. She is our only real source of evidence beyond a certain point in the night. The video I want to show her gives more of a look into the sequence of events of that night, but it doesn't tell everything," I say.

Misty looks confused. "The sequence of events? What do you mean? What happened?"

"I don't want to say anything until Ashley has seen the video. I need her genuine reaction. I want her to be able to give whatever insight comes to mind without being influenced," I say.

"You won't even tell me what's in this recording, but you expect me to give you authorization to show it to my traumatized child?" she asks, clearly offended and getting angrier.

Out of the corner of my eye, I notice Leona lurking just inside another room a few feet down the hallway. She's obviously been listening to our conversation and is now looking at her mother with red-rimmed, widened eyes.

"Mom," she says in a soft tone.

I pretend not to see her, wanting to know what she's going to do.

"With all due respect, Misty, she isn't a child. As I said in the hospital, she's eighteen years old. She isn't the same little girl who went out with her friends five years ago. She is an adult," I say.

"Mom," Leona whispers again.

"She might be eighteen years old, but you can't possibly really think that means she's an adult," Misty counters. "Not after everything she's been through."

"Legally, she is. Until a court has determined she cannot be perceived as an adult, that is exactly what she is. I know she's been through a lot, but that doesn't automatically mean she's been cognitively damaged or stunted. I know you want to protect her, but you have to give her the respect of acknowledging that she grew up in those years and can be an active part of this investigation," I say.

"Alright," Misty says.

"Mom," Leona says again.

She says it almost as if she isn't processing the change in the conversation. As though she's just barely hanging on and waiting for her mother to respond to her.

"Where is she?" I ask.

"In her bedroom."

I head up the stairs with Misty right behind me. I see the sign on the front of the door again, just as I had the first time I visited this room. Only this time, we don't just go past it. We pause out in the hallway and knock lightly.

"Come in, " Ashley says.

Misty steps into the room and gestures back at me.

"Honey, Agent Griffin is here. She has something she wants to show you and talk about."

Ashley nods from her desk. I notice one hand is lightly rested on the front of her computer, her fingertips just supporting it, as though she had been on the computer only seconds before we walked in.

I give her a "Hey, Ashley. How are you doing?"

She nods. "Fine. Glad to be here."

"It's good to hear that. I know this isn't easy, but I need to talk to you again about the night you went missing," I say.

"I already told you everything I remember," she says.

"Having gaps in your memory is completely normal," I reiterate. "But it doesn't mean you'll never remember. Sometimes all it takes is seeing or hearing something from that time for it to unlock the memories your mind might have buried. The investigation uncovered some additional details from that night, and I hope they'll help you put the pieces together."

"What details?" she asks.

"Before I show you, think again. You told me that you remember Allison and Vivian being there, and that the ground was cold and hard. You were at Sherando Ridge and set up camp for the night. Anything else?"

Ashley shakes her head. "No. I'm sorry. I'm trying."

Misty rushes to her daughter's side and squeezes her shoulders.

"You have no reason to say you're sorry. You didn't do anything wrong."

"No," I say. "Of course, you didn't. This isn't about you. Okay? You're not doing anything wrong. It's just important to me when I investigate to give people involved as much space and freedom as I can to make sure they are really remembering, not just building off something they heard or were told. I wanted to give you one more chance to remember something else before showing you the footage."

"Footage?" Ashley frowns. "Were there cameras near the campsite?"

"No," I tell her, trying to gauge the emotion that filled her face when she asked that question. "But there were some in the hospital where you ended up that night."

I watch her face, but there isn't even a flicker of recognition. Misty is the one who reacts.

"She was in a hospital? How did she get there? Who was there with her? When was she there? How was I not notified of this?" she demands.

"Ashley, there is security footage of you in the emergency room waiting room and just outside. I've seen it. Can you think of anything that might be on it? Anything you might want to tell your mother?" I ask.

"No," she says, her eyes slightly widened. "I don't remember being at the hospital that night. Why didn't they mention it when I was brought there?"

I shake my head. "Not that hospital. Will you look at the footage and tell me if it jogs anything?"

She nods, getting up from her chair to sit on the edge of her bed between her mother and me. I take my tablet out of my bag and hand it to her. The video is already cued up, so all I have to do is tap the center of the screen for the footage to begin. I purposely started it a few seconds before the group appears, to gauge her reaction and see if she seems to know what's going on.

Her eyes flick all over the screen, searching the chairs and corners, trying to figure out what she's supposed to be looking at. There's no response. No change in her expression. Even when Vivian, Allison, and Sean show up all but carrying her into the emergency room, she doesn't seem to realize what she's looking at.

"Is that... Vivian?" Misty frowns, her hand clasped over her mouth in equal parts concentration and shock.

I nod. "Yes."

She watches for another moment and gasps. "That's Ashley. They're dragging her into the hospital. Where did they find her?"

"Do you remember any of this?" I ask.

"Look at her," Misty snaps, flinging her hand in the direction of the screen. "Does she look as if she's in any condition to remember anything that was happening?"

I lift my eyes to her, staying calm and steady. "Misty, you need to let her watch and think."

"They just left?" Ashley asks.

I nod. "This stays pretty much like this for a while. I'm just going to skip ahead a little bit."

They watch the footage of Ashley getting up from the chair and walking out of the hospital.

"No one noticed," Ashley says under her breath, almost saying it to herself. She looks at me. "What then?" I show her the footage from the camera outside, and she looks at me incredulously. "Then what?"

"We don't know," I say. "There are no other cameras that caught anything."

"That's it?" Misty asks. "That's all you have? You have security footage of people who are supposed to be her friends dumping her at a hospital with who knows what kinds of injuries, then she just wanders away and that's it? You lose her after that?"

"We didn't lose her," I clarify. "That's why I'm here. I wanted Ashley to see this so that maybe she could remember something else."

Ashley shakes her head. "I don't. I don't know what happened." Her eyes go back to the screen and the empty corner of the sidewalk where she had just been sitting. "No one even noticed."

"I can't do this," Misty says, standing up sharply from the bed and storming out of the room. "I need to get some air."

"Why did they do that?" Ashley asks.

"Who?" I ask.

"Vivian and Allison. Why did they just leave?"

"They were afraid," I say. "Something had happened that night before this. Something really bad. Do you have any idea what I'm talking about?"

She shakes her head. "No."

"Okay. Give me just a second. I'll be right back."

"Can I watch it again?" she asks.

I nod. "Sure."

Walking out of the room, I pull the door most of the way closed behind me and start down the hallway to look for Misty. I hear her voice before I see her. It's low and muffled, a harsh whisper that says she wants the words out of her as fast as possible but for no one else to overhear them. Hers isn't the only voice. I follow them both to the top of the steps. Standing just out of sight, I look down and see Misty and Leona standing in the entrance to the downstairs hall.

Their heads are close together and I can see Leona's shaking as she rocks back and forth.

"No," she says. "No. No. No. That's not right."

"Yes, Leona. Yes, it is. That's what happened."

"No," Leona repeats. "It couldn't have. I don't understand. I don't understand what's going on."

"Listen to me. Your sister is home. That's all that matters. Do you hear me? Ashley is home."

I sink back into the hallway, then walk down again with heavy footsteps to announce my presence.

"Misty?" I call.

"Yes?" she responds, rushing up the steps. "Is everything alright?"

"There you are," I say. "We need to move forward with the next steps of the investigation. I wanted you to go over them with us."

FORTY-FOUR

MISTY FOLLOWS me back to Ashley's room, where we find her curled up on the bed, her back pressed against the wall and her knees to her chest. One arm wrapped around her legs holds them close while the other hand supports the tablet. She's fixated on the image on the screen.

"Ashley?" I ask. She doesn't move. I take a step closer to the bed. "Ashley?"

Her eyes snap to me. I almost expect tears in them, but they're dry. Instead, there's confusion and anger. It passes quickly and she holds the tablet back out to me.

"I don't know what happened after that. Just that I woke up in the house," she says.

I nod and sit beside her again. "That's actually what I wanted to talk with you about. You seem to remember the house better than anything else. Can you tell me more about it?"

She describes the house and the first moments she remembered being awake. Again, she talks about the man she called Wolf, but skirts around what he might have done to her. I don't need her to go into detail. I already know. At least, I have a good idea. The deeper dive into the details can come later.

"What do you think about taking me back there?" I ask.

Misty explodes beside me. "Absolutely not. Are you out of your mind? She just escaped that place and now you want her to just stroll back in there? Are you going to leave her alone in there with a big ribbon around her, too?"

"Misty, you need to calm down," I say.

"Stop telling me to calm down when you're saying you want to put my child in danger again."

"I wouldn't put her in danger," I say. "I would be there with her the entire time. Along with the other members of my team. A backup team would be on stand-by, ready to come in if we need assistance. There would be no point at which she would be alone or vulnerable."

"Seriously? Do you think that having you or either of those guys with her creates some sort of impenetrable force field? That it will create a shield around her that will deflect bullets?" she snaps.

"The chances of Ashley's captor's remaining there after she escaped are very low," I explain. "This is a high-profile case. Staying would just be an invitation. That's not how these types of criminals work. If there's a chance of identification, predators don't linger in the same place."

"No," Misty says. "No. You're not going to take her somewhere that has so many horrible memories for her. Even if it's empty, it's not safe. As you said, this is a high-profile case. I was already afraid enough when she was in the hospital. If you make her do this, you're just trotting her out and putting a target on her back. They will come for her. Don't you understand that?"

That strikes me. "They?"

"What?"

"You said 'they'. 'They' will come for her. Who do you mean?"

Misty stammers for a second, the question apparently having caught her off guard.

"Ashley was a young, healthy, smart girl. It wouldn't be easy to just keep her captive like that. I just assume it had to be more than one person," she says.

"She has only talked about one person," I point out. "This man she calls Wolf."

"To you," Misty says. "But she's said 'they' to me when we were just talking."

The words are thin and snipped as she squirms, obviously uncomfortable under my scrutiny. But I'm not going to let her off the hook that easily.

"So you didn't assume," I say.

"What do you mean?"

"You just said that you assumed there was more than one person, but then you said that Ashley mentioned it to you. So, did you assume there was more than one person who had her, or did Ashley tell you there was more than one person?" I ask.

Misty's mouth opens, then closes, bending down into a scowl.

"You're trying to put words in my mouth," she protests.

"No, I'm not. I'm actually trying to do the opposite. I'm trying to understand what you're telling me and to get as much information out of Ashley as possible," I say.

"She isn't a bottle of ketchup you can shake until you get to the last drop," Misty says. "She already said she told you everything she remembers. What else is it that she needs to do?"

"Keep trying," Ashley says.

Something is different about her voice now. It's not a dramatic shift. She hasn't suddenly slipped into a robotic monotone or developed an accent. The change is more subtle, but it's there. The words seem to have more weight. They're more anchored inside her when she says them. Misty looks over at her, but I can't tell if she's noticed the change or if she just didn't catch what her daughter said.

"What, honey?" she asks.

"We need to keep trying. I might not know every step that happened that night, but I know some things. And I want to help figure out the rest," she says.

"Honey, you've already done everything you need to do. You got yourself out and you told your story. That's the most anyone can expect from you. The rest is the responsibility of the police and the FBI. Let them do their jobs."

"I'm here because I didn't just let them do their jobs," Ashley replies. She scrolls back through the footage on the tablet again and pauses it, turning it to her mother. "You see her? You see that girl? Tell her to just let them do their jobs."

"Honey," Misty says in the slow, quiet tone I notice she uses when she's trying to calm Ashley. "All I mean is..."

"I waited for so long. I waited for someone to help, for anyone to come. No one ever did. If I kept waiting, I would still be there. I had to get myself out of there. I did their job then, and if I need to do it now, I will." She looks at the screen again, her face clouding. "To make it up to that girl back then."

"You have my word I am doing everything I can to do just that," I say. "I know going back to the house isn't going to be easy, but I'll be right there with you. The whole time. And if you change your mind while we're there, we'll leave."

"It's time for you to leave," Misty tells me.

"Mom," Ashley says.

"Dinner will be ready soon. We've given up enough of our time for today."

"I'll be back," I tell Ashley. "Thank you for watching that."

She nods as she hands me back the tablet. "Do you think Wolf is out there looking for me?"

Misty's eyes widen and snap to me, horrified.

"We'll find him," I say. "We just need to keep moving forward."

I GO RIGHT TO DEAN'S ROOM WHEN I GET BACK TO THE HOTEL.

"What's going on?" he asks, tugging his shirt on over his freshly showered head as he comes out into the hallway.

"Come to my room. I need to tell you about what just happened."

A few minutes later we're sitting in my room with the tablet on the table in front of us.

"Misty didn't know what happened with Vivian and Allison?" Dean asks.

"No. I asked the investigators not to disclose that yet. I don't want it to confuse other aspects of the investigation. Keeping those details confidential is our leverage right now. And Misty looked genuinely surprised when she saw them come into the hospital."

"She didn't want to know what happened," Xavier points out.

"She asked who the people were and where they found her," Ava says. "That's what Emma said."

"Yes," Xavier nods. "But she didn't ask what happened to her. She didn't want to know why they were bringing her to the hospital."

"Maybe she knew about Ashley's drinking," Dean offers. "It might not have been the first time something like this happened. It wouldn't be the first time a mother tried to paint a rosy picture of what her child was actually like when something awful happened to that child."

"Why would she do that, though?" Ava asks. "What would the point be of pretending Ashley was perfect? If Misty knew Ashley partied, maybe she knew people Ashley could have gotten wrapped up with."

"The same reason people tend to forget how horrible their relatives really were once they die. It can be hard to have negative thoughts about somebody you might not see again. For a mother whose child is missing, it can feel that acknowledging anything unpleasant or controversial about that child makes it seem as though she doesn't actually want the child back. Or as if it will somehow reduce the chances she'll get the child back," I say.

"As if she isn't showing enough sincerity to the universe," Xavier says.

"We've got to get her to that house," I say. "Misty pushed back against it so hard. Ashley is an adult. If she wants to go, she should."

"Do you really think that's a good idea?" Ava asks.

"I'm assuming you don't," I say.

"It's just that she was held captive at that house for five years. She went through horrible things there. And she escaped. Don't you think that could create a damaging situation for her?"

"You sound just like Misty," I say.

"Maybe it's something to consider," she says.

"And maybe you should consider I know better than someone who has no investigative experience. I wouldn't put Ashley in danger. I'm not suggesting she walk up to the front door and ring the doorbell if she sees her captor through the window. The chances of his still being in the place where she was kept are next to nothing. He's not stupid. And he's also not disconnected from the world. Ashley said herself that he watches the news and he keeps up with things. He knows her situation is being splashed on every network in existence. He's not just going to sit around and wait for the mob with the pitchforks and torches."

"That's not actually going to happen, Xavier," Dean says, quickly adding the disclaimer he and I both know needs to exist.

"Are you sure?" Xavier asks.

"Yes," Dean says out of the corner of his mouth.

"Can we arrange for it?" Xavier asks quietly.

"No," Dean says.

"The thing is, I sincerely doubt the house she could lead us to is the only place she's been kept this entire time. But getting there and seeing those surroundings could be a step toward finding where else she's been," I say.

"But couldn't you look at the house and find out all the same things without her there?" Ava asks.

"I could look at it," I say. "And I could research it. But, no, I couldn't find out the same things without her there. She's willing to do what needs to be done to find out what happened to her and stop it from happening to anyone else. I would think that if she is, other people would be, too."

FORTY-FIVE

"HEY," Dean says, coming into my room the next morning. "You slept late."

"Not exactly," I say.

"Two hours and fifteen minutes," Xavier says. "Give or take. Most likely between three and five-thirty."

Dean stares at him. "Please tell me you didn't embed a chip in her. Or bug her room."

"Why was 'embed a chip in her' the first thing out of your mouth?" I ask.

"I didn't do either one," Xavier protests.

"Then how could you possibly know that?"

He points at the table close to the window. "The assortment of food wrappers and room service dishes. Based on observing Emma eat and creating an average of the amount she eats over a set time frame, combined with the imbalance of real food versus vending machine food when considering the posted hours of room service, I'm guessing that is the approximate amount of overnight time spent not snacking."

"Some people read tea leaves, Xavier reads snack food wrappers and dirty dishes," Dean says.

"Well, now that I'm resigned to eating nothing but raw fruit and vegetables for the next few weeks, let's talk about what we're doing today," I say.

"I guess that depends on what Ava has to say when she gets back," Dean shrugs.

"Where did she go?" I ask.

"What do you mean where did she go? Didn't you send her somewhere?" he asks.

My spine stiffens. "No. I didn't. How long has she been gone?"

"About an hour, I guess," Dean says. "She slipped a note under my room door saying she had to go look into something."

"Under your door?" I ask. "Why would she do that?"

"Who else is she going to tell? You? She probably thought you would slip a note back that just said 'yay'," he says.

I roll my eyes at him. "Alright, I think that might be a little bit of an exaggeration. Things aren't that bad between us. I just need her to..."

"What?" Dean cuts me off. "Act like you never would have when you were her age?"

"By the time I was her age, I had already been an agent for a couple of years and taken down murderers and organized crime rings," I fire back.

"Because you didn't let anybody tell you who you were allowed to be or what you were capable of doing," he points out. "Because you took it upon yourself to disobey direct orders from your superior officers if you needed to."

"I haven't told her either of those things," I protest. "I've just told her to not interfere."

"And if someone had said that to you?" he asks. "If at the beginning of your career someone had tried to put you in a corner that way?"

"They did. Countless times," I say.

"And what did you do? You just sat there and took it?"

"We're not talking about me, Dean. We're talking about Ava."

"What are we talking about Ava about?"

I look up to see Ava standing at the door, gazing in at me.

Xavier leans slightly toward me to whisper. "Maybe we could talk about her grammar. That might be more constructive."

"The door wasn't all the way closed," Ava says, gesturing at it as she steps inside. "I heard everybody talking, so I thought I'd come in."

"What were you doing this morning?" I ask.

She smiles, clearly pleased with herself. "I went to talk to Ashley."

"You did what?"

"Oh, shit," Dean mutters.

Ava's smile drops from her face and she looks surprised at our reaction.

"You'd said Misty didn't want Ashley to go to the house and I thought..."

"You thought what? That you could convince her to change her mind? That you could go behind my back and interject yourself, and that would spontaneously make her agree to it?" I ask angrily.

"No," she says. "That's not what I meant. I just thought maybe there was another way that would accomplish all the goals."

"What goals?" I ask.

"Misty feeling that her daughter is safe and secure, but us getting the information we need to move the investigation forward," she explains.

"No," I say. "There is only one goal. And that's to find who did this to Ashley so we can get them out of society. 'We' don't need anything. I need Ashley to show us the house."

"I found out how to get there. That's why I went. I thought if she could describe to me how she got to the school and we were able to trace it back, we could find the house. She even drew a diagram of the house and as much of a map as she could," Ava says.

"If I'd wanted her to do that, I would have asked her to do it," I say through a stiff jaw and tightly held teeth. "The point was for her to retrace her steps and come to the house with me."

"Why?" Ava asks. "Why does she need to be there?"

"So we can see it through her eyes," Xavier says. "Emma needs to see what Ashley saw. And how she reacts to the surroundings. That would have told her more than a description and a piece of paper could."

"Xavier," Dean pipes up, backing up toward the door, "let's go downstairs and get some breakfast."

"We already had breakfast," Xavier says.

"Brunch."

"It's not late enough."

"Second breakfast," Dean says.

"Oooh, Hobbit style," Xavier says, moving toward the door. As he passes Ava, he pauses and looks at her. "The shovel, Ava. That's all I said. The shovel. Not the whole sandbox."

She watches him leave, stuck in those familiar few seconds of wonder before turning her attention back to me.

"I'm sorry, Emma," she says. "I was just trying to help."

"You were trying to get your point across and take over part of the investigation because you didn't like the way I want it handled," I say.

"I thought there could be a better way," she says. "I didn't think it was necessary for a traumatized victim to return to the place she was held and probably tortured for five years, especially when the perpetrator is still unidentified and at large."

She's forcing her voice to sound strong as she holds her ground, but I'm not impressed.

"She wasn't held there for five years," I say. "She was probably only there for a few days at the most."

"I thought she said that was where she was. Where she woke up and where she escaped from," Ava says.

"She said she woke up in a house. And yes, she escaped from that particular house," I say. "But that wasn't the house where she was kept for five years."

"How do you know that?" Ava asks. "She knew how to get out and get into town, but that could be as simple as sometimes they took her to the store. You know as well as I do there are kidnap victims who aren't always locked down. They get taken out and driven around."

"Because there's no electricity there," I say.

Ava looks slightly taken aback. "What?"

"No electricity. The area she described when she was first telling the story of how she escaped narrowed down the possible area of where the house could be located. Based on her description, it was clearly a farmhouse set on a good piece of land. The man who gave her a ride to the vigil the day she reappeared gave a clear account of where exactly he picked her up and what she said.

"Those details combine to roughly outline a general area where she realistically could have been. And in that area are several farms. Most of them are well-maintained and functional to this day. Three other houses in the general vicinity match her explanation of going across the field and out into the woods. Every one of them has been abandoned for more than a decade and a half. None of them has electricity.

"Ashley has mentioned on multiple occasions that Wolf watched the news. She knew to get to the school at the time of the vigil because she watched it with him. He couldn't have done that in a house that doesn't have any power. Ashley was moved. She doesn't want to admit it right now, but there was another place.

"But maybe even more important than all of that, you've damaged the relationship with Ashley."

"How did I do that?" she asks.

"I told her I want her to be involved. She's the only one who's going to be able to give us the information and insight we need to find this guy and bring the case to a close. Seeing what happened the night she went missing, and hearing me say that, was making her feel strong. It was empowering her. But your going over there to talk to her without me and asking her to tell you about the house rather than having her show us, you told her that we don't trust her. That she isn't important or capable.

"You isolated her further and took away her power again. This is a girl who was treated as someone else's property with no choices of her own. She was offered the chance to reclaim some of what was taken from her and turn the tables on Wolf and whoever else might have hurt her during that time. I asked her to trust me. Then you stuck yourself into it and took that away."

Ava stammers for a few seconds.

"I'm sorry," she finally says.

FORTY-SIX

THE DOOR OPENS and Xavier's head appears.

"Everything alright now?" he asks. "Did our diversionary tactic of dismissing ourselves under the guise of going for second breakfast give the two of you enough time to talk things out?"

"Thanks, Xavier," Dean says, gently pushing him the rest of the way into the room and looking at me. "They stopped serving breakfast. So, first breakfast is going to have to be enough."

"I wanted pancakes," Xavier pouts.

Dean looks between Ava and me, trying to measure the tension and figure out what to do next.

"Where do we go from here?" he asks.

"I'm going to get some coffee," I say. "Then we're going to go to the house."

"We are?" Ava asks, sounding almost hopeful.

"At this point, you've diminished their faith in me and potentially compromised Ashley's willingness to cooperate, and to stand up to her mother, who doesn't want her to have anything to do with the investigation. We do what we can and then we fix the rest later," I say.

"THIS PLACE IS HORRIBLE," AVA MUTTERS, LOOKING AROUND the dry, neglected front yard of the abandoned farmhouse.

"Savor it now," I tell her. "You'll see worse in your career."

The description Ashley gave of her escape from the house had us trekking through the woods and across an overgrown field I envisioned having grown crops for family who'd lived here. As I do any time I see an empty house that looks hastily deserted, I wonder what happened. What those last few moments were like before the door closed for the last time and the place was left to sit alone.

"There are tire impressions over here," Dean notes from the side of the house. "They're recent."

"Can you tell what kind of vehicle?" I ask.

"Not with any real specificity, but by the width and the depth, I'd say a truck," he says.

I nod, looking around. "Fits the atmosphere. People wouldn't be surprised to see a truck in a place like this. It would just look as if someone had decided to revitalize the house."

"Emma," Xavier calls from somewhere out of sight. "What constitutes breaking and entering when it comes to an abandoned house that has potentially recently been occupied? Do squatters' rights come into play?"

"Xavier, where are you?" Dean calls.

"Back here," he says.

We hurry to the back of the house and find him precariously balanced in front of an old-fashioned cellar door. He's holding his arms out to his sides as if trying to keep himself upright. One leg has cracked through the door and is on the cellar steps below up to his knee.

"What happened?" I ask.

"Well," he starts, looking down at the door, "I seem to be in a legally ambiguous situation. I wanted to look in that window up there, so I was going to climb onto the door. However, its structural integrity leaves a lot to be desired, and so it seems my foot has both broken and entered. But the vast majority of me is still on the outside, so I'm not sure of the precedent here."

Dean takes him by the wrist and helps him pull his leg out of the splintered wood.

"I think you're probably good," he says.

"Good," Xavier nods. "We'll fix the door later."

Dean pats him on the back, but I don't hear his agreement to the plan. Not that I doubt for a second there's a strong possibility of tools and lumber in his future.

"Why did you want to look in that window?" I ask, stepping back to get a better perspective of the window positioned above the cellar door.

"The curtain is different," he explains.

"They're all old white lace," Dean says.

"All white lace, but that one isn't as old. It was replaced a lot more recently than the others. Look at the edges that are together in the middle," Xavier points.

"They aren't yellow," I say after a few seconds.

"The lace yellows after coming in contact with the oils on human skin. That particular place on the curtain would be touched repeatedly when opening the curtains. But that curtain doesn't have any discoloration. It wasn't touched as much as the others."

"Come on," I say. "I want to go inside."

"I'd suggest the cellar door, but with the exception of my foot hole, it's chained," Xavier says.

"That's alright," I tell him. "We'll go through the front."

There hasn't been any sign of anyone in or around the house since we got there, but I still want to be prepared. I take my gun out of its holster and hold it down in front of me as I climb the steps onto the sagging, white-painted wood porch.

"Look," Dean says, nodding at the wood. "Are those drops of blood?"

The small reddish-brown circles stand out against the paint.

There isn't an exact pattern to them, but they seem to lead from the door down to the steps.

"That's what they look like."

"Ashley's blood?" Ava asks.

"She had some injuries when she went into the hospital, but none of them would have dripped like this. This looks like blood sliding off something and landing on the porch."

The front door is closed and I ensure my grip on my gun before approaching. The knob turns easily in my hand, and I push the door open into the still, quiet house. That means nothing. Silence right now doesn't mean there's no one inside. I step in cautiously, followed closely by Dean. Ava follows, each of the three of us with our hands at our weapons. Once we determine the room is clear, we wave Xavier in behind us.

"The floor," I say. "Do you see the discoloration?"

"Someone tried to clean something up," Dean says.

"It's a drag pattern," Ava observes. "Look at the edges. The center has a swirl pattern where someone tried to clean it using a circular motion." She gestures with one hand, simulating cleaning the floor. "But the edges still have streaks. Whoever was cleaning this didn't have enough time to get it done. Or they realized it was too difficult and gave up. Either way, the edges are intact and show a continuous sweep. There's no sign of anything passing back through the path. Something was dragged through here."

"Ashley is too small to have dragged a grown man," Dean notes.

"Then maybe it wasn't Ashley," I say. "Let's find out where the trail starts."

We follow the blood through the entryway of the house and to the dining room. A large wooden table takes up the majority of the center of the floor. There are chairs positioned around it as if a meal could be served at any moment. The only disruption is the chair at the head of the table. It's pushed aside and toppled onto the floor; as if someone shoved it out of the way.

Streaks of blood on its legs tell me something horrific happened to the person sitting in that chair.

"What did she tell you about getting out of the house?" I ask Ava.

"She said Wolf had left for a little while. He did that occasionally, but usually, she was locked up when he did. That time, he didn't lock the door. She thought it was a trick and didn't go anywhere at first, but then she got up the nerve to try and realized he wasn't there. So she ran," Ava says.

"He wasn't here?" I ask. "She didn't have to struggle to get out?"

"No. She said she just left."

"Then where did the injuries come from?" Dean asks.

"They could have happened earlier in the day. Or the day before," Ava suggests.

I nod. "They could have. That would have pushed her toward the edge and made her willing to take the risk. But if she left without any struggle, when the man wasn't even here, who was sitting in this chair? And who left that drag mark across the floor?"

We continue through the house, comparing Ashley's statements with what we see. The other rooms of the house look fairly undisturbed. There are a few personal belongings and some furniture. Some look as if they were left behind when the original family decided to leave. Others are newer. It's obvious someone was using this house on a fairly consistent basis, but only for a short term.

"What about the room with the new curtain?" Dean asks. "The one Xavier noticed."

We climb the steps and I pause at the landing, looking up and down the hallway to take count of the rooms and note which have closed doors. Those are the ones that represent the biggest threat. Only two of the doors are closed. We move to the first one, just to our left.

Opening the door reveals nothing but an old, dusty bed. It looks frail enough to collapse if touched. The smell in the room makes my throat itch. No one has been in here for a long time.

The next rooms are open and have the same partially-used feeling as the rest of the house. Finally, we get to the second closed door. By the positioning of it, I'm confident this is the room with the newer curtain. I don't know what I expect to find on the other side of the door.

I push the door open and we step inside. An eerie feeling comes over me when I see the single piece of furniture. A vanity pushed up against one wall, the mirror shattered. Everything else about the room is clean to the point of being unsettling. A sharp contrast to the dusty, pent-up stench of the other closed room: this one has the lingering scent of bleach.

I walk up to the vanity and look down at it without touching it.

"No dust. No fingerprints," I murmur. I look at the mirror. It's broken, but the pieces of glass have for the most part stayed in place. "Something hit the mirror pretty hard. This is the impact point. There appears to be a little bit of blood around the edges of a couple of these shards. We need to call a forensic team and have them take the pieces apart. There might be more under the glass."

I notice Dean crouched down beside the vanity, and walk over to see what he's examining.

"Blood?" he asks, pointing to a small red pool soaked into the wooden floor. "It seems strange someone would go to this extent to clean up a room, only to leave blood on the floor."

Ava comes over and kneels down to take a closer look. "That's not blood." She touches her fingertips to it and looks back up at me. "I think it's nail polish. It looks as though someone might have tried to get some of it up, but it had already dried."

"What the hell happened here?" Dean asks.

"Call the police. Get the team out here. While we wait, I want to see the cellar," I order.

Dean takes out his phone and starts the call while I head down the stairs. I put my gun away, confident no one else is in the house with us. I go to the kitchen and find the door I'm assuming goes to the cellar. There's a heavy slide lock across it, but despite its aged and worn look, it moves easily when I slide it open. It's obviously been used frequently.

I can hear Dean talking to the police on the floor above me as I start down the stairs. It's incredibly dark beneath me, and I reach into my pocket for my phone. Before I can get it out, a beam of light appears over my shoulder. Glancing back, I see Ava standing on the step above me.

"Thanks," I say.

She nods and I get my phone the rest of the way out, turning on the flashlight function so I can add more illumination to the space. There's a heavy, musty smell down here. I can imagine there's a section where the floor is still dirt. It's very likely that if we did much exploring, we would find long-forgotten baskets of root vegetables shriveled and putrefied in a corner somewhere.

I get to the bottom of the steps and shine the light around. It picks up crates and wood shelving units stacked with dusty glass jars and canned goods from generations past. Some old tools take up one wall, while discarded lumber and scrap metal hulks in another corner.

"The police are on their way," Dean announces, coming to the top of the steps. "Is there anything down there?"

"I'm not," Xavier replies. "I am distinctly not down there."

"It's just a cellar," I say. "Looks as if no one has been in it in a long time." Dean starts down the steps and I continue my slow turn to take in everything around me. "Wait."

Something isn't right.

"What's wrong?" Dean asks.

I look around again, and Ava follows the path of my beam with hers so we can see more of the space at once."

"This room," I say. "There's something off about it. The dimensions don't seem right. It shouldn't be this shallow." Something clicks in my mind. "Ava, turn off your light."

Her beam goes out and I turn off mine.

"Holy shit, that's dark," Dean mutters.

"Xavier, close the door up there," I call up. "You can be on that side of it."

"Thank you."

The door closes, fully extinguishing all light.

"No," I say. "*That's* dark."

"Emma, why are we standing in the dark?" Dean asks.

"The outside cellar door," Ava says after a few seconds.

"Exactly," I nod. "It's sunny out there. Xavier stomped right through that door, which means there should be sunlight coming in. But there isn't. Where's the door?"

FORTY-SEVEN

"How often did he make you go to that house?" I ask Ashley.

I expect her to look uncomfortable. Instead, she's almost stoic.

"We'd only been going there for a few months. We'd go for a couple of days at a time and then he'd bring me back to the first house."

"Where is the other house?" I ask.

She shakes her head. "I don't know. I was allowed to be in the car if we were going short distances, but when we were going to the second house, he kept me in the back of the truck."

"In the bed of a pickup truck?" I ask.

She nods.

"If she was in the bed of a pickup truck, how did no one see her?" Misty asks. "I pass trucks all the time on the road, and I can see when there's something in the bed."

"Do you ever notice those big locked boxes that are supposed to hold tools?" Ashley asks.

"Yes," Misty says.

"His didn't hold tools."

Misty stands, shaking her head. "Oh, my God. I can't believe this."

"The investigators found the passage between the upstairs bedroom and the walled-off section of the cellar behind the vanity. The wall was new, but that's a feature of the house that had to be designed into it," I say. "The structure and the stairs were built into it."

Ashley nods. "Wolf told me it had always been used to hide and transport people."

"So, he was familiar enough with the house to know about a hidden passage. He had to have known the family who owned it. That's helpful. Did you only ever use that passage?"

"If I was at that house, I was in that room or in the cellar. I got ready upstairs, then went down the steps into the cellar. They didn't let me go to the other parts of the house because they didn't want me to get near the doors or windows I could get out of," she explains.

"There's a window in that room, though," I say, all while silently noting that Ashley did indeed use 'they' instead of just 'he'.

"I couldn't get to it because of the bars."

"There weren't any bars."

She looks confused. "Yes, there were. There was a cage of metal bars blocking the window. I couldn't even open the curtains."

"A cage of bars? Attached to the window frame?"

"The walls on either side."

I get out my phone and call the detective in charge of the investigation still ongoing at the farmhouse.

"I need someone to go up to that room and put me on video," I say.

I wait a few seconds as they transport the phone up the steps, then a shaky video image appears. It's blurry and I can't tell what I'm looking at for a few seconds before it stabilizes.

"Hello, Agent Griffin," the officer says, waving at me.

I wave back. "Hello. Could you turn me so I can see the wall beside the window frame?"

"The wall?" he asks.

"Yes. Within a few inches of the side of the window." At first, the wall doesn't show any signs of anything unusual. Then I notice the slightest hint of a depression. "A few inches from the bottom there is a dip in the wall. Can you touch it?"

"Right here?" he asks, running his fingers over the paint.

"Yes. Does it feel different from the rest of the wall?"

"The texture's different. It feels like a hole that's been covered up."

"Can you go to the top of the window, the same distance out, and see if there's another one?"

"There is," he confirms.

"Alright. Thank you very much. Let me know if you find anything else."

I hang up and tuck my phone away.

"Someone removed the bars and sealed over the holes where the cage was attached to the wall," I tell Misty and Ashley. "They were trying to cover up what happened there."

"But why would they leave the broken mirror?" Misty asks.

"A broken mirror in an old house is innocuous enough. The fact that there was no sign of fingerprints isn't. Someone removed them on purpose."

"He didn't want anyone to know I was there," Ashley says.

"He? Wolf?" I ask.

She nods. "I had an appointment the day I left."

She says it so casually, as though she's talking about getting her hair done, but I know full well that's not what she means.

"An appointment?" Misty asks in a hushed, almost painful tone.

"Yes," Ashley says. "A regular. I don't know his name, before you even ask. I called him J. He liked having pictures and would come up with themes. Wolf would dress me up. There were props."

"I don't want to hear this," Misty says, curling away from her daughter, just the thought enough to make her sick. "I don't want it in my mind."

"Unfortunately, Ashley doesn't have a choice about whether it's in her mind or not. And the more we know, the better we're going to be able to figure this out," I say. "What can you tell me about J? His age? Ethnicity? Tall or short?"

I listen as Ashley describes him, jotting on my notepad.

"What else?" I ask. "What else can you tell me about him?"

"He was one of the ones I didn't mind as much," Ashley says.

"You didn't mind?" Misty gasps. Her reaction falls somewhere between horrified and disgusted.

Ashley's eyes slide over to her mother. She looks at her for a brief second, trying to figure out what the woman is thinking.

"It was my reality. It wasn't something I chose. It was chosen for me. What I could choose was how I dealt with it. Either I spent every second of my life hating it and being horrified by what was happening to me, or I could try to find some kind of good in it. Anything to keep me going for another day, just for the off chance that one of those days would come with the opportunity to get out. I didn't say I liked it. I didn't say it was fun for me. But he wasn't the worst," Ashley says.

I'm struck by her calm control as she's talking about what she went through. There's a blunt quality to it, but also something almost ethereal. As if she's pulled herself out of it and is talking about it as if it were something she'd only heard about.

"Tell me more about him," I say.

"Sometimes he liked to just spend time together. He would call it hanging out. As if we were friends. We'd play games or talk about what was going on in his life. He really liked to scratch lottery tickets. He told me he also did the numbers every week. That's something I want to do."

"Play the lottery?" I ask.

She nods. "It's something everybody does, right? Or at least, everybody over eighteen. That's what J told me. I wasn't allowed to scratch any of the tickets because I wasn't eighteen."

It sits heavily in my stomach that this man was concerned about not providing lottery tickets to a minor but not anything else that was going on in that hidden room in the cellar.

"You don't need to be thinking about things like that," Misty says. She sounds surprisingly harsh, but the tension on her face fades almost as soon as the words are out of her mouth. "I just mean you don't have to worry yourself so much about being an adult. Not yet."

"I'm eighteen," Ashley shrugs. "I've spent my whole life with people telling me what to do because I was a child. Now, I'm not under anyone's control. After what's already happened to me, what else could?"

"There's still danger, Ashley. There's still someone out there who could try to hurt you again," Misty says. "I can't stand the idea of something happening to you."

Ashley's expression doesn't change. The calm feels like cold water running down my spine.

"Really?"

FORTY-EIGHT

"WHAT ARE YOU DOING?" Dean asks, coming out onto the hotel room balcony to sit in the chair beside me.

"Getting fresh air," I tell him. "I'm also wearing my running shoes, so I'm counting it as part of the jog I missed this morning."

"I'll allow it," he chuckles. "Are you watching the security footage again?"

"Yes," I nod. "I've watched it about twenty times. I could probably recreate it."

"Let's not," he says. "Did you get any sleep last night?"

"Some. Look at this," I turn the tablet toward him. "This is right before Ashley gets up and walks away. Look right here."

I point to a spot on the road near the corner of the building.

"It's a puddle," he frowns. "Remember, it was raining for days before this."

"I know," I say. "Now, watch her carefully. Right before she gets up." We watch in silence and as she moves to stand, I point at her. "Did you see that? Watch again." I scan backward and play the few seconds again. "Right before she gets up, her head lifts and she looks in that direction."

"She's reacting to something," Dean says.

I nod. "She didn't just get up and walk away. She was responding."

"Alright. What does that have to do with the puddle?"

"Okay, watch it again. Right before she lifts her head, look at the puddle." We watch and I quickly pause the footage. "Do you see that shimmer in the puddle? I think that's a reflection of a car."

Dean leans closer and scrutinizes the still image. "It is. Someone drove up to the side of the hospital. That's what she's reacting to."

"Someone must have pulled up and said something to her. But when she gets up and goes around the corner, no car drives through. Which means it backed up. There's an entrance to that part of the parking lot not too far from that side. It's a service entrance, but whoever picked her up could have used it as a shortcut."

"He must be familiar with the area," Dean says. He looks at the footage again and makes an exasperated sound. "I wish we could see the reflection better. So we could figure out what kind of car it is. It looks dark, maybe blue or black. There doesn't seem to be anything special about the license plate, no graphics or anything, so that narrows it down a little bit. We just can't see what it says."

"How much sway do you think we have when it comes to getting vehicle records?"

"It's you, so... as much sway as you want to have before people figure out you maybe shouldn't?" Dean suggests.

"Fair enough evaluation. Okay, I need you to find out what kind of car everybody in Ashley's life drove at this time. Everybody among her family, her friends, her neighbors. All the people you can get your hands on, find out what they drove. Then we need to find out if there were any traffic stops, parking tickets, tolls, anything that night that would have documented where any of those cars was," I say. "We're going to do some process of elimination."

"Sounds good to me," Dean says. "Don't jog too hard."

I wave at him over my shoulder as he goes inside, and I keep staring at the screen, hoping something else will pop out at me. My phone rings, and I can't help but smile when I see that it's Sam.

"Hey, babe," I say.

"What about winter wonderland on the beach? How does that strike you for a wedding theme? Sandcastles that look like polar bears. Christmas trees decorated with starfish. Little baggies of graham cracker crumbs and white chocolate seashells as our favor."

I laugh. "It would definitely be unique."

"Unique is one of those words people say when they don't want to be really mean, but they can't think of anything nice, isn't it?" he asks.

"I think the little baggies of graham cracker crumbs sound very nice," I offer. "We could add tiny marshmallows and it could be a beach-themed s'mores kit, because I love your s'mores than anything."

"Xavier would be so ashamed that just came out of your mouth," Sam says.

"I am."

I jump, nearly dropping my phone. Xavier steps back slightly as if he's startled by my whipping around to look at him.

"What the hell, Xavier?"

"S'mores use milk chocolate. Sometimes dark, in extremely specific circumstances. Never, and I repeat never, white chocolate. Seashell shaped or not."

"How long have you been standing there?" I demand.

"Since Dean walked out of the room without me," he shrugs.

"Did he know you were in the room?"

"Probably not. He left me making waffles with Ava. She puts too much batter in and it leaks, but she flips it over anyway. I can't handle that," he says, walking out onto the balcony.

"I don't know if I like how easily he was able to sneak up on you," Sam says.

"I didn't sneak up on her," Xavier says. "I was here the whole time."

"Not reassuring."

"Why do you want to know about all the cars?" Xavier asks. "I can understand a couple of them, but why everybody's car?"

"I just want to narrow down the options," I say.

"The options for what?" Xavier asks.

"What is he talking about?"

I let out a sigh. "Hold on. I'm going to video call you. We might as well turn this into a full-on conference."

I hang up and call Sam with video so I can explain everything to both of them. I tell them about my conversation with Ashley and Misty.

"Are you saying you don't think they're telling the truth?" Sam asks. "You think this is...what, a hoax?"

"I don't know," I say.

"For what benefit, though? What would they get out of lying about her being missing? And where has she actually been? That's a whole lot of mass delusion if you think that she's been around, but the town is convinced she's been missing for five years," Sam says.

"I'm not saying I think she's just been hanging out, going to school, flipping burgers at the diner, and no one has noticed," I clarify. "It just doesn't add up. Nothing does. I can't decide which of the people around her I trust the least."

"Or her?" Xavier says.

I sigh, sliding through the pictures on my tablet to one I've been thinking about all morning. One taken of Ashley when she first walked out onto the soccer field and Misty ran to her. The one that shows Ashley's hand gripping her mother's arm as the two embrace, and the streaks of red polish on one of her nails.

FORTY-NINE

THE DOOR to the room opens and Ava comes in, looking frantic. Her face relaxes as soon as she sees Xavier.

"There you are," she sighs. "I swear, I took my eyes off him for two seconds."

"You go ahead," Sam says. "Seems you have a lot going on there. I love you."

"I love you, too."

"Think about the winter beach."

"I don't think I have any option but to think about the winter beach," I reply.

"Bye."

He laughs and his face disappears from my phone. I grab up everything from the small table on the balcony and head into my room.

"He's not a child," I tell Ava, putting everything onto the larger table inside and walking over to the coffee machine to make myself another cup.

It's a very vague step up from usual hotel coffee, but I'll take it. Maybe in a little while, I'll feel like walking down to the lobby to go to the much more elaborate coffee bar down there. They have several strengths of coffee, along with tiny creamer cups of half a dozen different flavors. Sometimes there are even teeny-tiny muffins in the acrylic cube display case.

I might be getting too familiar with this hotel.

"I know he's not," Ava says.

"Then don't talk about him as if he is one," I say. "He doesn't have any obligation to you. He doesn't even know you."

"He's standing right here," Xavier says. "And feeling somewhat like a metaphor."

"We were getting breakfast and Dean said he was going to come up here to see if you wanted to come down. You haven't been eating with us."

"Or maybe a simile," Xavier continues.

"I've been busy," I say. "If you haven't noticed, I'm investigating a rather complex and sensitive case."

"I have noticed," Ava replies, her voice getting sharper. "Just as I've noticed I was specifically told to be a part of this and you've done everything you possibly can to exclude me from it."

"You didn't say 'like' or 'as.' Definitely a metaphor."

"I've been investigating the way I always do," I say.

"Exactly," Ava says. "You've been doing it exactly the way you always do it because that's what you want. Have you considered for even a second that having me be part of the investigation has been about you, too?"

I whirl around to face her. "Of course, I have. That's the problem."

The answer explodes out of me and I instantly wish it hadn't. Xavier steps backward and reaches to his side to pick up the remote to the TV while I focus on sifting through the records and documents on the table. It's more so I don't have to look at Ava, and she seems to realize it.

"Emma, what did I do to you? I know there've been a couple of times in this investigation when you think I've overstepped, and I probably have, but you've been pushing back against me since the second we met," she says. "Is this some sort of test? You keep saying the Bureau is going to treat me rough, and I get that, but you seem to be starting it yourself. As if you're going out of your way to throw me under the bus for everything that goes wrong. Completely refusing to offer support or guidance. You refuse to tell me what you're doing and why, and then you get mad at me for trying to take the initiative because you're holding your cards too close to your chest. You're right, Emma. I don't know how to lead an investigation. And yeah, I'll admit that I've gone about some things the wrong way. But I want to learn from you. That's why I'm here. I'm not here for you to bully around."

Ignoring her isn't going to do me any good, so I look up at her.

"Look, I...I don't want to be replaced," I finally admit. "Okay? Is that what you wanted to hear?"

She shakes her head. "No. I don't know what you're talking about."

I let out a breath, running my fingers back through my hair as I drop down into a chair at the table and gather my words.

"When I started in the Bureau, I was twenty-three years old. Most people don't start that young," I say.

"I know," she says. "The average age for a new agent is about thirty, isn't it?"

"Yes," I confirm. "So, most people my age have only been working for a couple of years. I've had enough career packed into my almost ten years for two or three agents. But it's my life. It's what I chose a long time ago and what I've structured my entire existence around."

"I know," she says again. "I've been following your career. I've studied your cases."

"That. Right there," I say, pointing at her. "Do you realize how strange that is for me? How odd it feels to be at the age when I'm being studied? Or at least at the point in my career when that is happening? I don't feel old enough be there yet."

"But you've accomplished incredible things. They aren't trying to force you out because they teach your cases," Ava says.

"That's how it feels sometimes. There's always someone new. Someone fresh out of training who is ready to tackle the field. Someone who hasn't been shot and stabbed, choked, beaten. I worked hard to build this career. I've dragged myself through hard times and fought through moments when the Bureau was losing faith in me. Because this is what I'm called to do.

"But the hard moments have left their mark. I still have pain from some of my injuries. I have memories I really wish I didn't. And still, I don't want to give any of this up. But having Creagan put you with me makes it feel as though he's looking ahead to the new generation.

"I used to live right there in Quantico, but I moved back to my hometown a few years ago. Now I'm about to get married, and I think he thinks it's time for me to settle down. Which means taking what I've worked so hard to build and offering it up to someone else. I don't want that to happen. I see your potential, Ava. You're smart. You do take the initiative, and you've got a good eye for forensic evidence, which is a great skill to have. With some experience, you'll really take to this. I just don't want you taking my position."

"I would never do that," she says. She hesitates, then lowers herself into the chair beside me. She gathers her thoughts for a second. "I've never been great with people. You know how adults love to label children?"

"The great conveyor belts of life," Xavier chimes in.

"What?" Ava asks.

Xavier looks at her, surprised by the question. He grabs his head on either side and lifts, miming picking himself up, stands and moves over a few inches, then mimes putting himself down. Ava keeps staring at him, then turns a questioning look to me.

"Children being labeled and put on the conveyor belt adults choose for them so they can get processed through the factory of life," I explain. Her expression doesn't change. "It comes with time."

She nods. "Well, the label they gave me was introvert. I've always been awkward around people. My best friend always used to tease me for being both the coolest and the least cool person she had ever met."

"I know you're living in Harlan now. Where does she live?" I ask.

Ava looks down at her lap and shakes her head. "She's...she's not around anymore."

"Oh. I'm sorry."

She shakes her head again, a little harder this time. "It happened a long time ago. I would never want you to think I'm trying to step on your toes or get in your way at all. You have no idea how much I admire you. You intimidate the living hell out of me, both professionally and personally. That might have translated into my being too eager."

"You don't need to be intimidated by me," I tell her. "I'm sorry for being so harsh on you. You're right. I haven't been offering the support I should have been, and that's not going to give you the experience you need, either. You're going to be a strong agent, Ava. Don't let anybody make you afraid. But maybe follow your lead investigator a little better."

I smile at her and she returns it. I don't know if this counts as a breakthrough, but I feel I know her better now.

"Not to ruin this beautiful moment," Xavier says, "but do you think we should tell Misty the spring flag she still has hanging outside her house is no longer seasonally appropriate?"

I look over at him where he's sitting, the remote poised in his hand, staring at the TV.

"What are you talking about, Xavier?" I ask.

He gestures at the TV with the remote. "The news cameras keep focusing on the flag. It has butterflies and daffodils on it. Actually, I think those are jonquils. Commonly mistaken for daffodils, but easily distinguishable by their leaf shape and the distinctive characteristic of a hollow stem."

I get up and move quickly over to him to look at the TV. I was hoping I wouldn't see it, but there it is. Ashley's house fills the screen with a bright red "Breaking News" banner splashed across the bottom.

"What the hell is going on?" I ask.

"What is it?" Ava asks, coming over to us.

"We're at the house of Ashley Stevenson, the kidnapping victim who recently miraculously returned home after five years of captivity. Police were called this morning to respond to signs of vandalism on the house. Upon arrival, officers discovered the house had been breached and Ashley was attacked."

"Shit," I mutter, grabbing my phone and running for the door without caring if anyone is behind me.

FIFTY

"WHAT'S GOING ON HERE?" I demand when I get to the house.

"I'm sorry, this is a closed scene," a young officer says, one hand gripping her belt and the other held up toward my chest as though she's directing traffic and I'm an offending vehicle. "You can't go any further."

"Bullshit, I can't," I say, reaching into my pocket for my badge and holding it up so she gets a clear view of it. "Agent Emma Griffin. FBI."

Her face goes pale and then red, and she stammers for a few seconds. "I'm so sorry, Agent. I didn't recognize you."

"Where is the officer in charge?" I demand.

She points me toward the door and I duck under the police tape to go across the yard. Two large investigative trucks parked in the driveway blocked the view of the garage when I was out on the street and crossing the yard, but now I see the door clearly.

Bright red paint forms a "13" in the middle of the door, the long drips sliding down toward the pavement like blood.

"Agent Griffin," calls a detective with whom I've interacted several times before, as he comes toward me.

"What is this?" I ask before he even gets to me.

"The house was broken into and vandalized," he says.

"I can see that," I say. "Why wasn't I informed of what was going on? This is directly involved in my investigation. And where the hell were the officers assigned to monitor the house and the family?"

"I'm sorry," he says. "Everything happened so quickly. A neighbor noticed the graffiti and called emergency dispatch. When they got here, Ashley came stumbling out with a wound to her side. They found broken glass and other signs someone got inside."

"You mean the injured girl wasn't enough of an indicator of that?" I ask. "I want to know why I wasn't notified and had to find out about this on the news."

"The scene has been extremely chaotic. Two ambulances were necessary and the neighbors were all coming over here…"

"Two? Two ambulances?" I ask. "Who else was injured?"

"No one. A woman identified as Mary Grey, Misty's mother, collapsed and needed to be taken to the hospital as well," he says.

I let out an exasperated growl. "This is ridiculous. I should have been notified immediately. The scene better be thoroughly documented and all information sent to me. I also want a full explanation of why the surveillance team didn't stop this from happening."

"Are you leaving?" he asks as I turn away.

"I need to get to the hospital and find out if she is alright. I'm already behind," I say, storming back to my car.

WHEN I GET TO THE HOSPITAL, IT'S IN AN UPROAR, THE WAY IT had been the day Ashley reappeared. Media swarm the area in front of the doors. I have to force my way through to get inside. I flash my credentials to the security guard and head up to the floor where Ashley was kept before going home.

"Where is she?" I ask without stopping as I go past the nurse's station.

"Same room," they call after me.

"Convenient," I mutter.

As I turn down the hallway, I see Misty coming around the corner on the opposite side. She notices me and gasps.

"Emma." She rushes toward me, reaching out to latch onto my arm. "How could this have happened?"

I shake my head. "I don't know. I'm trying to find out. Catch me up on what's going on."

We hurry toward Ashley's room. I don't know what to expect, but when I get in the room, I find her sitting up in bed, her head rested back against a pillow. She has a line in her arm again.

"Honey, she's here," Misty says. "Emma just got here."

"Hi, Ashley," I say. "I'm so sorry it took me a while to get here. No one got in touch with me."

"You didn't call her?" Ashley asks, sounding stunned as she looks over at her mother.

Misty stammers for a few seconds, then gestures out through the door.

"I'm trying not to worry about you and my mother," she explains. "I thought it was the responsibility of law enforcement to ensure everybody who needs to be here is here."

Ashley nods and I step up between her and Misty.

"What happened, Ashley? Tell me everything. Was it Wolf?" I ask.

She nods, swallowing down the emotion that seemed to swell up in her throat.

"I was sleeping. A sound woke me up. It was a dog barking. It took me a minute to realize I was actually hearing it because I had been dreaming about a dog track. Isn't it strange, the kinds of things you dream about? What do you think that means? I was at the dog track and there was a dog named Wiseacre who I put my entire bet on."

Misty stiffens beside me, her arms moving to wrap more tightly around herself. I step closer to the bed, but she stays where she's standing.

"Alright," I say. "But what else?"

"The dog was in thirteenth place. But I was still rooting for it," she says. "I just couldn't let go."

"I mean this morning, Ashley. What happened this morning? After you heard the dog barking and realized you were awake."

"I didn't want to get up yet. I just wanted to go back to sleep. So I rolled over. But before I could fall asleep again, my window exploded. Glass went everywhere. I screamed and jumped up, and there he was. He tried to get me and cut me."

She indicates her side, then pulls the side of her gown around to reveal a bandage across a large portion of her pale skin.

"What did you do?" I ask. "How did you get away?"

"I pushed him away and ran out of the room. I went right to Leona's room. I figured Wolf would be right behind me, and her room is the closest. But he wasn't there. Leona was terrified when she saw me and we screamed for my parents until they came in. My dad ran outside to look for him, but he wasn't anywhere and the police were already there. Apparently, someone had called to tell them about the writing on the garage door. That must have been what the dog was barking about."

"But no one saw Wolf?" I ask. "No neighbors saw him come to the house or leave it?"

"No," she shakes her head. "We asked everybody, but no one noticed him."

"There's only woods behind the house," Misty says. "He could have easily gone into the trees and pretty much disappeared in a matter of seconds."

"What about your grandmother?" I ask.

"She was visiting," Ashley says. "She came over last night and said she had baby pictures and things she wanted to show me today. After the police came and were going through the house, she collapsed."

"She had a heart attack," Misty says. "All the stress of everything finally got to her."

"I'm so sorry to hear that," I say. "How is she doing?"

"She's alive," she says, brushing tears away from her cheeks. "Unconscious right now. They have her sedated and are going to leave her that way until they think her heart is strong enough for surgery."

"I think that's why I was having the dream about the dog track," Ashley adds as if the realization just dawned on her. "Before bed last night, Gran was telling me about how she used to go to see the dog races all the time. She loved betting on them."

Misty narrows her eyes at her daughter. "What are you talking about?"

"When Gran and I were talking last night, you were in the kitchen getting dessert, she was telling about when she was younger. She said one of her favorite things was going to the racetrack and betting on the dogs. She said it always made her want a greyhound as a pet. I love cats, but if I was to get another pet, maybe I'd try a dog. When she gets better, I'm going to go with her."

Her thoughts seem to be jumping around, but I attribute it to the stress she's under and the repeated trauma she's experienced.

"No," Misty says, shaking her head. "Your grandmother never would have gone to a place like that."

"She did," Ashley says. "I guess there are things about her before you came along you didn't know." Her eyes snap over to me. "Emma, have you ever been to Vegas?"

"Las Vegas?" I ask, as if there is another Vegas that might be a viable option in this scenario. "No."

"I want to go there. I hear it's so much fun. All the bright lights and shows. And of course, the casinos. I've heard some people go there and lose a lot of money, but they just can't get enough of it. This will make sure I have plenty to bring me with me, though."

"What do you mean?" I ask.

"When I sue the police department," she says. "They were

supposed to be watching and they weren't. So, this happened to me, and my grandmother had a heart attack because of it. That should be a decent payout. I'll probably put some of it away, but I'm booking a high roller trip. We'll just hope I have better luck there than I did with Wiseacre."

She laughs slightly and I look over at Misty.

"Where are John and Leona?" I ask.

"John went to get me coffee and Leona is with her grandmother. They have her in the next hallway so we can be with both of them," she says.

I nod. "I need to call the rest of the team and let them know what's going on. If you'll excuse me."

I step out of the room and call Dean to give him a brief overview of what's happening. As I'm getting off the phone, I get to the room where Ashley's grandmother is under care. Even from outside the partially open door, I can hear sobbing. I step inside and find Leona sitting beside the bed, her head buried in the bedding beside her grandmother. She's holding the woman's hand and crying so hard her body shakes.

"I don't know what's happening, Grandma," she whispers. "I don't understand why she's here. She can't be. I saw her standing there bleeding and I just..."

She dissolves into sobs again.

"Leona?" I say, getting closer.

She gasps as she lifts her head. "You could have knocked."

"I'm sorry. I heard you crying and wanted to make sure you're alright."   •

"No, I'm not alright. Do you see my grandmother?" she asks.

"I do. I heard and I am so sorry. But they have her under really good care," I say.

"Spare me," she mutters.

She stands and starts for the door of the room, brushing past me. Something catches my eye on the bedside table and I go to look at it.

The gold bracelet has a plaque in the middle, embedded with small colored stones.

"Don't touch that," Leona snaps.

I look over at her, surprised she's still in the room. "Is this your grandmother's?"

"Yes. She's worn it as long as I can remember. It has our birthstones in it."

"It's beautiful."

I take another look at the bracelet, then walk out into the hallway to go back to Ashley's room. Leona goes in the opposite direction, but my attention isn't on her anymore. As I approach Ashley's room, I see John coming down the hallway.

"Hi, John," I say.

"Agent Griffin," he says. "Good to see you. I know having you here will reassure Misty. She was very agitated this morning."

"I can imagine," I say. "Can I speak to you for just a second? About Ashley?"

He nods. "Absolutely. How can I help?"

"I've just noticed something and I wanted to know if it means anything to you."

"Alright."

"A couple of times now, Ashley has mentioned things like playing lotto or going to a dog track. She was just talking about how she wants to sue the police and use the money to go to Vegas. Every time she talks about it, Misty seems to get really uncomfortable. I know it's an unusual thing for her to be focused on right now, but the mind works in strange ways sometimes. It might be an escape method for Ashley to think about exerting her adulthood through activities like that. But Misty seems really distressed by the idea. Is that just her protectiveness worrying about Ashley, or does it mean something else to you?"

John lets out a breath, his shoulders dropping as he looks down into the coffee cup in his hand.

"Misty always worried it would pass down to the girls. Leona seems to have escaped it, but maybe Ashley isn't so lucky," he says.

"I don't understand."

His eyes meet mine and I see a wisp of sadness and something like longing in them. It's like looking at the aftermath of memories.

"Misty has a gambling addiction. She's been in recovery for a long time, but it got very bad for a while. We actually met in a rehab center that treated addiction."

FIFTY-ONE

"It looks like a nice facility," I say, biting the end off a carrot stick. "Not one of those get-back-to-nature retreats or anything, but for what it is, it seems good. A lot of the staff is made up of volunteers from the medical community who want to help people battling their addictions."

"Is it only for gambling addiction?" Dean asks, taking a bite of his sandwich.

This might not be the topic of conversation I'd usually like to have during a summer picnic, but it will have to do. I spent most of the day at the police station and at Ashley's house, trying to piece everything about this morning's attack together. I didn't realize I hadn't stopped all day until Dean, Xavier, and Ava showed up with a picnic for dinner.

We're taking advantage of the long summer day to eat outside, but I'm feeling far from leisurely. The whole time we've been sitting here, I've been researching the rehab center John told me about. It's hard to imagine Misty there. But knowing about that time in her life helps give me more insight into some of her reactions.

"No. The center treats a variety of addictions and compulsive behaviors. They use a lot of social engagement and group therapy settings to encourage accountability. The thought is that the patients will learn to rely on friendships, enjoyable activities, and common interests, and not want to let their friends down, which will help to create strong support systems. Because they don't all share the same addiction, they are supporting each other in the same even playing field of overcoming the basic idea of addiction rather than the objects of their addictions. That's how Misty and John met. They were in social groups together," I say.

"I'm surprised to hear a facility like this would condone romantic relationships between patients," Ava comments.

"They don't," I say. "John mentioned that. They actively discourage any kind of romantic or sexual relationship. But the two of them were able to get away with more because Misty was pregnant, so people didn't suspect anything happening with them."

"She was pregnant with Ashley?" Dean asks.

"Yes," I say, nodding. "Leona was three. She was staying with Mary while Misty underwent treatment. He said it especially helped because one of the nurses was pregnant, too. So they would commiserate with each other and the nurse would give her a little bit of special treatment because of it. He actually showed me a picture of them with their bellies. One of the other nurses took it and apparently printed out a copy of it to give to Misty when she left the facility."

"And he happened to be walking around with it?" Dean asks.

"No. Years ago Misty almost relapsed. John took a picture of the picture so he could have it on his phone and use it as a reminder to her of what she overcame and where she didn't want to return. He asked me not to tell Misty he'd told me. She's really sensitive about it," I say.

"Are you going to keep it to yourself?" Dean asks.

"I think so. At least for now. I don't see any reason to mention it to her yet."

"You know, I never thought of gambling as an addiction the same way I think of something like alcoholism or smoking. Those are seen in patterns in families, but it never occurred to me that something like gambling addiction could pass down to another generation. But it clearly did. Ashley has a strong compulsion toward gambling."

I nod. "I know some of it is wanting to act like an adult, but it's such a draw. She was talking about that with more intensity than she was about her grandmother, who is a few rooms away after barely surviving a heart attack. The only thing she talked about concerning her grandmother was the basic facts about her collapsing. She was much more animated about going to dog tracks and their going together when she gets better. She even said her grandmother wants a greyhound as a pet and that she might want to try one, too. She's a cat person, but thinks a dog might be an option."

"A cat person?" Ava asks. "Did she tell you that?"

"Yeah," I shrug, taking a bite of my veggie-stuffed pita and cramming the wayward ends into my mouth. "Why? What's wrong?"

"I didn't tell you this because I didn't want you to get mad. But I talked to Leona," she says, cringing.

"What did you find out?" I ask.

"Use the shovel well," Xavier says to Ava in a solemn voice.

"I asked her about Sean and what their relationship is and was. She told me that they are seeing each other and have been for years. They've always tried to keep it under wraps a bit because they don't fit into each other's worlds."

"But what about Allison?" I ask.

"She didn't know about that," Ava says. "But one thing she mentioned was that it was hard back then, because he had a cat and she is extremely allergic. She even hated getting into his car because he would let the cat ride around with him. There was so much fur and dander, it was miserable for her. If she had that kind of reaction to just being near a guy with a cat, there's no way that the family would own one."

"I thought I remembered seeing a picture of Ashley with a cat, though," I say.

Ava nods. "It was one of the pictures the news used to publicize her case. Just a random childhood shot. That cat belonged to a friend of hers."

This gets my mind turning. Things I've heard Ashley say start to bubble up to the surface of my thoughts.

In the hospital, she asked for a banana split with extra pineapple.

She wanted lemonade with lunch.

Wiping off my hands, I pull out my tablet and find archives of the local newscasts. I listen to the statements Misty made leading up to the vigil.

"What's going on?" Dean asks.

"I don't know," I say. "But let's see if I can find out. Thanks for the picnic."

I get up and start toward my car. A few steps away, I turn back to them.

"Ava, talk to the police who investigated the house. Find out everything they know. Ask if they tested the blood in the mirror and on the living room floor. Then tell them to search under the front porch. They'll probably need to dig," I say.

She smiles softly and nods.

I run the rest of the way to the car and jump in, headed straight for Mary Gray's house. Before I left the hospital earlier, Misty told me that was where they would be staying once Ashley was discharged. She didn't want to stay at the house that had already been invaded.

There's a light glowing on the front porch when I pull up to the address Misty gave me. I ring the doorbell and a bewildered John answers.

"Emma. I didn't expect you here tonight," he frowns. "We're just settling in."

"I know," I say. "I'm sorry to barge in like this, but I need to speak with Ashley."

He hesitates, but then agrees and steps aside to let me in.

"She's in pain from the stab wound. She went right upstairs to rest when we got her here."

He leads me to the room and gestures to the closed door.

"Thank you," I say.

He walks away and I knock.

"Yes?" Ashley says from the other side.

"It's Emma," I say.

"Come in."

I open the door just enough to slip inside and close it behind me. Ashley is curled up in a chair near a bay window that looks out over the lawn. The curtains ripple in a soft breeze coming in. There isn't a single shred of fear or worry in her eyes as she sits there.

"The doctors didn't want to keep you overnight?" I ask.

She shakes her head. "They stitched me up and said I would probably do better recovering at home."

I nod and walk closer. "There are a couple of things I wanted to ask you about. Just some things that confused me and I wanted to straighten them out."

"Okay."

"Thanks. Could you tell me again how you were able to get out of that house?"

"It was the only time I ever saw the door to that room open. It must have been a mistake, but I took the opportunity. I ran and I went out the front door."

"And Wolf didn't notice?"

"He was too busy preparing for my appointment later. I told you that that client liked themes, so Wolf must have been in the room putting up the props and scenery," she says.

"And you heard about the vigil on the news because he would let you watch it with him. Which means you weren't at that house for very long. You must have been somewhere else just a couple of days before then."

"Yes."

"Tell me about the nail polish."

Her head tilts the side curiously.

"Nail polish?"

"You said the room with the vanity was where you got ready. And the vanity mirror wasn't broken when you left."

"No."

"Someone was injured in that room. The mirror has blood on it. They went in and removed every piece of evidence that could relate to you, but they weren't able to fix the mirror. Maybe they didn't have time, maybe they thought people would think that it was just because the house is old."

"You keep saying 'they,'" Ashley points out. "I told you it was Wolf. He must have killed J and cleaned up everything to stop him from being able to tell anybody I was there."

"When we were first searching the room, we found a stain on the floor. It was red nail polish. As if a bottle had tipped off the side of the vanity and spilled. Before it could get cleaned up, it had dried most of the way. In the pictures of you right when you got to the vigil, you have on nail polish. But just one nail. And only a little bit."

"I was doing my nails when I noticed the door," she says.

"No," I say, shaking my head and sitting down in the chair across from her. "I don't think that's how it happened. It wasn't all the way dry when somebody tried to clean it up. Most of the way, but there was still enough moisture in it to pry part of it up. Which means that you were there just a few minutes before that room got cleaned. Whatever happened in that room, you were there. You saw it."

She stares at me silently for a few seconds, then turns serenely to look out the window.

"Do you think I'll be able to go to the beach soon? I would love to build a sandcastle."

"There was a picture of the family at the beach building sandcastles on the news. Along with the picture of you holding a cat, which I know wasn't your pet. Leona is allergic to them. You never owned a cat," I say.

Ashley glances over her shoulder at me and lets out a soft laugh.

"I must be remembering wrong."

"Ashley," I say, sliding to the edge of the seat and meeting her eyes. "I need you to tell me what happened in that house. You didn't just walk out. Something happened that morning. What was it?"

"I told you, the door was open and I left."

There's no anxiety, no tension in her words. Just smooth, soft delivery.

"The break-in this morning. You said the window in your room broke and he came in. How is that possible? You were on the second floor. He could have climbed up onto the roof of the porch, but how could no one have noticed him? And you say he didn't even chase you? He went through all that effort to vandalize the garage and climb into your room, but he gave up after cutting you once?"

Ashley shrugs one shoulder. "I came to him on Friday the thirteenth. Maybe the bad luck is just catching up with him."

My stomach turns and my heart drops in my chest.

"The day you went missing wasn't a Friday," I say. "But you were born on Friday the thirteenth."

She looks toward the door to her room and gestures for me to get closer. As if she needs to tell me something. I lean toward her. She puts her mouth so close to my ear that I can feel the heat of her breath trail down the side of my neck.

"Maybe I'm just the girl who cried Wolf."

FIFTY-TWO

I'm up for the rest of the night, digging through every bit of documentation and evidence I've gathered through this investigation. I watch the same footage over and over. I read every news article and look through every police report. I go back to the statements every member of Ashley's family gave the day she went missing and compare them to what her friends said that day, and with each new version of their stories after.

The traffic violations and vehicle registrations Dean was able to find for me give me more insight, but there are still gaps. Still so many questions with answers just out of my grasp. Ashley's words crawl down my spine and leave me with an ever-tightening band clenched around my chest.

As soon as the sun comes up, I'm at the hospital. The administrator isn't happy to see me, but I don't care.

"I need to know who handled Ashley Stevenson's DNA test," I tell him. "Who took her blood and who processed it."

"The sample was taken by the doctor on duty that night. It was supervised by another doctor and by a detective. It was then sent to the lab at Gunther Memorial."

I've been pacing across his office, but those words stop my feet.

"Gunther Memorial?" I ask.

"Yes," he says. "They have an on-site lab used for processing blood samples for DNA testing as well as a variety of other purposes. It's regularly used by the police department."

"And it was sent before the transfer request came," I say.

His expression looks like that thought hadn't even occurred to him.

"Yes," he confirms.

"Damn it."

Without further explanation, I run out of the office and head out of the hospital. My phone is already ringing when I get behind the wheel.

"Dean," I say when he answers. "Remember the rehab center I showed you? I need you to look on the website for me and find the staff page. There's a nurse who was recently honored for twenty years of volunteering there. Her name is Jessica Blanchett."

I wait for a few seconds while he searches.

"Alright, I found it. She's a nurse with a special interest in helping those with addictions live healthier lifestyles. Recently marked twenty years volunteering her time at River Bend. When she isn't volunteering, she uses her exceptional nursing skills and compassionate nature to care for patients at Gunther Memorial Hospital."

"Shit," I mutter. "Okay, I need you to do something for me."

"Name it."

"Work with Ava and figure out how to get our hands on court records, arrest records, anything that will tell us when Misty went into River Bend and for what. John made it sound as if it was voluntary, but I don't think it was. Figure out why she was there. Then see if you can track anyone else who was sent there in the two years before she went."

"Anything to narrow it down?" he asks.

"Look for links to her time there. People who were sent by the same judge or with similar charges. Talk to the judges if you can.

That might be easier than getting subpoenas for the court records," I say.

"Where are you going to be?"

"Gunther Memorial," I say. "Then to the courthouse."

I get to the hospital in record time and ask for Jessica Blanchett at the information desk. The man behind the desk directs me to the fifth floor and I ride the elevator up. I have no intention of talking to her. Not yet. I just need to see her. To make sure I'm on the right track.

It's not a track I want to be on. It's making me feel sick and it's sending prickly, painful heat along the back of my neck and through my chest. But it's slowly falling together.

One glance at Jessica tells me it's the same person. I already knew it was, but seeing her changes things. She's distinctly older than in the picture with Misty that John showed me. Not just because of the years that have passed. This is the kind of age that comes from what a person's been dragged through over those years.

I watch her for a few moments, then leave.

My next stop is the courthouse. I go to the Department of Vital Records to access public documents. Scanning through the weeks surrounding the day Ashley was born, I find exactly what I was expecting to. Or, more precisely, don't find it.

It takes two more days for us to gather all the information from the judges and the rehab center. Every moment of those days, I'm on edge. I'm waiting for the next phone call, the next alert. I visit Ashley each day, but she tells me nothing else. It's more of the same. More memories rattled off from the statements Misty made, more carefully crafted recollections.

On the second day, she sits next to Leona on the couch and I notice the older sister swallow, the color in her cheeks draining away. She looks as if she's going to be sick. Ashley's hand moves in a slow crawl across the cushion toward Leona's and when her fingertips touch the back of her hand, Leona stands and rushes out of the room.

"She's just scared," Misty says, trying to comfort Ashley. "This has all been a lot for her."

When the information finally comes, Dean, Xavier, Ava, and I sit around it, scouring it for any detail that might fit. I haven't told them what I'm thinking yet. I can't seem to make the words roll down my tongue. Once they are out, there's no putting them back; I don't know if I'm ready to take that step. Soon. Once I know.

It doesn't seem real. I want it to be what the girls told me. As horrible as the stories have been, I want the timeline to be true. But there's a voice that's missing. One that's been here the whole time and yet none of us has heard it. That's where the problem lies. I just have to get to the answer.

"This man," I say, pointing at the record in front of me. "He was in the center twice."

"Not when Misty was there, though," Ava says.

"I know. But that's the point. He was there when Jessica was there. His charges line up. I need to call John."

"Why?"

"He's going to be able to get me information no one else can."

"About the center?"

"About Misty."

An hour later, I'm sitting in a rock garden outside the hospital with John. I've been as careful as I can to skirt around what I think is happening while still letting him know how important it is for him to get me the information I'm asking for.

"But we weren't married when she was in the center. We didn't get married until I got out a few months after her. I wouldn't be able to access her financial records from then."

"You were in rehab for months after she got out. I'm assuming when you were discharged, you didn't have a whole lot to your name. Didn't have a great job to go back into or somewhere to live. Right?"

"That's right," he says, sounding uncomfortable at the memory.

'So, you probably moved in with Misty. When she put you on her bank account it helped you get on your feet," I say.

"Yes," he says.

"Then you have access. It's the same bank account as before you were listed on it. Now that you are, you can request statements. I know I'm asking a lot. But I need you to do this. It's critical," I say. "I really don't want to have to go through the time and the effort to convince the courts to request the information. That could take weeks that we don't have."

"Do you really think it will tell you what you need to know?"

"Yes," I nod.

"Then I'll do it."

FIFTY-THREE

"CAN I HELP YOU WITH SOMETHING?" Jessica Blanchett asks me when she comes around the side of the nurse's station.

The nearly twenty-four hours it took for John to get me the financial records from the bank was enough time to sift through everything else and find the pieces of my theory. Now it's just a matter of making sure those pieces fit together.

"Yes," I say. "Actually, I think you can. You work at River Bend rehabilitation center, right?"

"Yes," she says. "I volunteer at the center as much as I can."

"That's very admirable," I say. "Can I ask why you started doing that?"

"My brother had problems with addiction," she says. "I knew from a very young age I wanted to help people who are struggling."

"I can understand that," I tell her. "I'm working with a family right now to investigate a disappearance. Do you remember a patient you worked with eighteen years ago, Misty Gray?"

"I can't discuss the patients I work with," she says.

"I'm not asking for any details," I say. "I just want to know if you remember her. If it helps, I already know the two of you were rather close. I've seen the picture of you two comparing your pregnant bellies."

She takes a breath. "I remember her. It was so sweet. I couldn't believe a person like her had ended up in that center. And I hated myself every time I thought that. That's the kind of thinking that alienates people with addiction problems from the rest of society. It's as though we think they should be degenerates or some sort of lesser humans. But I couldn't help it. That was what I thought when I met her. She was kind and shy. Nervous. It was obvious I was going through a lot and didn't want to talk to people about it."

"But the two of you bonded over being pregnant," I say.

"Yes," she says. "We were just a couple of days apart. We were going through it together. I don't have any sisters or close girlfriends, so it was nice having somebody I could talk to."

"She gave birth here, didn't she?" I ask.

"Yes," Jessica says. "After her discharge."

"Were you there for her labor and delivery?"

"I was," she says. She's starting to get warier of me.

"That must have been really special," I say. "Being able to go through that together and watch her give birth. But if you were only a few days away from your own due date, why were you still working? I would think you would be on maternity leave by then."

"I wasn't at my due date quite yet."

"Oh, Misty delivered early?"

"Not dangerously so, but enough that she was there before I went on leave. I was very glad to be able to witness that with her," she says.

"What about you?" I ask.

"What do you mean?" she asks.

"Your child. What did you have? A girl or a boy?"

"Oh," she says. "A boy."

"Do you have any pictures? I don't have any children, so I get my fix from other people."

"No," she says. "I don't have any pictures with me. I'm sorry. I'm not understanding what you need from me."

I smile at her. "It's okay. I've got everything I need. Thank you for speaking with me." I start to turn away, then turn back. "That cut on the side of your face looks as if it was pretty serious. What happened?"

Jessica lifts her fingertips to rest on the healing wound that covers one corner of her forehead and goes into her hair.

"I'm just clumsy," she tells me. "I tripped and hit my head on the corner of a table."

I smile again. "I hate it when things like that happen. You should have seen me the last time I moved. I was a mess of bumps and bruises. Anyway, I hope it feels better soon. Thank you again."

By this point, my car seems to know the way to the other hospital without my even having to steer it. I get inside and go directly to Mary Gray's room. I'm not expecting anyone to be there; I'm surprised to see Leona and Ashley sitting beside the bed. Ashley's holding her grandmother's hand, but Leona seems more focused on her sister, her body curled slightly away as she watches her carefully.

"Ashley," I say.

She turns to me and smiles. "Hi, Emma. I was here having my stitches checked, so I thought I would stop in and see Gran."

"Grandma," Leona whispers.

"I was just telling her tomorrow is Friday the thirteenth. I hope everything will be okay. You never know what might happen on that day. Right, Leona?"

Leona jumps up from her chair and runs out of the room, her hand over her mouth as if she's going to throw up.

"Ashley," I say carefully. "We need to talk."

"It's so funny how she acts like that. When we're at home she tells me everything."

"Ashley?" Misty comes to the door and looks in. She's surprised to see me. "Oh, Agent Griffin. Hi. I didn't realize you were here."

"I was just stopping in to check on your mother. How is she doing?"

"Better," Misty says. "Still not out of the woods. Come on, honey.

We need to get going. We have that therapist appointment this afternoon."

"Therapist?" I frown. "I thought you didn't want Ashley speaking with a therapist."

"I changed my mind. I think it would do her good to talk through what happened to her and try to get past it," she says.

"Can I have a word with her just really fast?" I ask.

Misty glances at her watch. "We don't have the time. Maybe tomorrow."

They leave, Ashley glancing over her shoulder at me before heading down the hallway. I walk over to the bed and look down into Mary's face before checking the table. The medical ID bracelet is still sitting there. I pick it up and turn it over, reading the inscription before running my fingers over the stones.

One sapphire, two pearls.

FIFTY-FOUR

This is the part of every investigation I hate the most. I feel held down, trapped in place and unable to do what needs to be done. There are still steps that need to be taken. Evidence that needs to be gathered. I don't want to go through it. I don't want to wait. Every second that passes could make everything so much worse.

I spend every one of them trying to push the investigation through. I need to put the final pieces into place. To ensure the excavation under the front porch of the farmhouse is complete. To get the results of the blood test on the mirror.

Friday the thirteenth dawns, and a heaviness settles over me. I'm not superstitious. That belief was even more grounded by the events at Arrow Lake. The date has never meant anything to me except for the times I would curl up with a bowl of popcorn and watch scary movies with Bellamy when we were younger.

Now it's different. I can feel something crawling along my skin. Taunting me. The rain dripping down from the sky is too appropriate. Too on-the-nose. It makes everything feel more closed in.

I spend the morning fighting with the detectives and judges, trying to get them to release more information to me. Even with everything I already have, they won't budge. There are steps that need to be taken, legal channels that have to be followed to get what I need. They're right. I know they are. Some of the information I need will only be useful if it's acquired through those legal processes.

But that means nothing to me at noon, when my phone rings and I hear Misty sobbing on the other end.

"She's gone."

"What do you mean she's gone? What's going on, Misty?"

"Ashley's gone. I can't find her."

"Stay where you are. I'll be right there."

I don't even remember the drive to the house. When I get there, Leona and Misty are in the front yard. Misty is holding her daughter by the upper arms, trying to keep her under control as the girl thrashes and cries.

John comes out of the house holding his phone. He looks at me, his face like stone.

"Leona, you need to calm down," Misty says. "You need to calm down. We're going to find her."

"No!" Leona screams. "No. She's not here. She never was. She's gone!"

"Stop talking like that," Misty says. "Everything is going to be fine. Daddy is calling her friends. She's probably just out with Vivian and Allison. Everything is going to be fine. Do you hear me?"

Leona finally breaks free of her mother's grasp and starts to run. She trips, crashes to the ground, and crawls through the mud before getting her feet under her again and running for her car.

"No!" Misty screams.

John scrambles down the porch steps, nearly falling. He's still in his pajamas, his hair disheveled, as though he was trying to sleep the entire day away.

"Call the police," I tell him. "Then call Dean. You have his number, right?"

"Yes," John says.

I nod. "Call him. Tell him to have Xavier find me."

I know Xavier still has the tracker on my phone. He'll be able to locate me no matter where I am.

"Where is she going?" Misty asks.

"*You* need to tell *me* that," I say.

She looks at me with a bewildered expression. "What do you mean?"

"I think you know exactly where Leona is going. And you know why. Why don't you show me, so we can end this?"

"I don't know what you're talking about," Misty says. "Everything was fine this morning and then all of a sudden Ashley was gone and Leona completely panicked. She has been really on edge and hasn't been able to accept that her sister is back. This pushed her past her limit. I don't know what's going to happen."

"Misty, this is enough. You need to stop now. The police and my partner are going to be on their way. You really don't want either one of them to get to her before you do. This may be your only chance to save the children you have left."

Half an hour later, I follow Misty's car into the overgrown parking lot of an abandoned factory. As we drive past the broken, weather-faded sign, I can't help but notice the name of it.

WiseAcre Inc.

We drive around in loops for a few moments. Misty is stalling. I don't know what time she's waiting for, but I'm not going to play her game anymore. I stop my car and get out, running toward the hulking remains of the factory.

Misty follows close behind me, resigned to the reality that she isn't going to stop me. She leads me inside through a collapsed door. We haven't gone far onto the old factory floor when I see a figure standing in the middle of the room.

"Ashley!" Misty calls out.

Ashley whips around but says nothing. Even from a distance, I can see the tears streaking down her face.

"Honey, we were all so scared. What are you doing here?" Misty asks. When there's no response, Misty starts to get visibly unnerved. The smile she plastered on her face is fading, worry filling her eyes. "Where is your sister?"

That's all it takes.

"I don't know!" The words explode out, filling the crumbling space. "I don't know where my sister is. Maybe she's in one of the machines. Maybe she's in the river. Maybe in the dirt."

"Stop it," Misty says.

"Maybe she's in all of them. Parts of her in the gears. In the vats. Do you think there might still be chemicals in them? That would help the process along, wouldn't it?"

"Stop," Misty repeats, her voice starting to unravel. "Stop it now. Tell me where Leona is. Tell me now."

The scream of pure rage and agony that rips out of a girl too small and young to make that kind of sound rattles off the rusted machines. Her eyes burn into Misty, the tears flowing unchecked.

"That's all you care about, isn't it? It's all you've ever cared about. Never me."

Her hands clench and unclench at her sides. Teeth clenched, her breath seethes in and out. I step in front of Misty to try to break her fixated stare.

"Focus on me," I say. "Just look at me. Do you see me? It's me, Emma. Just focus on me, okay?"

She looks at me and I see the emotion shift. She nods.

"Good. Good. Can you show me where Leona is?"

She turns without a word and I follow her across the dirty floor to a set of spiral metal steps. We climb up them and she points down into an empty water reservoir. Leona lies at the bottom on a pile of debris. One leg is twisted and broken and I can see blood on her face. I hear a groan.

"She's alive," I say. "We need to get help for her."

Ashley faces off with her mother.

"She came here looking for me, didn't she?" she asks.

"We didn't know where you went," Misty says. "You were just gone. She was worried about you."

"No. She came here to see if I really had crawled out of the grave she put me in."

Misty recoils. "Stop it. Don't you say things like that!"

"She already knows, Misty. And so do I." I turn to the girl I've been calling Ashley. "Lyla. Have you heard that name?" She shakes her head. "It's yours. It has been since you were born." I gesture toward the top of the steps. "Leona didn't know. She didn't know about you."

"This is ridiculous," Misty says. "What are you going on about? This is Ashley. My daughter. Ashley Marie Stevenson."

"This is your daughter, but it's not Ashley. I noticed your mother's medical ID bracelet. Leona mentioned it had birthstones for her grandchildren in it. There were three. One for January, two for June."

"I lost a baby," Misty says. "I told you that."

"I know," I say. "And in a way, you did. But not how you say. The daughter you raised, one of the June babies, was actually a twin."

Misty looks angry, but a smug look crosses her face.

"You have no way of knowing us," she says. "You can't access my medical records."

"No," I say. "I can't. But I can access death records. They're public. And there's one for Lyla Jane Gray. Your infant daughter. You hadn't married John yet, so she didn't have his last name. Ashley didn't get his last name until she was almost a year old, did she?"

"This is completely outrageous," Misty snaps. "You have no idea what you're talking about."

"I do, Misty. The death record is for a stillborn twin. Only, the morgue has no records of receiving or disposing of any infant remains on that day, or any of the days in the week before or after June thirteenth. That's because there weren't any. Because your daughter Lyla wasn't stillborn. She was born healthy and strong, just like Ashley.

"And then she went home with your nurse. Jessica Blanchette. She had been pretending to be pregnant for months, ever since she took care of you when you were sent to rehab for your gambling addiction, rather than having to serve jail time after being caught with a hell of a lot of pills. Tell me, was that the plan all along? Did you know while you were in that rehab center that you would sell your baby daughter to her? Or were you as fooled as everybody else was with her fake pregnancy?"

"I don't know what you're talking about," Misty says.

"Of course, you do. John showed me the picture of the two of you with your pregnant bellies. How long did it take until you found out your boyfriend was in that facility a year before you? That they met before you racked up a huge debt to him and then made it infinitely worse by losing the drugs you were supposed to sell?"

"So, you sold me instead," Lyla says.

"I've seen all the transactions. I know how it happened. Just tell me, for my peace of mind, that that man isn't your children's father," I say.

"No," Misty says, shaking her head. "He died before I found out I was pregnant."

"Why did you lie to your husband about when you lost a baby? Why didn't you tell him the twin died, the same story you told your mother?" I ask.

The tears are falling freely down Misty's face now. She's stammering, but somehow holding it together.

"I didn't want him to know. I begged my mother not to tell him. He was in treatment longer than I was. We weren't really serious until after he got out. I hadn't told him I was pregnant with twins. It wasn't something we talked about. My life was finally starting to turn around. I told my mother I didn't want to start our life together in pain." She turns to Lyla. "But I was still mourning. I needed to be able to grieve for you."

"To grieve for me?" Lyla screams. "You're the one who caused this. You're the one who put me in his grasp! He called me 'thirteen'.

That's all he ever called me. I used to spend all my time dreaming of my family. Wondering what you were like. Imagining that you were looking for me. That you loved me and were going to find me one day."

Misty shudders. Lyla continues.

"Things didn't start getting really bad until I was around twelve. Before then, I knew they weren't my parents, but they took care of me. I didn't realize until then they were grooming me. They were raising me like livestock. That's when I found out the truth. Where I actually came from. And the thing was, I didn't even know then how horrible you really were. Not until Ashley disappeared. He used to make me watch the news with him so he could laugh about Ashley. About you.

"He wanted me to know that what I thought about you was wrong. He wanted me to know where I really came from. That I was used as collateral. Payment so you could go on with your life. But even then, I convinced myself to have compassion for you. I told myself you were manipulated and mistreated by them just as I was. That you wouldn't have made that choice if you didn't absolutely have to.

"I wanted to find you again. I wanted to be part of a family. If I could give Ashley back to you, it would be what you wanted. But then I found out what you really did. That you and Leona murdered her. She didn't go missing. She hasn't been lost for five years. She's been dead. Leona told me. She thought I had come back from the dead to torture her for what she did. And now that's exactly what I'm going to do."

She takes a step toward her mother, but I stop her. "Lyla, no. Not for them."

"No!" Misty says, crumbling in a heap of sobs. "Leona didn't do anything. It was me. I did it. The only one to blame is me."

"Stop," Leona's voice comes from below us. "Mom, stop. You can't take the blame for this. You've covered for me for long enough. It was me."

I look down and see Leona grimacing as she tries to pull herself up to sit with her back against the metal container. She looks up at us. "I didn't mean to. Ashley was always the favorite. She was always the one who did everything right and was popular and beautiful. She got away with everything.

"I got so tired of it. I was always living in her shadow. No matter what happened, she wasn't blamed for it and everything went her way. That night, I was supposed to go out with Sean, but he called me at the last minute and said he couldn't go. I still wanted to go out and do something, but Mom said I had to stay home and help her because Ashley was out.

"Later, Sean came over and apologized for not seeing me. He gushed all over me and told me how special I was, how much he loved me. Then he told me what happened with Ashley. That he had been with her and the other girls, and she was drunk out of her mind. He wanted me to go pick her up and bring her home so he wouldn't get in any trouble.

"Of course, I did it. I was so mad at him and so hurt, but I was so wrapped up in him. I guess I still am. As soon as I saw her, I was so angry, I couldn't even see straight. I brought her out here to sober up. But she started rubbing in my face that she was hanging out with my boyfriend and his actual girlfriend while I was home. She kept saying she was only thirteen and was already getting more attention than I ever had.

"I snapped. I picked up a piece of metal. I really just wanted to scare her, but it cut her. Right across the side. She stumbled and fell over the edge into this water reservoir. I tried to save her. But I couldn't. I called Mom and told her Ashley went missing."

"Leona," gasps Misty. "You?"

She seems shocked to have the truth finally come out, but at the same time it seems she's known somehow all along, just kept it buried deep under the surface.

"I'm sorry, Mom." Leona is crying now, and so is Misty, and even Lyla has tears shimmering in her eyes.

"I thought," Misty says, "I thought that if—if I gave Ashley the love I should have given Lyla all those years that somehow, some way, she would feel it. I know you missed out on it, Leona. I'm sorry. I'm so sorry, for both of you."

Neither Lyla nor Leona answers.

FIFTY-FIVE

"MARY IS GOING TO BE FINE," I tell the group gathered around me. "Misty knew her mother was going to tell me about the twin, so she had to do something to keep her quiet. Her medical alert bracelet said that she was allergic to quinine. It's easy to access, undetectable, and results in organ breakdown and heart attacks in those who are allergic to it," I say. "She just didn't expect her mother to survive."

"What about the man she sold Lyla to?" Bellamy asks.

"His name was Frederick Smith. Nowhere near a Wolf, I have to admit. They found his body behind the house he shared with Jessica. Lyla told me when Misty started making statements on the news about Ashley's disappearance, he wanted to capitalize on it. He wanted to extort money from her by using Lyla as a pawn. After an entire lifetime of being used and manipulated, she wasn't going to take it anymore.

"She decided she was going to benefit from it herself. Thinking about getting out and finding her family was enough to give her the strength to fight back. Jessica was helping her get ready for her appointment that day. She smashed her head in the mirror, which knocked her out. It wasn't enough to kill her, but she wasn't the one

Lyla was particularly focused on. Jessica had always been kinder to her. Lyla was after Frederick.

"He was stabbed thirteen times. That wasn't a coincidence. Apparently, Jessica regained consciousness and realized what had happened. Shecleaned up all the evidence of Lyla and took Frederick's body. The knife Lyla used came from the kitchen. They found it under the porch. That was why the blood didn't extend far. She dropped it through one of the rotten boards."

"I can't believe she lived through that," Sam mutters. "Poor girl."

"She has a long road ahead of her," I say. "But at least now there's something at the end of it, and all the people who failed her are paying for it." I look at Bellamy, with Bebe cradled in her arms. "Twice now mothers were involved. I don't understand."

She looks down at the baby. "I can't explain it. Nothing Misty did was right. I won't even for a second condone it. But Leona was her daughter, too. I would do anything for Bebe. She was just pushed to a place I hope to never find myself in."

THREE DAYS LATER I'M SITTING ACROSS FROM LYLA AT THE hospital, where she's finally getting the treatment she really needs.

"How did you know?" she asks. "I felt from the very beginning you didn't believe me."

"It wasn't that I didn't believe you," I say. "And I didn't know for sure. But there was something that was tugging at me."

"How?"

"There's something you should know about me."

I tell her the story of my father and Jonah, and everything I went through with them.

"I guess that makes me the evil twin," she says sadly.

I shake my head. "No. I don't think there has to be a good or a bad."

"It sounds ridiculous, but I miss Ashley. I never knew her—not after birth, anyway—but I feel as though a part of me is missing. I wish I could have known her."

"That doesn't sound silly at all," I say. "You two have a special connection. And I might not be able to tell you much, but I know someone who can. Give me just a second."

I leave the room and come back a few seconds later with John.

"Hi, Lyla," he says, tears in his voice.

We sit down together and start the process of building a relationship he never got to have with the stepdaughter he never knew existed. He wants to be her father, to give her the love she never had. It will take time. I know that. But they need each other now.

"How is..."

"Your grandmother?" John asks. "It's okay. You can say that."

"How is she?" Lyla asks.

"Better. She's awake. She's healing well. I've told her everything and she can't wait to meet you. She says she has missed you your whole life. She didn't know where you were, but she said she never believed in her heart that you were really dead."

Lyla hangs her head and I see a tear drop onto the table in front of her.

"I can't wait to spend more time with her. I want to help take care of her."

Suddenly, a light explodes in my brain.

"Excuse me," I say. "You two keep talking."

I get to my feet and start out of the room.

"Are you okay?" John asks.

I nod but don't answer as I run out of the room. I wrench my phone out of my pocket and call Sam.

"The grandmothers," I say.

"What?" he asks.

"The girls working on Windsor Island, Gabriel, the member of The Order who was helping Dad. Every single one of them either used the excuse, or had the excuse used for them that they were going to take care of their sick grandmothers right before disappearing, being used, or dying. That's the connection."

"What are you saying?" he asks.

My mind is spinning at lightning-speed.

"All of them link back to the Dragon."

AUTHOR'S NOTE

Dear reader,

I hope you're enjoying the ride with Emma so far and loved *The Girl and the Unlucky 13*.
Be sure to checkout the next book as I'll be wrapping up season two of Emma and many of your questions will be answered!
Thank you for continuing to go on great Emma adventures with me.
Please, leave me a review if you can spare a moment of your time.

My promise to you is to always do my best to bring you thrilling adventures.
I hope I have fulfilled that. I look forward to you reading my next novel!

Yours,
A.J. Rivers

P.S. If for some reason you didn't like this book or found typos or other errors, please let me know personally. I do my best to read and respond to every email at aj@riversthrillers.com

ALSO BY A.J. RIVERS

Titles are now available on Audible. Type https://www.audible.com/author/AJ-Rivers/B0833HF2GL in your web browser to browse Audible now. Not an Audible subscriber, type https://www.audible.com/pd/Bo8FXNYXFD try a free month today.

Made in the USA
Columbia, SC
11 October 2023

24310172R00214